Group Therapy

BB EASTON

For Judd.

Prologue

Lou

I HATE HOW HAPPY she looks. Hopping and skipping around a bonfire in the middle of the woods like some kind of fucking fairy princess. Her and all the other half-baked hippies who live here. The noises they're making are horrible. Howls and yelps and random, interpretive drum solos. Someone's shaking a turtle shell on a stick, for fuck's sake. This is what passes for music around here.

A pair of cymbals crash together out of nowhere, but I don't even flinch.

I don't have the energy.

"Luna, come dance with us!" my mother calls, beckoning me with long, fluid arm movements.

She has always been a little bohemian, but ever since my dad ... well, she's gone off the fucking deep end. Her golden-brown skin is swirled with silver paint. Locks of her thick, dark hair are wrapped in copper wire and pierced with hoops and dangly crystals. Her armpits look like Chia Pets. And her tits are bouncing around like a couple of newly liberated bitches, free of the patriarchy and all its underwired confines.

Returning my attention to the sketchbook in my lap, I flip up the hood on my black sweatshirt and frown at my drawing. Rotting flesh requires so much shading. I curl up under the tree I'm leaning against and drag my pencil in short strokes across the paper, but something's not quite right. It needs more … dried blood? Exposed bone structure?

I glance up and find my subject again—Leif, the commune leader. Sorry, I meant, *artist colony* leader. Evidently, these people are more offended by the term *commune* than their own repulsive body odor.

Leif blows into a wooden tube that has to be at least four feet long, producing the same groan-like baritone noise as a constipated elephant. He takes a deep breath and blows again, so hard that I think his eyes might pop out of his head.

That's it. That's what's missing.

I flip my pencil over and erase Zombie Leif's right eyeball, redrawing it a few inches lower, dangling from the socket.

Much better.

I guess the constipated-elephant call was some kind of hippie bat signal because the drum circle suddenly goes quiet and all eyes turn toward Leif.

He spreads his arms and smiles, slow and wide. His long hair is pulled back in a low ponytail, and his face is kind, I guess. But there's something about that grin that gives me the fucking creeps.

"Beautiful. That was truly beautiful, my fellow conduits of Spirit. Did you feel the silvery glow of the moonlight bathing us in its radiance just now? It's as if the entire cosmos stopped by to help us welcome these three new souls into our communal family. Crystal, George, Luna … welcome to Indigo Hills."

My heart slides all the way down into my guts as every scruffy, unwashed face turns toward my mom and cheers. She

2

beams at them one by one, soaking up the adoration as she reaches for her new husband's reluctant hand.

George isn't from the commune either. In fact, it's possible that he's even more out of place here than I am. Picture a grumpy old man from Long Island, New York, suffering silently in an ill-fitting tunic and a few yards of love beads. That's my stepdad right now. I would almost feel sorry for him, but he agreed to this bullshit. He's enabling my mother's grief journey or midlife crisis or nervous breakdown or whatever the hell this is, and because of that, I'm going to be finishing high school in some backwoods, Appalachian hillbilly town, hundreds of miles away from all of my friends.

Nobody fucking cares what I want. What's best for me. Not my mom. Not George. And definitely not my dad.

Turning her Zen goddess smile toward me, my mom motions for me to come stand with them. To pretend to be a happy little family for her stupid new friends. Her bangles jingle like celestial wind chimes as she flicks her fingers at me.

I ignore her and erase a chunk of Zombie Leif's ear.

"Through the sharing of our habitat, our hearts, and our ... animalistic bodies"—Leif's voice drops an octave on that last part. *Gross*—"we will become one."

I peek through the split ends of my jagged emo haircut and watch as Leif takes my mom's free hand. She blushes and drops her eyes. I roll mine as hard as I can.

George glances between the two of them with a scowl.

Leif continues, "Alone, you were but stardust, floating on the breeze. But together ..." —he takes George's free hand too, which, based on George's face, is an unwelcome surprise— "...we're an entire pulsating nebulous."

"Nebula," I hear myself blurt out. "It's fucking neb-u-lah."

I stand up, brushing the leaves and pine needles off my ass, and stomp off in the direction of my unfortunate new home.

My chest aches, and tears sting my eyeliner-caked eyes as I think about how much I've lost in such a short amount of time. How badly I want it all back. My dad. My home. My mom—the way she used to be at least. Not this tofu-boho-chic version of her. And the worst part is, my parents are the ones who took it from me. All of it. We were a perfectly normal family until my dad … did what he did. And then, when remarrying the first guy who paid her any attention didn't make her feel better, my mom dragged us all to an artist colony in the North Georgia Mountains to "find" herself. That's all she cares about—herself. What about me? What about *my* self? What about what I need?

Footsteps crunch through the leaves behind me as George calls my name with that thick New York accent, "Lou! Wait up!"

I stop a few feet away from an RV with a psychedelic paint job, parked on the edge of the woods, and blink back my tears. Spinning around, I fold my arms across my chest and straighten my spine.

"If you're here to lecture me about giving this place a chance—"

"Givin' it a chance? Are you kiddin' me? I hate this place." George leans over and puts his hands on his knees, trying to catch his breath.

"What are you talking about? You guys love it here. You're literally wearing Birkenstocks right now," I snap.

George straightens his back with a grunt. "Ya mother loves it here. I love air-conditioning and gluten and ESPN and not living in a goddamn recreational vehicle that looks like the inside of one of Ringo Starr's bad acid trips." He tosses a hand in the direction of the RV parked behind me. "That's what I love."

"Then why are we still here? I wanna go home!"

"Because look at her." George turns his head and gazes lovingly over his shoulder at the bonfire.

I glance in that direction and find my mom standing off to the side with Leif. She tips her head back and laughs at something he said, lightly touching his arm.

It makes my blood boil.

"I've never seen your mother so happy."

"I have," I spit.

"Hey." The sincerity shining out of George's eyes and the deep V of concern between his furry gray eyebrows make me want to cry even worse than before. "I know it's been a hard coupla years, kid. Ever since your dad—"

"I don't want to talk about it," I manage to say around the lump forming in my throat.

George holds up his hands. "Okay, okay. Look, I know I'm not him, all right? But if I were, I'd tell you to get the hell outta here as soon as you graduate. Go to college, Lou—and I mean a real college, not just some art school. Look around."

George gestures behind him toward the rest of the compound, but this time, my eyes land on a spot over by one of the cabins. A naked hippie couple is standing on a tarp, smearing paint on each other with their bare hands. The man leans over to scoop some more aqua blue out of the bucket, but he slips and falls, taking his partner out at the knees. They both crash to the ground, laughing and rolling around until they go still. I can't tell whether they passed out from head trauma or if they were just so stoned that they forgot what they were doing.

"This is what happens to middle-aged artists, Lou— borderline homelessness and chlamydia. Is that what you want?"

I glance back at him and shake my head.

George's eyes soften. "Listen, I know you like to draw in your little notebook or whatever, but you need to forget about that, okay? Get yourself a nice job with a pension, a corner office, maybe one of those coffee machines with the little … the little plastic cups that you drop in. So bad for the environment. You understand what I'm saying?"

I survey the hedonistic wasteland around us and nod, my anger boiling away to reveal the sadness that's always there, just below the surface.

"Attagirl. Come here …" George slips the notebook out of my hand and pulls me in for a hug.

I don't like how much I like George's hugs. He's grumpy and old, and he always smells like McDonald's, but when he hugs me, it's because I need to be comforted, not the other way around. Not like my parents. They were affectionate, but I always got the feeling that their hugs were more for them than me.

I feel a whoosh of air and hear a rustle of pages as George covertly tosses my sketchbook into the pitch-black woods.

Then, with a clap on my back, he whispers, "Hey, do me a favor and don't tell your mother we had this little talk, okay? She'd have my balls for breakfast with a side of quinoa."

Lou
Twelve Years Later

8:00 a.m.: Drama Llama Kim

MAKE EYE CONTACT.
  Lean forward.
  Uncross your legs.
  Back straight.
  Don't chew on your pencil.
  Now you're tapping it. Stop that.
  Fuck. I forgot to listen.

The surgically enhanced blonde sitting across from me, Kimberly, arrived for her appointment fifteen minutes late, which gave me just enough time to work up a nice, anxious sweat.

"… and then that bitch had the audacity to say that I took her spot! I was like, 'Honey, if this is *your* spot, then why is *my* Audi parked in it right now?'" Kimberly looks around, clutching a tiny little Louis Vuitton purse/wallet thing in one hand and a still-steaming Starbucks cup in the other, and scoffs, "Where am I supposed to put this? *The floor?*"

"Here." I take her pumpkin-spice-autumnal whatever—which, judging by the lavalike temperature, must have been purchased around the same time that Kimberly was supposed to be here—and place it on the desk behind me.

Kimberly frowns. I can't tell if she's unhappy about the distance between her and her twenty-dollar beverage or if she just caught a glimpse of the pit stains that have already formed under my arms.

The furniture in my office is nice, so I know it can't be the decor. Kimberly and I are facing each other in a pair of brown leather armchairs—the fancy kind with brass grommets and feet carved to look like giant chicken talons. Behind me is a desk so big and sturdy and wooden that I'm pretty sure if it had been on the *Titanic*, both Rose and Jack would have fit very comfortably on it and would have lived happily ever after with a brood of beautiful babies and annual Irish riverdancing parties. The wall to my right has two massive bookcases, filled with gorgeous, old, leather-bound psychological texts that list things like *feeblemindedness* and *idiocy* as actual clinical diagnoses. There is one shelf that contains a collection of brightly colored textbooks and manuals that I brought from home, but the rest of those dust-collectors came with the office. And behind Kimberly is a wall of windows overlooking Peachtree Street—the north end of Peachtree Street, where people carry dogs in their purses and can afford therapy, not the south side, where the muggers put cigarettes out on your face *after* they rob you at gunpoint. I should know—that's where I went to college.

8

When I graduated from Georgia State University a few months ago, the department chair, Dr. Callahan, said he could get me a postdoc fellowship at the most prestigious private practice in the city. He made it seem like he was doing me this huge favor, pulling alllll the strings, but now that I'm here, I'm starting to understand why Atlanta Psychology Associates had an opening in the first place.

"So, Kimberly ..."

Eye contact.

Lean forward.

Smile.

Not too much.

Pencil down.

"How was your week?"

"Ugh. Where do I even begin?" Kimberly cuts her longing gaze from the seasonally decorated cardboard cup on my desk over to me. Then, she lifts her hand, ready to begin listing her grievances on her inch-long Swarovski-encrusted nails. "Let's see. On Monday, I found out that my hairdresser gave me *synthetic fucking extensions*." She emphasizes those last three words with so much disdain that she might as well have said *scorching case of herpes*. "I paid for Indian temple hair, Dr. Sterling, not the plastic shit that grows out of a My Little Pony's asshole."

I always invite my clients to call me Lou. I don't like the idea of establishing a power differential when I'm trying to relate to people on their level—"join" with them, as Carkhuff calls it—but the clientele here just ignores me. Honestly, I think they prefer saying Dr. Sterling because it sounds more expensive.

"Then, my Botox girl froze me worse than Teresa Giudice's bank account. She knows I have an audition coming up too. I mean, look at this!" Kimberly's eyes bore into mine as her mouth opens maybe an inch. Big enough to talk, but not big enough to eat a sandwich without cutting it up first. "This is my surprised face!"

I feel my eyebrows rise, as if my face were trying to help Kimberly's face by modeling the expression she's going for, but

I immediately pull them back down, furrowing them in what I hope reads as pensive compassion.

"What am I supposed to do now? I haven't worked since *Boss Wives of Atlanta* got canceled. I want to be a serious actress, Dr. Sterling. I'm not Drama Llama Kim anymore."

"There." I lean forward, pointing at Kimberly with my pencil. "There it is."

I feel it, the joining that Carkhuff talks about. That was the most vulnerable Kimberly has ever been with me. She opened up, identified her fear, and is finally ready to take responsibility for her life. This is big.

While maintaining eye contact, I steeple my fingers under my chin. " 'I'm not Drama Llama Kim anymore.' I think that statement really captures the central issue that you're dealing with. What I hear you saying is—"

"What I'm saying is that they're trying to destroy me, Dr. Sterling! They're trying to destroy meeee!" Kimberly's face might not be able to express her feelings at this moment, but the high-pitched wail at the end of that sentence definitely makes up for it. She stomps over to my desk and snatches up her beverage, self-soothing by sucking fall-flavored comfort from the tiny hole in the plastic lid.

Giving her a minute to calm down, I angle the clipboard in my lap so that she can't see what I'm writing. Then I add today's outburst to my running list.

The only baggage I have is Louis Vuitton!

You wouldn't understand. You probably eat carbs!

They're trying to destroy me!

Once Kimberly returns to her seat, clutching that Starbucks cup like it's a Primetime Emmy Award, I take the box of tissues off my desk and offer them to her.

"Oh, please." She waves them away, dabbing the corners of her eyes with her fingertips, careful not to put one out with her inch-long bedazzled nails. "I had my tear ducts Botoxed too. Crying is for peasants."

9:00 a.m.: Winnie the Wine Mom

"Yoga? *Meditation?* Let me tell you somethin', Dr. Sterling. You and Deepak Whatever-His-Name-Is can both go straight to hell because that's exactly where you're headed. You know who does yoga? Terrorists—that's who. I am a good Christian woman. I came here, lookin' for Zoloft, and you're tryin' to convert me to Islam!"

10:00 a.m.: Teen Angst Adelynn

"Shh! God." Adelynn shushes me after spending ten minutes engaged in a text conversation while I tried—and failed—to break the ice. She doesn't even look up when she does it. She just keeps tapping on that glowing screen while my mouth hangs open, her painted black thumbnails moving so fast that they almost disappear.

I'm tempted to yank that damn phone out of her hand and dunk it into my coffee, but what would be the point? We do this every week. She doesn't want to be here—her news anchor mother just makes her come because she's embarrassed that her daughter wears black lipstick and dog collars to school—and there's nothing clinically wrong with her either unless *broodiness* has been added to the American Psychiatric Association's *Diagnostic and Statistical Manual of Mental Disorders* without my knowledge.

So, I decide to let it go. You can lead a horse to water, but you can't make it talk to you about what's going on at school.

Sliding the legal pad out of my clipboard, I flip to a clean page and spend the next half hour drawing a decaying teenage girl texting her boyfriend.

Zombie Adelynn doesn't look very happy. The corners of her mouth and her one remaining eyebrow are pulled down in a scowl because her fingertips have rotted off, and you can't use an iPhone without fleshy digits. The bones just clink against the glass. Poor thing. I think I'll call this one *A Fate Worse Than Death.*

11:00 a.m.: Angry Bill

Angry Bill punches a hole in my Sheetrock. Again.

Security escorts him out. Again.

I dump the bagel out of my brown paper lunch bag and breathe into it until my heart rate returns to normal—*again*—but this time, I inhale a sesame seed that must have fallen off the bagel, and now, it's lodged in the back of my trachea forever.

1:00 p.m.: Nervous Nicole

"I tried using earplugs to see if that would block out the snoring, but then I was like, *Oh my God, what if there's a fire and the smoke detectors go off and I don't hear it because I have earplugs in and Frank doesn't hear it because of his snoring, and then we all burn to death—*"

"Nicole—"

"Or worse, what if the neighbors call the fire department because of the fire that we don't even know is happening and they come and break out the downstairs windows and get me and Frank out, but by the time they get upstairs, little Jack and Hannah have already died of smoke inhalation—"

"Nicole, if I may—"

Nicole is wringing the hem of her long cardigan with both hands now, like it's a dirty dishrag. "Or the roof could fall in on them, like at the end of *Edward Scissorhands*, or that backdraft thing could happen, like in that movie *Backdraft* or—"

I raise my hand this time. I actually raise my hand, like I'm in kindergarten. "Nicole, I'd like to point out that—"

Nicole's pressured speech slows to a rolling stop when she sees my hand go up, but the force behind the words is simply too strong. It's as if her weekly therapy session is the only opportunity she has to purge the death spiral of negative thoughts in her mind, and if she doesn't get them all out in fifty minutes or less, she'll die.

I continue to nod as I write in my legal pad, looking up every few seconds to make eye contact while resisting the urge to grimace when she says things like, "I was so afraid someone was going to break into the house and steal the baby and put her on the grill and grill her that I got rid of the grill and also the oven, but I think she's too big to fit into the microwave."

I tear the page I was writing on out of my legal pad, fold it in half, and hand it to her with a sympathetic smile. "I'm afraid our time is up."

"What's this?" she asks, confused enough that I'm able to get almost two complete sentences in.

"My recommendations. Just … read it when you get home."

2:00 p.m.: Aggressive Celeste

I duck as a ceramic mug goes flying past my head. It shatters against the wall behind my desk as the thrower of the mug, Celeste—a wellness-brand ambassador, which I think is code for wealthy octogenarian's wife—screams like a banshee and storms out of my office.

I turn to see my Georgia State mug lying in pieces on the floor while the remnants of my lukewarm coffee slither down the textured gray wallpaper toward it.

Celeste returns a second later, completely composed, to retrieve her Chanel clutch. After tucking it under one arm, she turns toward me, shoulders back, chin up, and says, "Same time next week."

I shrug in defeat. Not that it matters. Celeste wasn't asking, and she wasn't waiting for my response either. By the time my shoulders fall, she's already out the door.

I slump back in my chair and stare out the window, treating myself to a few moments of deliciously bad posture before I go pick up the shards of my favorite mug. That's something nobody tells you about psychotherapy. You assume it's going to be mentally challenging, maybe even emotionally draining, but nobody prepares you for the sheer physical exhaustion of having to monitor, control, and inhibit what your face, back, legs, arms, and hands are doing at all times for eight hours straight.

While people scream at you.

And throw ceramic projectiles at your head.

Okay, so maybe there are a few things nobody told me about this job.

My desk phone rings right in my ear, forcing me to use my muscles again way too soon. I lift my hand over my head and pat the desk behind me until I find the receiver.

"Dr. Sterling."

2:50 p.m.: The Notorious E.I.C.

Speed-walking down the Atlanta Psychology Associates hallway, I tuck my sweaty vintage blouse—not vintage, as in the aesthetic, but vintage, as in I found it at a thrift store and assumed that the previous owner had purchased it out of a Sears, Roebuck and Co. catalog, using a rotary phone—into my plaid menswear pants while discreetly trying to clear that damn sesame seed from my throat.

I look down at my feet and am reminded that I opted for Chuck Taylors today instead of heels.

Shit. Is that what this is about? The dress code?

I push a few random braids and my feather extension down into the dark, wavy mess that is the rest of my hair, hoping that they'll stay hidden at least until my meeting is over. Then, I stop directly in front of the last place I want to be right now and stare at the plaque on my supervisor's door.

GROUP THERAPY

ERICA ITO-COHEN, PhD

I take a deep, shaky breath and lift my fist when a voice barks at me from the other side, "Don't knock when I call for you."

Inside, a small, severe woman with a sharp, angled bob sits behind a desk even bigger than mine. I hustle in and sit across from her, feeling like I've been called to the principal's office. Only this is worse because the woman behind *this* desk holds my entire career in her clawlike hands.

In the state of Georgia, getting your doctorate is only the first step to becoming a licensed clinical psychologist. You also have to pass a licensing exam, which I'm studying for; do a yearlong postdoc fellowship, which ... you've seen how well that is going; and you have to submit a letter of recommendation from your postdoc supervisor, who, in my case, just so happens to be The Notorious E.I.C.

Dr. Ito-Cohen glances with disapproval first at me and then at her Apple watch.

"Sorry it took me a minute." *Sit up straight.* "I had to—"

"If I wanted to hear the excuses of a millennial, I wouldn't have taken all that birth control in the '90s," E.I.C. snaps.

I can feel my heartbeat in my neck.

"This matter is urgent, so I'll be quick. I need your help. Dr. Ramos was in a terrible accident during his lunch break—"

"Oh my God," I gasp. "Is he—"

"He'll live, but he has a very important client coming in right now, and you're the only..."—Dr. Ito-Cohen looks me up and down and then arches an eyebrow in disappointment—"...*psychologist* with an opening."

"Oh." I swallow. "Okay."

Dr. Ito-Cohen opens her desk drawer and pulls out a handful of M&M's. Popping several into her mouth, she continues talking, a little faster than usual and crunching on random syllables. "The editor in chief at Snowden Publishing House is a dear friend of mine. She called me, at her wits' end with an author whose writer's block is ruining her publication schedule. She asked if we had any creativity specialists on staff who could cure him."

"But we don't—"

"I told her yes," E.I.C. cuts me off before shoving another handful of M&M's into her usually poised face.

I feel the blood drain out of mine.

"You." Dr. E.I.C. points one skinny claw at me. "You're my new creativity specialist."

I cough so hard that I finally dislodge that damn sesame seed. "Me? But I—"

"You're ... *artsy*," she says, gesturing vaguely at my appearance.

"Sure, but I don't—"

"This isn't up for discussion. I need a warm body, and right now, you're the only one with an opening."

My mouth snaps shut, and her face softens fractionally.

"I'm counting on you, Dr. Sterling. This case is important to me."

"Okay."

"It's personal."

"I understand."

"What I'm saying is, it's going to be very hard for me to write you a letter of recommendation if you fuck this up."

I swallow my shock and force myself to nod as I desperately try to remember my training.

Don't react. Validate her feelings. Restate the problem in your own words.

"What I'm *hearing* is, this editor is actually some asshole from your past who's come crawling to you in her time of need, and you want me to make you look good."

I deeply, deeply regret that statement the second it leaves my mouth. I can actually feel my own asshole pucker as I brace for E.I.C.'s wrath. She opens her mouth to ... I don't even know ... scream at me, fire me, feast on my soul, but then her pointy little jaw closes again, her mouth settling into a thin, hard line.

Man, she must really be desperate.

Dr. Ito-Cohen reaches across the desk, and instead of ripping my still-beating heart from my chest, she yanks a thrift store price tag from the armpit of my blouse and hands it to me.

"Do *not* make me regret this."

I walk back to my office in a trance, clutching that price tag as if it were a death sentence. It might as well be. If I don't convince some high-profile author that I'm a distinguished creativity specialist and miraculously cure his writer's block, E.I.C. is going to flush the last ten years of my life, plus my entire future, down the fucking toilet.

This day just keeps getting better.

April, our receptionist, bounces down the hall toward me, looking every bit the TikTok superstar she aspires to be. Dewy twenty-year-old skin that looks filtered, even in real life; pants that are extremely high-waisted yet baggy enough to allow freedom of movement while she records herself doing choreographed dance moves when the waiting room is empty; toxic positivity—she's got it all.

"Hey, girl! Here's the file for your new client." April beams, handing me a manila folder.

"Thanks." I muster a smile and accept the file in her hand before ducking into my office.

April follows me. "Ooh, you should Google him before he gets here, so you can pretend like you know who he is. Famous people love it when you already know who they are."

I take a bite out of the half-eaten bagel on my desk and glance at the name on the file.

Then, I choke.

As I dig deeper through the contents of the folder, my mind begins chanting one word over and over while simultaneously losing its grip on reality.

No, no, no, no, no, no, no.

My eyes fly over every word, every line, hoping something I see will prove that this can't be the man I think it is, but it's all there in black and white.

17

NAME: THOMAS O'REARDON

DATE OF BIRTH: 6/14/91

ADDRESS: 128 KNIGHTSBRIDGE, LONDON
SW1X 7LJ, UNITED KINGDOM

"Apparently, he's kind of a big deal." April twirls a shiny lock of hair around her finger.

I lift the trash can and spit the hunk of bagel into it.

"Kind of a big deal?" I sputter, wiping the crumbs from my lips with a shaky hand. "*Kind of a big deal?* Thomas O'Reardon isn't just *kind of a big deal*. He's the next fucking Stephen King! His books are dark and romantic and terrifying and brilliant and … and …"

I yank my bottom drawer open and thrust a hand into my shapeless, crocheted shoulder bag. Pulling out a tattered, dog-eared paperback, I thrust it into the air with the back cover facing April. "And he looks like *this*!"

April's perfectly contoured face brightens as she reaches for Thomas's latest number one *New York Times* best-selling psychological thriller. His publisher obviously knows he's beautiful. His headshot takes up half of the back cover and seems to get bigger with every book he writes.

I should know—I own them all.

"Dude, he's super hot for a millennial."

I snatch the book back and protectively cradle it against my chest while trying not to hyperventilate.

April furrows her perfectly microbladed eyebrows at me. "You're, like, really freaking out."

"It's Thomas O'FuckingReardon!" I squeal.

April only blinks in response.

"He's like … okay, he's like Harry Styles but for books."

"Oh my God, I love Harry Styles," she gasps, recognition finally dawning on her vacant face. "It's the hair for me."

I clutch my copy of *Ruby Lies* tighter as icy-cold dread grips my throat and squeezes with both hands.

He's coming here. Right now. He's coming—

April waves her hand in front of my face to snap me out of my trance as an angelic male voice calls out from the lobby, "Hello?"

An angelic *British* male voice.

Fuck me.

Paralyzed from the nose down, I shift my eyes to April and feel them widen in panic.

April holds her hands up, as if I'm some unpredictable, caged beast, and walks slowly backward toward the door, reciting inspirational quotes from Instagram memes the entire way. "Hey, girl, you got this. You are enough. You can do hard things. Just ... don't be weird."

The second she leaves, a switch inside my brain flips from Inactive to Hyperactive. Suddenly, all I can see is messes. Little messes everywhere.

I begin cleaning frantically. I clear the entire left side of my desk into my trash can, laptop and all, as my office phone starts to ring. I hit the speaker button so that I don't have to stop my manic tidying. "Please tell me it's not him."

April's disembodied voice floats through the speaker, sounding even girlier than usual. "Dr. Sterling, your three o'clock is here." Then, she lowers her voice to a whisper and adds, "He even sounds like Harry Styles!"

I drop a handful of shattered mug shards into the trash. "Just ... keep talking. I need two more minutes."

"Oh, really?" April coos.

I can almost see the flirty little smile on her face. Thomas must be standing right in front of her. He has that effect on women. Lots of women, if the tabloids at the grocery store checkout aisle are to be believed. Not that I read them. Not that I buy them and take them home and kiss his picture and scribble out his date's face and then glue a picture of myself over her picture and cut the whole thing out and tape it to my bathroom mirror. Nope. Not me.

"You want me to clear your schedule for the afternoon, so you can devote your full, undivided attention to Mr. O'Reardon?"

"Please don't," I say out loud.

I flip the zombified sketch of Adelynn over to reveal a fresh page on my legal pad.

"How do you think your four o'clock is gonna take that?" April muses. "You know he's been in a bad place ever since he did *Detective Pikachu*."

"Ryan Reynolds? Really?" I rummage through my desk drawer until I find an old peppermint.

"You're right. Mr. O'Reardon is our number one priority. I'll send him right back."

"Nice. Thanks a lot, April." I hit the speaker button again to end the call, smear on some lip balm, and fluff my hair. Cupping my hand over my mouth, I exhale into my palm just as Thomas O'FuckingReardon darkens my doorway.

Lou

3:00 p.m.: Thomas O'FuckingReardon

I FREEZE WITH MY hand cupped over my mouth and nose as the face that was just smashed against my boobs—the face that, at this very moment, is propped up on my nightstand and prominently displayed in at least eight places on my bookshelf so that it is the first thing I see every morning and the last thing I see each night—raises a single angular eyebrow at me.

"Sorry ..." His astute, calculating eyes dart around the room, collecting data in a few milliseconds, before returning to the strange young woman in the thrift-store blouse with a feather in her fucking hair. "I'm looking for Dr. Sterling."

His accent … God help me. I can't do this. I can't fucking do this!

"I'm …" I clear my throat and pull my shoulders back, which, I realize too late, makes it look like I'm thrusting my tits in his direction. I retract them immediately, but now, I probably look like I'm doing some kind of pop-and-lock dance move, and—*oh my God*—my armpits are leaking and he's waiting for me to say something and—

"I'm Dr. Sterling," I blurt out, shoving a hand toward the seat Celeste vacated not even twenty minutes ago. "Please, come in." Wobbly baby-fawn legs carry me over to the armchair in front of my desk as crippling panic twists my face into a smile fit for a sewer clown.

Thomas looks at me the way one might look at a person wearing a vest made out of dynamite—like his instincts are telling him to run, but his brain is forcing him to cooperate without making any sudden movements.

Slowly and without a shred of expression on his reserved, chiseled British face, Thomas enters my office—thus sucking all the air from the room—and lowers himself into the chair across from me with the stealthy grace of a hostage negotiator.

Fantastic. Great start, Sterling.

Thomas crosses his long legs—*he's so tall*—and rests his elbows on the grommeted Italian leather armrests. His fingers lace together, where they meet in the middle, and I note how many Xs his body is making right now. Three-quarters of what people say is nonverbal, and at the moment, Thomas's body language is screaming, *I don't trust you*, with a dash of, *Come any closer, and I'll scream.*

Make eye contact.

Lean forward.

Uncross your legs.

Not that much! Jesus, Lou.

I snap my thighs together as a prickly heat climbs up my neck and into my cheeks.

Thomas's expression looks exactly the same as the one on his book cover. Guarded but amused. Serious yet prone to mischief. Cocky but with every reason to be. And unfortunately, my body responds the exact same way that it does to that photo—by pumping all the blood out of my brain and into areas that do *not* fucking need it right now.

He is a human being. He is here for help. Speak to the human. You can do this.

"Hi, Thomas." I smile, focusing every bit of my attention on those two simple black pupils. They're the only ordinary, non-intimidating thing I can find to look at on this man. "I'm Dr. Luna Sterling, but you can call me Lou."

"How old are you?" he replies bluntly.

I blink. "Excuse me?"

Those crystalline eyes—so sharp, so severe—travel over my eighty-seven-dollar outfit before returning to mine, demanding answers.

"I thought I'd be seeing someone … older."

"And wiser?" I add. I hoped it would sound like a joke. It didn't.

"No offense …" He looks around my office—probably searching for clues as to where the real Dr. Sterling went and what the hell this twenty-eight-year-old dumbass is doing in his place—and wrinkles his perfectly straight nose. The gesture is so cute that I'll have no choice but to forgive him for whatever completely offensive bullshit he's about to say next. "But I was told I'd be seeing an expert."

There it is.

"Specialist," I correct.

"What?" With his accent, the word comes out more like *wot*, and it's almost as cute as that damn nose wrinkle.

"A creativity *specialist*," I say.

"Right …" He doesn't even try to hide the skepticism in his voice as his dark, discerning eyebrows furrow in the center.

"You don't seem impressed."

Oh my God! Why are you being so defensive!

"I'm five months behind on my deadline ... *Lou.*" The sound of *my* name coming out of *that* mouth would probably have caused me to spontaneously combust if it hadn't been laced with so much condescension. "I'll be impressed with anyone who can help me at this point. It's just that when my editor called last week and said she was sending me to see America's premier creativity expert—sorry, *specialist*—I just imagined I'd be seeing someone who looked a bit more like Dr. Phil and a bit less like ..." Thomas's eyes travel down the length of me, settling on my thirty-five-dollar Converse before making their way back up to my mortified face. His expression is unreadable, but if I had to guess, I'd say it looked like someone had whispered a joke in his ear and he was trying not to laugh. "You."

Now, my face is flushed for an entirely different reason. I pull my shoulders back and force myself to make eye contact, ignoring the deafening drumbeat of blood rushing in my ears.

"I might look young and ... *non-Dr. Phil-ish*, but I'm almost the same age as you. So, if thirty years is enough time for you to specialize in the art of thriller-writing, then perhaps twenty-eight years is enough time for someone else to specialize in, oh, I don't know, creativity."

Jesus Christ, Lou! Simmer down!

Thomas lifts his interlocked fingers to his lips as he studies me with narrowed eyes.

He can probably see how fast my heart is beating just by looking at the pulsating vein popping out of my forehead right now.

Oh my God. I'm gonna pass out.

Breathe, bitch. Breathe!

"What's your medium?" he finally asks.

"Excuse me?"

"I assume you must be an artist to have developed such a *specialty*." He sizes me up. "Pottery? Watercolor? Taxidermy perhaps?" With a single finger, he draws an invisible line up and down between his ear and shoulder.

Hesitantly, I reach up and touch my hair in the same spot, my fingers sliding down the length of my feather extension. A mortified heat floods my face.

Oh, I am so turning those books around tonight. Thomas O'Reardon, you are facing the wall from now on.

"No?" He smirks. "Photography then? Oh God, not poetry."

"Pencil," I manage to reply without breaking the one I'm holding in half.

"Pencil?" he scoffs.

"Yes, pencil. Now, if you don't mind, can we please—"

"I'd like to see this riveting pencil work." Thomas pulls out his phone and looks at me expectantly. "What's your Instagram?"

What?!

"I … don't have an Instagram account."

"Bollocks." He begins tapping the screen. "All twenty-eight-year-old artists have an Instagram account."

"I hardly see how that's any of your—"

"Got it." He looks up at me and beams with pride.

I thought I loved his pensive smirk, but if I could wake up to a full-on Thomas O'Reardon grin every morning, I would never wish for anything ever again. But the giddy swell in my chest immediately deflates when I remember that he is now my fucking client. The only time I will ever see him smile like that— or see him at all—is on Fridays from three to three fifty p.m. Period.

Thomas turns his phone to face me, and there, staring back, is my goddamn Instagram page—@lunarrrrt. My face, my internal organs, my hope of ever becoming a professional adult liquify and slide down my pant leg into my burgundy Converse low-tops. I'd rather him stumble upon a collection of poorly lit naked photos of me on the toilet than sit here and have to watch him look at every piece of art I've ever poured myself into.

"Clever name. It's like Luna and art, but—"

"With a little growl. Yeah." My gaze lands somewhere on the carpet next to his spotless black dress shoe, which probably cost more than my rent. I try not to watch as Thomas's self-satisfied smile morphs into a frown so deep that I can't decide if he's going to need a trash can to barf into or a priest to bless the images away.

After what feels like the longest twenty seconds of my life, Thomas shakes his head and releases a full-bodied laugh at my expense.

"What?" I snap, fighting the urge to crawl under my desk and die.

"I thought *I* was mental." Thomas turns the screen toward me again, revealing a zombified portrait I drew a few years ago. "Is that George Washington? Bloody brilliant."

"No." I snatch the phone out of his hand and slap it facedown on the desk behind me. "It's Alexander Hamilton."

Thomas grins again, but I will not be disarmed this time.

"Forgive me." He chuckles with a hand over his heart. "I didn't recognize him without his … nose."

"It's an honest mistake. Shall we begin?"

"Yes. Please." Thomas uncrosses his legs and leans forward, resting his elbows on his knees. "You can start by telling me where you came up with those gloriously morbid images."

My breath hitches, and my heart skips one, three, ten beats as I find myself assaulted by Thomas O'Reardon's wide-eyed singular interest. I feel like an ant being roasted under a magnifying glass, but I don't even mind because it means I get a better look at the sun.

I swallow and say, "We're not here to talk about me," with absolutely zero conviction behind my words.

And he knows it.

"*We* might not be, but *I* am." He tilts his head in the direction of his phone on my desk. "That … is what I need. Where do you get it?"

"What?" I ask. "My inspiration?"

He nods, eyes alight. I don't want to indulge him, but his posture is so open now. The Xs are gone, replaced by the rapt attention of a good listener. Nobody fucking listens to me around here, but for some reason, Thomas O'Reardon is now hanging on my every word.

"Fine." I sigh in defeat, cueing up the rehearsed, abbreviated, safe-for-human-consumption version of my trauma.

Everyone who has suffered a loss has this story locked and loaded. The version they can recite on autopilot. The version they share with coworkers and casual acquaintances and nosy bartenders who ask too many damn questions.

"My dad died when I was twelve, and the only thing that really made me feel better was normalizing it, you know? Reminding myself that everybody dies. Because if everybody dies, then losing my dad wasn't some unfair tragedy; it was just ... a normal part of life."

Thomas doesn't show overt sympathy or nod in understanding, but the tiny crease between his eyebrows and the downward pull on the corners of his mouth say enough. He waits for me to continue, and something occurs to me. Other than Adelynn, who doesn't speak to me at all, I think this is the most a client has ever let me say before cutting me off.

I smile, both at the novelty of having someone's undivided attention and the ridiculousness of what I'm about to admit. "My way of normalizing death was to imagine what everyone around me would look like if they were zombies." I shrug. "It sounds weird, but it made me feel better. And drawing what I saw in my head seemed to help even more. It gave me something to do with my hands, kept my mind occupied... ...." I drop my eyes and let out a small laugh. "I guess I just never stopped."

"So"—Thomas smirks, his impassive face finally coming back to life—"how would *I* look as a zombie?"

Devastating.

"Disgusting. Truly. I'd decapitate you as a public service."

I inwardly cringe at my unprofessional joke, but Thomas laughs anyway. Even his laugh is controlled, refined.

"You are not what I was expecting," he says.

Warmth blooms in my stomach, but I force myself to shake off his spell, sit up straighter, and rest my pencil-holding hand

27

on my clipboard. "I told you about me. Now … where do you get your inspiration?"

"If I knew that, I wouldn't be here, would I?" Thomas crosses his arms over his chest.

Another X. Shit.

"Um, okay. Let's start at the beginning. What inspired you to write your first book, *Blood Oath*?"

"You've done your homework."

Thomas rises from his chair and walks over to the bookshelves beside me. He stands with his hands in his pockets, casually perusing the titles as he speaks. I was relieved when he put some distance between us, but now that he's facing away from me, I'm able to freely admire the rest of him, which is even crueler. Thomas is the picture of cool confidence in his charcoal-gray slacks and moss-green sweater, pulled on over an untucked white tee. They are the clothes of a very wealthy man, worn with the ease of a lazy day off. In fact, everything about Thomas projects coolness—his posture, his effortlessly disheveled thousand-dollar haircut, his eerily calm demeanor—everything, except for the fact that he can't even look at me right now.

"Honestly?" he continues, sliding a first-edition copy of the *Diagnostic and Statistical Manual of Mental Disorders* out a few inches before pushing it back in. "It was a bad date. I took a girl to the cinema to see some revolting horror film—*Curse of Doom*, something like that. I hoped she'd be so terrified that she'd rather get off with me for two hours than face the nightmare on the screen." He chuckles, but there's no humor behind it.

"Did it work?"

"It did not." Thomas glances at me out of the corner of his eye before quickly returning his attention to the outdated books on my shelf. "Film should have been called *Cockblock of Doom*. She laughed through the entire thing."

Thomas slides a book out called *The Anal Phase Explained* and arches an eyebrow before putting it back. "That night, I went home and began writing the scariest story I could think of. A tale so terrifying that it would have any girl trembling in her date's arms."

"So, your motivation was sexual." I swallow as soon as the words leave my mouth.

"You're a student of Freud," he muses, sliding a dexterous finger down a spine that I wish were my own. "Isn't all motivation sexual?"

"No." I aim the word mostly at myself for salivating over the person I'm supposed to be helping.

Thomas looks at me over his shoulder.

"I'm more of a Maslow girl," I say with a smile, forcing myself to stand and walk over to him.

Thomas watches me approach without blinking, and I can practically see his defenses going back up with every step I take closer. I'm invading his space and …

Fuck, he smells amazing. What is that? Fabric softener? No, all his clothes are probably dry-cleaned. Cologne? God, he smells like the ocean. Not the way the ocean actually smells, but the way the ocean feels like it should smell. Crisp and bright and cool. Refreshing. How can a person smell refreshing?

I resist the urge to bury my face in his cashmere-covered chest—barely—as I slide a more modern textbook off the shelf. Flipping it open, I easily find the brightly colored diagram I'm looking for.

"Abraham Maslow believed that people's motivations are based on what he called a *hierarchy of needs*," I explain.

Thomas's eyes shift to the image on the page—a large pyramid, divided into five horizontal levels.

"If your basic needs aren't being met, like food and water..."—I point to the bottom level of the pyramid, labeled *Physiological Needs*—"...then that's going to be your motivation."

I try to block out the scent and warmth radiating off of the man standing only inches to my left as I continue my lesson. Looking at him is out of the question.

"Once your physiological needs are met, then you can focus on Safety and Security Needs, like shelter, employment, access to medical care." I slide my finger up to the next level on the pyramid, once again feeling the weight of Thomas's rapt attention.

"Once those are met, you move on to Social Needs, like love, belonging ..." My finger hovers under the final word in the description while I silently pray for the earth to open up and swallow me whole. When it doesn't happen, I exhale a single syllable, "Sex."

I peek up at Thomas, and it's as if my lungs no longer need air. With one glance, I'm suspended somewhere between life and death. I've taken my last breath, but my heart keeps beating, probably loud enough for everyone in the office to hear. Thomas is looking at me with that book-cover smirk again, but this time, it's as if he's in on my secret. As if those really are the same eyes that have been watching over me every night. The same lips that twist in delight when my hand disappears under the covers. The same ears that have heard me gasp his name a thousand times.

But they're not.

And unless I want to lose my only hope of getting licensed, they never will be.

I drop my gaze back to the book, blinking away everything I think I just saw.

"Now that those needs are *fulfilled*"—I swallow. *By a different supermodel every week, according to TMZ*—"you've leveled up." I slide my finger up to the fourth tier. "Your new motivation is Esteem—status, respect, and accomplishments—which, evidently, doesn't inspire you very much."

Thomas exhales sharply. "You know what I need to do, don't you?"

I peek up at him and wince, my heart thrashing against my ribs like a caged bird. "You're not gonna like it."

"My publisher flew me all the way to America for this, so if you know what my problem is—"

"We have to knock you down a level," I blurt out.

"What?"

I close the book and take a deep breath, meeting his confused stare. "You said it yourself—Social Needs, specifically *romantic* social needs, are what inspire you to create, so—"

"You want me to go back to being a sexless loser." Thomas blinks, his mouth parted, as if I'd just socked him in the stomach.

"You don't have to be a loser, but..."—I clutch the book to my chest—"yes."

Thomas crosses the room and flops back into his chair. No more Xs. Just a pair of lifeless arms that drape over the armrests, as if he landed that way after being mortally wounded by my recommendation.

"What am I supposed to do?" he asks, facing my empty chair. "Join the priesthood?"

He doesn't look away when I sit down, but he doesn't make eye contact either. He just kind of stares through me.

"Maybe just don't have sex while you're writing," I suggest with an apologetic tone. "Olympic athletes do it all the time. It really works."

"Celibacy," he huffs. "Is that all?"

"Actually ... no." I cringe. "I also think you should find someone that you want to impress again, like the girl from your date—some unattainable muse. It could be a celebrity, a supermodel—it doesn't matter. That longing is what drove you to create before. It could work again."

Thomas finally looks at me, but when he does, I wish that he hadn't. His features are hard, his sharp blue stare colder than a metal blade. All traces of the cocky smirk I wake up to every morning are gone, replaced by a glare that has me questioning everything I just said and my entire life in general.

Thomas O'Reardon is here, in your office, and you managed to make him hate you. Brava, bitch.

Thomas shakes his head and gazes once again at my bookshelf. The break in eye contact makes me physically sag in my seat with relief.

" 'Write about what you want the most and experience the least,' " he says, almost to himself. Then, with more acceptance than anger this time, his eyes flick back to mine. "That's what my creative writing professor used to say."

I hold his stare, along with my breath, as Thomas's jaw flexes and his nostrils flare.

"Social Needs," he finally grinds out.

I press my lips together and nod.

"Fuck."

Thomas and I don't speak as I walk him back to the lobby. When he makes a beeline for the exit, I head toward the check-in desk on the left.

April watches us from the other side of the Plexiglas window with unbridled excitement.

I slide his file to her through the open slot at the bottom. "April, please put Mr. O'Reardon down for the same time next week."

Thomas pauses in the doorway and turns around. "April, please warn Dr. Sterling's other clients that she's an evil, morbid sadist."

As soon as he exits, I drop my forehead onto the window, feeling like I just ran an emotional marathon. Backward. With heels on. In the dark.

April taps the Plexiglas beneath my smooshed cheek with one perfectly manicured fingernail. "How'd it go?"

I press a thumbs-up against the glass as I notice an old man approaching the window out of the corner of my eye.

"Excuse me, miss," he says to April. "May I please change my appointment? I'd like to see the sadist."

Thomas

I DROP THE KEYS to my rented car and my rented flat on my rented foyer table next to a rented bowl full of fake fucking rented fruit and sigh. The dull thud of metal landing on wood is the only sound in this sterile, soundproof prison. In any other major city, you can't get away from the noise. No matter how expensive the hotel room or how many floors up you are, the sirens and jackhammers and car horns slither their way in through the windows and the vents, creating the white noise of civilization that reminds you that you're never alone. Not really.

In this flat, I can hear my own fingernails growing.

I walk down the marble hallway into the sitting room, which doesn't look like it has ever actually been sat in, and open the door to the balcony. The din of the world nineteen stories below greets me like a pet waiting to be let in.

I leave the door open, welcoming the noise, as I turn and face the opulent emptiness that will be my home for the next six weeks. A pointless purgatory. If I couldn't write this manuscript in six months from the comfort of my own home, what the hell makes them think I'm going to be able to do it in six weeks here? I don't even know why I agreed to come. I should have just wired the million-dollar advance back to my publisher when my first deadline expired or after my first extension or my second. I know when I'm on the cusp of a breakthrough, when a few more weeks might make all the difference, and this is not one of those times.

This feels permanent.

I glare at my laptop, lying on the counter separating the kitchen from the sitting room. The idea of opening it and staring at a blinking cursor on a blank page makes me want to chuck it into the abyss nineteen stories below, so I cross the room, grab the slender source of all my problems, and stomp down the hallway. I realize it is irrational to villainize an inanimate object, but fuck this thing. It's going in the office, where I can shut the door on it and refuse to acknowledge its presence for the next month and a half—at which point, I will go home, say that I tried, and finally, irrevocably admit defeat.

I place the device on a polished wooden desk next to a floor-to-ceiling window and pause, recognizing the street that my therapist's office is on in the distance.

"We have to knock you down a level."

Her words echo in my mind as I flop into the ergonomically advanced, environmentally sustainable desk chair and swivel toward the window.

It's not enough that I can't write. Now, I can't even have sex to take my mind off the fact that I can't write.

As much as I loathed her recommendation, I have to admit, I did love watching her blush when she said it.

Before I know it, my mobile is in my hand, and I'm swiping through Dr. Sterling—Lou's—Instagram all over again. She really is a brilliant artist. The way she manages to capture her subject's humanity by stripping it away is unlike anything I've ever seen. I wonder what she'd charge for a portrait. Whatever it might be, I'd pay double, quadruple, just to find out what she sees when she looks at me. Which features would be lost to the rot. Which would endure. Would I still look like the smug, successful prick the rest of the world sees me as, or would she find the emptiness lurking just below the surface?

There are no self-portraits or selfies of any kind on her page, so I find myself Googling *Dr. Luna Sterling Atlanta* out of curiosity. I tell myself it's because I want to verify her credentials—she seemed far too young to be an expert in her field—but when I see her photo on the Atlanta Psychology Associates website, I know I'm completely full of shit.

I just wanted to see her again.

The ghost of her scent tickles the recesses of my brain as I stare into those haunting honey-colored eyes. When Lou stood next to me at her bookshelf earlier, she was so close that I picked up a hint of warm, smoky incense trapped in her wild, dark hair—something mystical and earthy. It occurred to me then that she seemed more like a witch doctor than a psychologist— a beautiful young witch doctor, who draws gruesome zombie portraits with precision yet blushes when she says the word *sex*.

If the word alone affects her that much, I'd love to see—

Instantly, my mind conjures an image of Lou lying naked on her back. Her dark hair spills across the bed like waves on a midnight sea. Her breathing turns to panting, her back arches on a strangled cry, and as she whimpers through her release, a pink flush washes over her glistening, golden skin.

"Fuck," I hiss, setting my mobile facedown on the desk.

I scrub a hand over my jaw, wondering when I became such a shitty excuse for a human being. My publisher is paying for me to get top-notch therapy on another bloody continent, and I'm more interested in shagging my psychologist than taking her advice.

Picking up my mobile again, I quickly navigate away from Lou's headshot and over to my web browser, where I search *Abraham Maslow's Hierarchy of Needs*.

I find the exact same textbook Lou showed me in her office and click the Buy Now button. I even pay an exorbitant amount for next-day shipping just to prove to myself that I'm taking this seriously.

As I walk back into the sitting room, now filled with the sounds of a foreign city on a Friday night, I decide to finally reply to the text my agent sent earlier, asking how my first session went.

Not terrible, I type back.

And much to my surprise, it's the truth.

Lou

"GIRL, JUST ADMIT IT. The fact that he was an asshole made him, like, fifteen times hotter." Dee wraps her smirking lips around the curly straw spiraling out of her fishbowl margarita.

On Fridays, I usually meet my friends from grad school—Dee, Courtney, and Beth—at The Yacht Club for drinks. It's a shitty bar with a fancy name and the only place in the city where you can get a margarita served in an actual fishbowl with two paper umbrellas, at least three citrus fruit skewers, a random flavored Popsicle, and an entire bottle of off-brand Mexican beer sticking out of it for less than the price of the aspirin you'll have to beg your roommate to go buy for you the next morning when he wakes you up to tell you that you're half-naked on the kitchen floor. *Again.*

"Fine. It made him hotter." I slump back against the splintery wooden booth seat and rub my temples with both hands. "If that's even possible."

My eyes drift to the far side of the room, where a collection of metal trays with paintings of animals dressed like pirates and boat captains adorns the exposed brick wall.

"I can't do this," I mumble. "I can't be his *therapist*. I can't even be in the same room as him without ovulating."

I sit up, tearing my eyes away from a hummingbird in a three-cornered hat, and look to Courtney. Dee is no help in these kinds of situations. Or any situation really.

"Honestly, the way this fellowship is going, I don't know if I should be anybody's therapist," I admit before sucking down almost half of my toilet bowl–sized beverage through a twisty yellow straw.

"Oh, honey," Courtney coos with her sweet Southern accent and her big brown eyes. "What's goin' on?"

"My clients only have rich-people problems. I was trained to treat actual disorders, not … FOMO." I dig a Swedish Fish out of my drink with two hooked fingers and pop it into my mouth. "I think they gave me all their reject clients too. One of the desperate housewives I saw today had her phone out the entire time, so she could watch her housekeeper on the nanny cam. What am I supposed to do with that?"

"See? This is why I got a postdoc working with kids," Dee chimes in. "I keep tellin' you, kids are where it's *at*. They don't care if you smell like Fireball at ten a.m. You can take a nap under your desk while they color and call it 'autonomous art therapy.'" She makes finger quotes in the air around those last three words. "And when they show out, all you gotta do is give 'em *the look*."

Dee demonstrates her scariest, most threatening face. She's right. That shit is terrifying.

Courtney recoils in horror before turning back toward me. "Okay, or … maybe you could switch to behavior modification. I'm lovin' my fellowship so far. Y'all, when my clients don't follow the treatment plan, I get to spray 'em in the face with a water pistol."

"Shut the fuck up." I cough-laugh so hard that I almost choke on the rubbery red fish I was chewing. "You do not."

"It's just a little squirt gun." Courtney wrinkles her nose like a bunny.

"Gangsta." Dee shakes her head in disbelief.

I shake my head, too, but it's in disappointment. "Freud failed me."

Courtney leans forward, a mischievous little smile on her sweet, churchgoing face, and whispers, "Also ... I learned how to classically condition Brian to hand me his credit card every time I click my tongue. He doesn't even know he's doin' it."

Dee chuckles. "Hell yes. You do what you gotta do, right? For example, this weekend, I reverse-psychologied myself into some very mediocre head," she says, sweeping her nonexistent hair over her shoulder with pride. She used to have shoulder-length dreadlocks, but she buzzed them off while we were pulling all-nighters, trying to finish our dissertations, and never looked back.

"With Alcoholic Mike?" I ask.

"Bitch, that was two weeks ago," Dee snaps. "This was Vasectomy Mike. Keep up."

I smirk. "Sorry. I forgot that you only date unavailable, middle-aged white guys named Mike."

"Or Matt," Dee corrects me with a scoff. "*Anyway,* so I was all like ..." Dee switches to an innocent Valley girl voice and bats her eyelashes as she giggles. "*Do* not *go down on me. I can tell you're thinking about it. Stop iiiiit. Oh my God, you are* so *bad.*"

Courtney and I burst out laughing as the missing member of our quartet slides into the booth across from me. Beth has the build and personality of a former high school linebacker who wasn't good enough to go pro and became a boot camp drill sergeant instead.

"Sorry I'm late. I think I tore my meniscus in that last session." Beth yanks the beer bottle out of Courtney's margarita and begins chugging it.

"Oh no. What happened?" Courtney asks, looking her over as if her meniscus might be located somewhere above the table.

"You know how I like to use physical analogies with my life-coaching clients? Well, today's theme was mental flexibility," Beth says with a belch.

"You busted out the Twister mat again, didn't you?" I ask, trying to squelch my smile.

Beth points Courtney's now empty beer bottle directly at my face. "I did what had to be done, Sterling. Get off my jock."

As if summoned by the word *jock*, our server, Mark—a bearded redneck in a camo trucker hat and a Hooters T-shirt with the sleeves cut off—appears out of thin air. "Hey, Beth. What can I get for y—"

"Two Fuck Me in the Graveyards and a bathtub full of Bengay, stat," she barks, eyeing the bottle sticking out of my margarita now.

"Add some fuzzy handcuffs, and you just described my Tuesday night." Mark high-fives me with a chuckle as my friends choke on their beverages.

"Hey, boo," Mark says, and I know what's coming before the words even leave his mouth. "I need your half of the rent, like, yesterday."

I give him an irritated smile. "I'm on it."

"Okay, but, like, what does that mean?" Mark asks, lazily dragging his finger across the edge of the table.

"It means, I just need to move some things around."

"Oh, you need to *move some things around*, huh?" Mark turns his back to the table and twerks for emphasis.

I throw my paper umbrella at him like a dart, hoping the pointy part will stab him in the ass but no such luck. It bounces off like a quarter.

"As much as I'd love to keep doing this, I gotta go," I say, sucking down what's left of my drink as Mark dismisses me with an air kiss and sashays toward the bar.

"The fuck, Sterling? I just got here." Beth pouts.

"She's going to get some booty," Dee says. "Look at that face."

I roll my eyes. "Actually, I'm going home to eat a box of Lucky Charms and drink for free, but thanks for pretending like I have a sex life."

"Hold up. When was the last time you got some?" Dee asks.

"I don't know." I shrug. "I had that summer thing with Tristan."

Dee sprays a fine mist of blue margarita all over the table as she chokes on her laughter. "That summer thing? We physically shoved him into your Uber after he hit on you at the bar!" She points toward the splintery counter at the back of the room, draped with fisherman netting. "We made you take him home, and then he puked on your carpet and came in your hair!"

I cross my arms and slide further down in my seat. "Not in that order."

"Face it, woman," Dee says, arching a smug eyebrow. "You're not gonna be able to help this fine-ass author man until you take care of your dick problem."

"She has a point, hon," Courtney chimes in with an apologetic smile. "It's like how, on an airplane, you have to put on your own oxygen mask before you can help anybody else."

I poke a mystery piece of fruit at the bottom of my glass with my straw and sigh. "I'm not saying you're wrong. It's just … where would I even find somebody? All I do is work and study and hang out with you guys."

"No more excuses." Beth slams her palms down on the table and leans across it, making me jump. "Think, Sterling. I guarantee that you know at least one guy who would bang you out right now, no questions asked."

I glance at all of their expectant faces, but my mind is blank.

"We can always grab you somebody from the bar again." Dee chuckles.

"No!" I shout. "No. I … I think I know a guy."

"Attagirl!" Beth reaches across the table and slaps me on the arm. "Now, go on. Make us proud."

I nod and suck down the last dregs of my margarita, needing every drop of liquid courage I can get.

"I gotta go too," Courtney says with a bashful little smile. "Brian and I just started watchin' *Outlander*." She waggles her eyebrows on that last word to let us all know that *Outlander* equals sexy time.

We groan in cringey unison.

I don't know what happens after that. One second, I'm slurping bottom-shelf tequila through a straw, and the next, all of us are holding our credit cards up in the air like mindless robots.

"Thanks, ladies!" Courtney twiddles her fingers at us as she slides out of the booth. "So sweet of y'all to pick up the check!"

Dee shakes her head as Courtney bounces away. "Stone-cold gangsta."

Lou

THWUMP, THWUMP, THWUMP.

I never knew the rhythm of my headboard hitting the wall could sound so … *sad*. I'll admit, between finishing my PhD and prepping for this fellowship position, it's not something I've gotten to hear all that often, but when I have, it's been more like the rapid *WHAM-WHAM-WHAM-WHAM-WHAM* of a jackhammer than the polite knocking of an anxious Girl Scout.

I could have called a handful of guys from the bar whom Dee and Beth had forced on me in the past, but after the last one, well, *you know* … I decided to go in a different direction. Someone older. More distinguished. Someone intelligent, with shared interests.

I realize now that I might have overcorrected a bit.

I glance across my bedroom at the cap and gown still hanging from my closet door in an attempt to make myself feel better about the situation.

See? You're not fucking your professor. You're fucking your former *professor. It's totally different.*

This is what grown-up professionals do. They have no lives or hobbies, so they sleep with their colleagues out of convenience and desperation. This is progress. This is normal adult behavior.

The only other sound in my room besides the *thwump-thwump-thwump* is the ever-present din of sirens and car horns and dogs barking outside. The inner-city noise here has always been comforting to me. It's like this subtle, constant reminder that I'm not at the commune anymore. That I really did make it out of there.

I glance over at my window—the source of the sound—but my blinds are closed. A series of vertical shadows slash across the white vinyl slats, reminding me that there are a dozen steel bars bolted to the other side. Instead of distracting me from my shame by the outside world, this view only adds to it. Not only am I fucking my former professor—who might possibly be twice my age—but I'm also still poor.

Eager to wrap this particularly regrettable decision up and begin repressing it as quickly as possible, I lift my hips and try not to sound as phony as I feel when I moan, "Oh, Peter. Yes. Right there."

"Peter?" His delicate missionary thrusts—pokes really—come to a complete stop as my partner lifts his graying, albeit handsome, head and scowls at me in disapproval. "Luna, we've talked about this. You're to call me Dr. Callahan when you're in my office."

"Your what?"

"Shh …" He smooshes an authoritative finger against my lips. "I know it's difficult with this much passion burning between us, but we must try to remain quiet. These university walls are paper-thin."

Oh … my fucking … God.

The *thwump-thwump-thwump* resumes, and I stare at my ceiling, trying as hard as I can to make it collapse on top of me with my mind.

It could be worse. You could have puke on your carpet and cum in your hair.

A little role-playing never hurt anybody.

Maybe if you go along with it, he'll hurry up and finish. This is taking forever.

Just then, I hear Mark come home from his shift at the bar. The sound of the front door slamming closed behind him gives me an idea.

"Dr. Callahan," I gasp dramatically, "it sounds like the Social-Emotional Assessment class just let out. We don't have much time."

"You're right," he whisper-shouts. "We'll have to be quick!"

I grasp the headboard and grit my teeth as he begins pounding into me like a caffeinated jackrabbit—the *thwumps* now accompanied by the *snap-crackle-pop* of his joints—for all of five seconds before he jerks, goes frighteningly still, and collapses on top of me.

I lie there, motionless, for a few seconds before I finally lift my hand and tap what I really hope isn't a cadaver on the shoulder. "Dr. Callahan?"

Suddenly, Dr. C lurches off of me like I just pressed a pair of defibrillator paddles to his chest and yells, "Time is of the essence!" He rolls off the bed and begins yanking his clothes back on with a surprising amount of agility.

"We can't risk being seen together on campus," he insists, shoving his socked feet back into a pair of brown loafers that look to be at least five years my senior. "I'll leave first."

I sit up, clutching the sheet to my chest, but before I can come up with my next line, Dr. Callahan gives me a quick peck on the forehead and exits my bedroom with the stealth of a secret agent.

As soon as I hear his putty-colored sedan sputter out of my driveway, all the tension in my body releases at once, like the snapping of a rubber band. I fall backward onto my pillow and stare at the ceiling, wondering how it's possible to feel even more sexually frustrated than I was before.

With a heavy sigh, I roll onto my side and pull the top drawer of my nightstand open.

A soft, comforting *buzzzzzz* comes to life in my hand, which I promptly slide under the sheets.

I close my eyes and try to re-create the scene from a few minutes earlier in my mind. Only instead of Dr. Callahan hovering over me, it's ...

I let my head fall to the side and open my hooded eyelids just enough to find my muse.

My Walmart bookcases sag under the weight of a decade's worth of textbooks and notebooks and case studies and assessment manuals. What won't fit on their shelves is piled high on the desk under the window. But one shelf—one perfect little shelf—directly across from my pillow has room to spare. Instead of being crammed together in rows so tight that a diamond might form from the pressure, there are only eight books on this shelf. Eight pristine hardback thrillers, each standing upright with their covers on display, but one is turned around backward.

The one front and center. The one with the largest author photo on the back.

A familiar pair of eyes, shrouded in mystery yet sparkling with brilliance, watch me through the vertical and horizontal slashes of shadow and light filtering in through the window. A sinister, self-satisfied smirk tugs on his full lips, like he enjoys seeing other men fail to please me. He enjoys watching me crawl back to my fantasies of him night after night, knowing that his chiseled face is the first one I see every morning and that his whispered name is the one on my lips every night.

"Thomas ..." I pant, slamming my eyes shut as that rubber band begins to tighten again.

I picture that perfect face hovering over mine as my back arches off the mattress. I picture the genius behind it—the man who dreamed up the most fantastical, frightening, spellbinding stories I've ever read—and salivate over the things he could do to me with a mind that wicked. Then, I picture his permanent smirk darken into something feral and ferocious and utterly fucking unhinged as he watches me come undone beneath him.

I suck in one last breath before a whirlpool of pleasure grips my body and pulls me under. The outside world disappears as a delicious, pulsating darkness swallows me whole. I cling to it for as long as I can, and I swear, from somewhere far away, I hear the sound of a book crashing to the floor.

Thomas

IT HAS BEEN SIX days, twenty-two hours, and fifty-nine minutes since I called my therapist an evil, morbid sadist and walked out of this waiting room. Not my finest moment. But I've had some time to think about it—six days and twenty-*three* hours, to be exact—and as much as I hate to admit it, Dr. Sterling—Lou—was right. About everything.

That doesn't make her recommendation any easier to follow, however. The silence in that flat and the silence in my own head as I struggle to come up with even a single viable idea would be a lot more tolerable if I had a cute American companion around to help drown it out.

"Mr. O'Reardon," the bird behind the counter calls out.

She eye-fucks me as I approach, glossy lips spreading wide, further proving that Lou's assessment of my motivational problem is one hundred percent accurate. Ten years ago, I would have killed to have a girl look at me like that. It quite literally drove me mad. I attended university all day and stayed up all night, feverishly writing *Blood Oath*, oftentimes falling asleep at my desk and waking up for class a few hours later with indentations the shape of computer keys marring my face.

But now that I get those looks on a daily basis, well, here I am.

I walk down the short hallway to Lou's office, dreading whatever *delightful* recommendation she's going to have for me today. I'm also dreading what's expected of me as soon as I pass through that door. It would be a lot easier to bare my soul if I were talking to someone who looked like a seventeenth-century monk or a bored, middle-aged barman who's only pretending to listen while he covertly glances at his watch for the ninth time. I can't talk to *her*. I can't even look at her without thinking of ways to make her blush again.

I step through the doorway of Lou's office and watch as she drops what appears to be a broken mug into a small bin. She's wearing a dress this week—a cream-colored button-up, belted at the waist to accentuate the curves I didn't need to know she had—and her long, wild hair has been tamed into shiny, smooth waves, aside from a few braids and that bloody feather, of course. She looks like she spent some time getting ready today, and selfishly, I hope it was on my account.

Fuck. I should ask for a different therapist.

I rap my knuckles on the doorframe and watch as Lou's stunned face lifts and brightens.

"Thomas!" She greets me like she's elated to see me, but after the way I behaved last week, I can't imagine why that would be the case.

My publisher must be paying her well.

I furrow my brow at the thought, which causes Lou's smile to falter.

"Oh, um, please ..." She extends a hand toward the chair nearest the door. "Have a seat."

Lou picks up her clipboard and walks around to the chair in front of her desk. Her legs wobble slightly, and I notice that she's wearing high-heeled boots and tights this week instead of trainers and trousers.

Interesting.

She takes a moment to go through what I now realize must be some kind of ritual. Just like she did during our first session, Lou straightens her back, crosses and then promptly uncrosses her legs, clutches her pencil tightly, lifts her chin, and finally makes eye contact.

Her irises are the color of honey. I find it fitting because even though this woman is almost intimidatingly beautiful—and equally intelligent—there is a sweetness about her, a warmth that I imagine most people don't look hard enough to see.

I fold my arms across my chest as I settle in and notice the corners of Lou's mouth turn down as I do.

She clears her throat and sits up even straighter. "So, have you made any progress since last week?"

"No," I state bluntly, hating the way her hopeful smile deflates on that one word.

"Oh, well, that's okay. We're just getting started." Her smile returns, but this time, it's forced. "So, last week, we identified what motivates you to write and came up with some ideas about how you can—"

"Grow my hymen back?"

A snort bursts out of Lou, followed by a quiet cackle as she lifts her clipboard to cover the lower half of her face.

Her reaction is adorable, but I resist the smile I feel tugging on my lips. Smiling feels like flirting, and if she flirts back, I know I won't get a damn thing out of this trip to America, except for a life-threatening case of blue balls and a terminated contract from my publisher.

"*No,*" she says, schooling her features as she sets the clipboard back down on her lap. "We came up with some ways to *rekindle* your desire to write."

I arch an eyebrow at her sexy choice of words but don't reply.

"What I mean is, last week, we looked at internal factors contributing to your writer's block—what motivates you—so this week, I'd like to explore some possible external causes."

Lou crosses and promptly uncrosses her legs again.

Do not look at her legs. For fuck's sake, she's trying to help you. Make eye contact and keep your daft, inappropriate mouth shut, and after this appointment, you can switch to the ugliest therapist in the office.

Lou sits up straighter, fidgeting with her pencil. "Okay. So, um ..."

New plan. You're freaking her out. You have to talk.

She taps her pencil on the clipboard twice before clutching it tightly in her fist again. "Have there been any significant changes in your personal life since you completed your last book?"

"No."

Good. That was short. To the point.

"No new relationships or ... breakups?" She drops her eyes, as if bracing for my response, and my chest swells at her apparent interest in my relationship status.

I think of a hundred different flirtatious comebacks to that question, but I manage to inhibit all of them and answer with the simple truth. "Not if I can help it."

Lou's eyes lift to mine, and the relief I see in them makes not smiling really fucking hard.

"What about your living situation?" she asks. "Any changes there?"

"Not unless you count being shipped off to America and given six weeks to write a manuscript or return a million-dollar advance."

Lou coughs suddenly, as if that dollar amount caught her off guard. I guess nobody filled her in on the details of my little publishing problem. "Yeah, besides that," she rasps, glancing at a spot on her desk, where I assume her mug used to be.

I feel the sudden urge to jump up and find her some water, but I suppress it, just like every other urge I've had since I got here. "Then ... no," I respond instead. "No changes."

Lou clears her throat. "Okay, so your primary residence is still in England?"

"London. Yes."

"And have you lived in your current home long enough to write a few books there?"

I nod. "A few."

"So, you had a writing routine established." Lou sticks her thumbnail between her teeth and squints at me, as if she's working out a puzzle. "Have there been any changes to your writing environment? You weren't going to a coffee shop that shut down or anything like that?"

"No."

"What about your family? Any significant changes or stressors there?"

Suddenly feeling warm, I stand and remove my jacket. The shirt I'm wearing—a simple gray tee—must lift a few inches when I do because I notice Lou's gaze drops to my lower stomach before darting over to the wall behind me. She points to a coatrack by the door, unable to look me in the eye.

And she's uncomfortable again. Well done.

I turn my back and walk across the room, feeling an immediate sense of relief as soon as she's out of my line of sight. With every step I take farther away from her, my ability to express myself begins to return. "Nothing has changed," I say, hoping to end this incessant line of questioning. "Nothing has happened."

"Why do I get the sense that you're disappointed about that?"

Lou's question gives me pause. I hang up my jacket and allow myself to really think about what she said.

With my feet still facing the wall, I take a deep breath and say out loud the thing I've come to fear most over the last six months. "Because if nothing caused it, then there's nothing to fix. I'm just ... empty. Out of ideas. Out of inspiration. I had a good run, you know? Can't complain. But"—I force myself to turn and face Lou, whose features mirror the sadness I didn't realize I'd been carrying—"I think it might be over."

As if beckoned by her stare, my feet carry me back to the empty chair across from her. I sit, unable to tear my eyes away from the heartbreak I see reflected back at me.

Then, suddenly, Lou blinks, as if intentionally clearing the emotion from her face and replacing it with something neutral. Focused. And possibly a little pissed.

Leaning forward, Lou laces her fingers together between her knees and pins me with a direct stare. "Let me ask you something, Thomas." Her tone is assertive. I wasn't expecting that. "If you really believe that it's over, that you're never going to write another book again, then why did you agree to come all the way to America for therapy?"

I lean back in my seat and think for a moment. "I don't know. Curiosity, I suppose."

Lou cocks her head to the side again—a gesture I'm beginning to suspect means that she thinks I'm full of shit. "And maybe a little hope?"

I shrug, causing Lou to raise her eyebrows at me in annoyance.

"You want this to work—I know you do. If you didn't, you wouldn't be here right now. But for that to happen, you're going to have to talk to me."

I open my mouth but find myself rendered speechless by the realization that she's right. Again.

"Now, a minute ago, when I asked about your family, your immediate reaction was to physically escape from the question."

Is that what I did?

I look over my shoulder at my jacket on the coatrack.

"So, spill it," she says, obviously fed up with my coy bullshit.

I laugh and shake my head. "Now, you sound like Dr. Phil."

"And now, you're changing the subject."

I hold my hands up in surrender. "All right. Fine. What do you want to know?"

"Whatever it is that you've spent the last five minutes *not* telling me."

I sigh and tip my head back, staring at the ceiling as I gather my thoughts. I tell stories for a living—or at least, I *did*—but I've never told this one. I'm not even sure where to begin.

"How about this? You're a man of words. Why don't you start by giving me one word to describe your family, and we'll go from there?"

"Smothering." The adjective falls out of my mouth before I have a chance to even consider another.

I don't look at Lou, but I can see her dark head nodding slightly in my peripheral vision. "How are they smothering?"

I focus on the light fixture overhead. It's turned off. I didn't notice before, but the entire room is lit by natural light from the window and a tall lamp in the corner behind Lou's desk. It's ... nice.

"I have two older sisters—Maggie and Rose. They've always treated me like a human baby doll. I'm confident that if I hadn't moved to London the second I graduated, they'd still be trying to spoon-feed me to this day."

"And your parents?" Lou asks.

I struggle to formulate a response over the sound of a pencil scratching my every word onto a piece of paper. I'm a fucking *New York Times* best-selling author—this shouldn't be so hard.

"They ... don't like each other very much."

"What does that look like?" Lou asks quietly.

Scritch, scratch, scritch.

"It looks like ... *nothing*. They don't talk or even sit in the same room, if they can help it. I assume they must have loved each other at some point to get married, but by the time I came along ... you would have never guessed it."

I glance down at Lou, and the sadness I picked up on earlier is etched into her features again. Before, I assumed that she was mirroring something I was feeling, but now, I'm not so sure. This feels personal.

"My father has mistresses," I say without thinking. Lou's eyes lift to mine. "Always has. I remember a few of them calling the house when I was young. I hated those phone calls. Mum would get so clingy afterward. She used to crawl into bed with me at night and hold me while she cried."

Lou flinches and closes her eyes, as if what I said physically hurt her. I think back to what she shared about her father dying when she was young, and I wonder if she had the same experience. If her mother curled around her like a boa constrictor in the middle of the night and cried herself to sleep too.

Lou's eyes open and bore into mine. "Smothering."

I nod.

The room is so quiet that I hear her swallow.

"I imagine an experience like that could make someone grow up to fear adult relationships," she says.

Something in her eyes tells me that statement might be more autobiographical than hypothetical, but I don't press her about it. In fact, I don't want to talk about it at all.

I cross my arms and lean back in my seat. "I wouldn't call it a fear so much as a general aversion," I say, trying to lighten the mood. "I've seen the marriage brochure. I'm not interested."

Lou nods. Not in sympathy, but in solidarity. I can't look away from the story in her eyes. I want to know the beginning, middle, and end.

I want to know who smothered her.

A moment passes between us—a second, maybe two— where our eye contact goes from being conversational to … something else. The appropriate amount of time before someone looks away or clears their throat has come and gone, and yet here we are. A thrill shoots up my spine when I realize that Lou is defying social norms to hold my stare. That this attraction, connection, whatever it is, isn't one-sided.

Lou drops her gaze first, blinking down at the clipboard on her lap as a rosy pink floods her cheeks. And just like before, I feel a rush of relief as soon as our eye contact is broken, as if I can think again. Breathe again.

This is not fucking helpful.

Lou shifts in her seat and picks up where we left off. "It sounds like your father seeks comfort from other women, and your mother seeks it from you, the baby of the family. How has she been ever since you moved to London?"

"Fine, I suppose. The same." I shrug.

Lou's eyes narrow before sliding down to my crossed arms. Glancing back up at me, she says, "How are *you*, Thomas?"

The concern I hear in her voice makes my chest ache.

"I'm empty, Lou. How are you?"

Lou smiles. It's not a smile of pity or politeness; it's bashful and beautiful and completely fucking inappropriate, which only makes me love it more.

Glancing down at her notepad, Lou scribbles something quickly and bites her lip.

"What?" I ask.

"Nothing."

"What did I say?"

Lou lifts her eyes, and they sparkle like gold. "You ... wrote a poem."

"What? That?" I gesture to her paper with a laugh. "Yeah, Dr. Seuss would be so proud. Perhaps I should sign it for you. It's the only thing I've written in months."

Lou's eyes light up. "Oh my God. Really? Would you sign my copy of *Ruby Lies* too?" She gestures over her shoulder toward her desk, and a chuckle bursts out of me.

"You've read my books?"

Lou slaps a hand over her mouth in pure, undiluted mortification, and it's the cutest thing I've ever seen. Of course she reads psychological thrillers. It fits her perfectly.

"I am so sorry," she mumbles into her palm. "I just went full fangirl. That was so unprofessional."

"No." I chuckle, shaking my head. "I'm the one who owes *you* the apology."

She blinks. "For what?"

"For behaving like a proper tosser."

"Can you repeat that in American, please?" she asks, lowering her hand to reveal a hesitant smile.

"Douche bag. Asshole. Entitled prick."

Lou laughs, and I realize with a pang of guilt that I don't want another therapist. I want this one. In two sessions, she has me speaking in bloody rhymes. Maybe she can help me after all.

"You've been fine," Lou says. "Trust me. Most of my clients just come here so they have someone to scream at once a week."

The thought of people mistreating this woman makes my blood boil. "I don't want to be one of those clients," I snap before regaining my composure. "I'd much prefer to be the brooding, emotionally repressed sort."

"Well, mission accomplished," Lou quips, pressing her lips together.

Perhaps it's the ever-present ticking clock in my mind, telling me that our session is almost over, or maybe it's the thought of spending another week in soundproof solitary confinement, but something in the finality of her tone makes me panic.

"Let me make it up to you," I blurt out. "Let me"—I look around her office, stalling for time, searching for inspiration. My eyes land on her desk, and I remember her coughing fit earlier— "buy you a drink after this. With my sincerest apologies."

Lou looks as surprised as I feel.

Buy her a drink? Did you just fucking ask her out?

Lou's eyes are wide as she begins stammering through the politest of rejections. "Oh, wow. Um ... God, Thomas, I ... I wish I could, but ..."

I stand abruptly, eager to put her out of the awkward misery I've just inflicted upon her. "Right. Of course. I'll just..."—I jerk my thumb in the direction of the door—"see you next week."

I take two steps toward the exit when I hear rustling behind me.

"Thomas, wait!"

I turn and find Lou standing in front of her chair, clutching her clipboard to her chest.

"I can't ... I mean, I'm not allowed ... but ... um ..." Her gaze travels over to her bookshelf, and it occurs to me that she's the one searching for inspiration now. Whatever she finds on that shelf must do the trick because her eyes suddenly light up and flick back to mine. "I can see you in a group!"

"A group?" I ask with a frown. "Like a group dinner?"

"No, like ... group therapy."

Group what?

That's not exactly the response I was hoping for, but ... I do think I need to see her more than once a week if I have any hope of finishing this book on time. Or even starting it. Or not going mad in that silent nineteenth-story box of shame.

"What *kind* of group therapy?" I ask, eyeing her sideways.

"Any kind!" She beams a little too brightly. "All kinds. What kind do you want? Depression, anxiety, anger management, meditation ..."

I have a hard enough time expressing myself to Lou when we're alone. The idea of having to do it in front of her *and* a half-dozen American strangers makes me want to book an early flight back to London, but when I look at her hopeful face, I can't even pretend like I'm not going to go. I'd probably go to group electroshock therapy if it meant I could spend more time with her.

"Creativity!" she blurts out. "You wanna do a creativity group? Let's do a creativity group!"

"All right." I nod, taking another step toward the door. I need to go before I manage to bugger this up any worse than I already have.

"Great!" Lou says. "I'll have April contact you with the details. Oh, and, Thomas?"

I pause in the doorway.

"I think you should rent a treadmill." When my eyebrows pull together, she elaborates. "That's your homework for this week. Repetitive, mindless physical activity is great for creativity."

"Okay ... well, see you next week."

I cross the threshold and exhale as soon as I make it to the hallway. I don't know how I could have possibly made that session any more awkward, but somehow, Lou finds a way to beat me at my own game.

Her voice echoes down the hallway behind me with one final recommendation. "And don't forget to keep it in your pants!"

Lou

"OKAY, SO LET ME get this crooked ..."

Mark, Dee, Courtney, and Beth are huddled around me in our usual booth at The Yacht Club, staring at me like I just sprouted a third eye—and not the nice, symmetrical, cosmic kind. It's the kind that's all bulbous like a frog's and sticks off the side of your head and won't stop fucking blinking.

Mark continues his delicate summary of my dumbass idea for the benefit of everyone at the table. "Daddy Harry Potter asked you out, and you said—"

"Group therapy?" Dee interrupts with a scowl.

"I ... I didn't know what else to say!" I stammer. "He looked so rejected when I told him no."

"Well, *I* think it makes perfect sense," Courtney says with her sweet-tea twang, patting the back of my hand. "It's like when I was in high school. My parents wouldn't let me date, so if I wanted to see a guy, it had to be, like, a group thing."

Beth slurps from the rim of her fish-bowl beergarita and pins Courtney with a bewildered stare. "You mean, like an orgy?"

Courtney's cheeks flush. "Sometimes."

Beth left our graduate program after getting her master's degree. She felt like life coaching would be a better fit for her than clinical practice. That decision alone makes her the smartest person at this table.

Swiveling her brute-force attention over to me, Beth asks, "Do you even know how to do group therapy?"

"Yes." I shrug, trying to ignore Courtney's polite wince. "Theoretically."

Beth arches a bushy brown eyebrow at me.

"I mean, I've taken classes. How hard can it be?"

Dee snorts.

"What kind of group did you tell him it was?" Courtney asks.

I pull the skewer out of my margarita and rip a hunk of indistinguishable fruit off with my teeth. "All kinds," I say with my mouth full, hoping no one can understand me.

Pineapple? No, mango. Wait … a potato soaked in cran-apple juice.

"All kinds?" Dee's nose wrinkles up on one side. "The fuck does that mean?"

"I don't know!" I shout, still chewing on some unidentified alcohol-soaked food substance. "I messed up, okay? You guys have to help me!"

Mark turns his Bass Pro Shops hat around backward and scratches his short, scruffy beard. "Okay, so you have to do all kinds of group therapy … somewhere … soon."

I nod and swallow.

He thinks, Courtney thinks, Beth thinks, Dee chuckles at me and shakes her head while sucking blue margarita through a curly straw, and I hold my breath.

Mark's eyes suddenly light up. "Why don't you do it here? We're only open from twelve to nine on Sundays."

"Really?" I ask, searching his big brown eyes for any signs of bullshit. "Oh my God, Mark. Sunday mornings would be perfect! Thank you!"

"Nuh-uh." He wags his finger at me. "*You* get Sunday nights. I'm already teaching yogalates here on Sunday mornin's."

And just like that, my spirits sink lower than the neckline on Mark's tank top. "Sunday nights? After you close? What time would that be? Like, ten o'clock?"

He shrugs. "Beggars can't be choosers. Take it or leave it."

I sigh. "Fuck it. I'll take it. Thanks, Mark."

Courtney furrows her perfect little eyebrows. "Don't you need to check with the owner or somethin'?"

Mark chuckles. "He's spending his midlife crisis in Costa Rica, honey. I'm the boss now." With that, Mark skips off to his other tables, cowboy boots click-clacking across the sticky hardwood floor.

"Okay"—I turn to the girls—"we have a day, a time, and a location."

"*We?*" Dee asks. "What *we?*"

"We." I gesture in a circle around the table. "I said I offer *all kinds* of therapy. How can I do that without all kinds of therapists? I need you guys. Pleeeease?"

They glance at one another while I give them my best, pitiful puppy-dog eyes.

"Beth"—I shift toward the easiest member of the group to sway, seated diagonally across from me—"you can bring your Twister mat and be as hands-on as you want—I don't care."

Beth pulls the beer bottle out of her fruity blue concoction and taps it against the side of my fish bowl. "I got your back, Sterling. Ride or die," she says before downing what's left in one swig.

"Beth, thank you." I turn to the petite blonde sitting across from me, sipping on her curly straw as nonchalantly as possible. "Courrrrt, come on. It'll be fun."

Courtney sighs and gives me a tight smile. "Okay, fine. But only 'cause it'll look good on my letter of recommendation."

"It totally will."

I think.

Finally, I turn to the woman next to me, who is pouring a mini bottle of Cuervo Gold from her purse into her margarita.

"Fine," Dee says without looking up, "but you're buyin' from now on." She screws the cap back on and pins me with a threatening stare. "And I want top shelf, ho."

"You can have all the shelves. Any shelf you want. Starting now." I pull out what little cash I have in my purse and toss it onto the table before grabbing my bag and cell phone. "Thank you, guys. Seriously."

"Where are you goin'?" Beth asks while simultaneously sliding what's left of my drink over to her side of the table.

"Ooh … you goin' to bump uglies with Dr. Callahan again? Get it!" Dee does a few body rolls in her seat for emphasis.

"Actually, I'm going to my mom's birthday party, but thanks for that visual."

"Hey, maybe you'll get some booty there." Dee points her empty mini bottle at me with a wink.

"If by *booty*, you mean, *scabies*," I say, sliding out of the booth, "then … yeah, maybe."

Lou

IT'S, LIKE, A SEVENTY-DOLLAR Uber ride from Atlanta to the Indigo Hills Artist Colony, so I don't make the trek that often. At least, that's what I tell my mother when she guilt-trips me for not visiting more.

I also tell her the reason I don't have a car is because I can't afford one, which is only partially true. The rest of the truth is that I don't *want* a car because I know that the second I find myself in possession of one, my mom and stepdad will expect me to visit this god-awful place more than triannually, which, quite frankly, is already two times a year too many.

It's not that the commune isn't beautiful. It is—in its own rustic way. Nestled in the foothills of the Appalachian Mountains, the Indigo Hills Artist Colony is a quaint, colorful little collection of cabins and RVs and gardens and orchards, which is under constant threat of being reclaimed by the surrounding forest. It almost feels as if the lean-to buildings and outhouses clawed themselves right up out of the dirt.

Take this table, for example. Outside, in the common area, there is a "table" large enough to seat twenty, but it's really just the trunk of a massive oak tree that got struck by lightning and split in half. The folks here took the two halves, laid them open end to end, jacked them up off the ground with the stumps of other fallen trees, and called it a table. It's wobbly. It's splintery. It's sticky with sap. And I'm sure it houses an entire swarm of termites. But it's not nearly as icky as the sleazeball sitting at the head of it.

Leif, the self-appointed leader of this "intentional community," stands up, clearing his throat as he smooths a hand over his graying hair, which he wears pulled back in some kind of leather-wrapped ponytail. He then clinks his artisanal, hand-hammered spork against a misshapen, hand-molded ceramic drinking cup. Actually, it doesn't clink at all. It thuds.

Thud, thud, thud.

"A toast to the soul of the hour," he announces, lifting his cup in the direction of my mother, seated to his left. His cult-leader–like smile never ceases to give me the creeps.

"Not so many moons ago, this celestial spirit was plucked from the cosmos and *thrust* into the physical realm. *Thrust* into a physical body. *Thrust* into a patriarchal caste system ..."

Please take a moment to imagine what Leif's hips are doing to punctuate this speech.

I glance at my stepdad just in time to see him roll his eyes. George is ten years older than my mother, but as gorgeous and youthful as she is in all her barefoot, boho-chic, wire-wrapped-dreadlock glory, he looks like he could be her dad. He's been putting up with Leif's advances toward his wife since they got here twelve years ago, but what George lacks in muscle mass and, well, hair, he makes up for in sheer, uncontested devotion to my mother. Leif doesn't stand a chance.

Yet he persists.

"But she broke free of that bondage and followed her ample, heaving heart straight to me. I mean, *us*." Leif sweeps his arms out, gesturing at the table full of dirty hippies—his precious devotees.

Now, it's my turn to roll my eyes.

"Happy birthday, Crystal." Leif's teeth glisten as he grins at her like she's next on the menu. "Your spirit shimmers like the gem that shares your name."

God, could he be any cheesier?

The hippies all cheer and raise their glasses as my mom blushes and pretends to be humble. She knows she's the prettiest one here. Hell, she's the prettiest one anywhere. Twelve years spent living in the woods would make most people devolve into furry, smelly, hunched-over little Hobbit-like creatures, but not Crystal. She looks like a supermodel on day three of a weekend-long music festival. She even has a few sprigs of grass in her hair, like she's been lying in a meadow, casually high on shrooms, contemplating the meaning of life all afternoon. It's not fair.

People like to say that we look alike, but to me, looking like your mother isn't a compliment. It's validation of the fact that the stress of grad school has aged me to the point that I now resemble a fifty-year-old mountain dweller.

Okay, a fifty-year-old mountain dweller who looks thirty-two.

Leif finally sits back down, and George, to my absolute horror, stands up next.

He raises his glass and tries to smile, but the frown lines in his face are so deep that it just looks like a less severe scowl. "To my dear wife," he begins, his New York accent just as thick as the day we arrived here. I think he hangs on to it in protest. "I'm so happy that you, uh, made another circle—what's it called? Revolution? Orbit? That's it. You made another orbit around the sun. And, uh …"

George looks to me for help, but all I can do is wince and shrug.

"You know ... your, uh, essence? It just grows ... and grows ... and, uh ... ah, forget it."

George sits down with a *humph*. My mother squeezes his hand with a warm smile.

Hippies cheer, glasses thud instead of clink, and the party begins. My mom and her friends leap up to go grab their obscure, indigenous instruments and frolic around the bonfire while I stay behind, pushing vegan soy cake with nut butter around on my plate. I make the mistake of taking a bite, out of curiosity, and now my throat feels like it's been coated in almond-flavored glue.

I reach for the pitcher on the table, but a voice to my right stops me.

"Unless you wanna be chasing little green men through the forest in about forty-five minutes, I'd steer clear of the punch."

I turn and smile as George takes the seat—er, *stump*—next to me. He returns my smile, but it fades a bit as his eyes drift toward the bonfire behind me.

"Listen, I need a favor."

Here we go again.

"George," I sigh. "We've talked about this. I don't have any money."

His eyes snap from my mother back to me. "But you got yourself a big-girl job now."

"Yeah, and I also have a PhD's worth of student loan debt to pay back."

His face falls.

"Ugh. Sorry. What do you need?"

"The intanet!" George shouts before looking around to make sure nobody heard his little outburst. "I mean ..." He lowers his voice to a whisper. "The intanet. I haven't seen a Mets game in over a decade. I heard you can watch 'em from the clouds now. On the telephone? I don't know. I don't know how it works, but I need it, Lou. I'm dyin' here."

"You want a cell phone? With a data plan and everything?"

My heart sinks. I want George to be happy, but until I get licensed, I'm basically just an intern—with the pay stub to prove it. I might be able to call myself a doctor, but I barely make enough to cover half the rent in a shitty part of town, my delightful new student loan payments, and alcohol, let alone a second cell phone bill.

George must be able to tell that I'm trying to figure out a way to let him down easy because before I can say no, he goes in for the kill. "You know, sweetheart, if money's such a problem, you can always move back here. We kept your bunk just the way you left it."

My mind flashes back to the inside of the three-by-six-foot hole in the wall I called a bed for the three years that I lived here. My parents have a private bedroom in the back of their RV but not me. I got a glorified coffin in the hallway. I can still see the 2000s emo band posters and zombified hippie portraits that I taped to the ceiling inside.

"No!" I blurt out, yanking myself back into the present and away from that patchouli-scented mobile home from hell. "No. It's fine. I'll get you a phone, okay? I promise."

George grins and spreads his arms, and just like always, I fall into them. Nobody hugs me quite like George.

In fact, nobody really hugs me at all anymore.

That thought disappears as George holds me at arm's length and gives me a look I don't trust. "Hey, I need ya to do one more thing for me."

"George, come on."

"Relax." He grins. "I just need you to distract Leif while I piss in his kombucha."

His eyes are alight with joy as he hops up from his stump and waddles off toward the bonfire.

"Fuck it," I mumble to myself, tossing back two half-empty glasses of punch before I follow him down the hill.

Lou

I CAN TELL IT'S morning before I even open my eyes. The backs of my eyelids glow orange, and somewhere far away, I smell coffee brewing.

Good. Coffee tells me that I am not in fact on a rowboat in the middle of the Atlantic, which is what I would have guessed based on the way I feel right now. Everything is moving. Including the questionable vegan fare in my stomach from the party last night.

Maybe I fell asleep in my old bunk, and George is driving us to freedom. Or the closest McDonald's.

A shadow falls over my face, blocking out the light filtering in through my eyelids. Then, I hear the creak of a chair, the *click-click* of a retractable pen, the clearing of a male throat.

As soon as I open my eyes, I regret it. Deeply.

Dr. Callahan is sitting two feet away from my face. Eyes wide, fascinated. Clipboard at the ready.

"Quick," he says, "tell me everything you were just dreaming about before you forget."

"Hmm?" I groan, groggily taking in my surroundings.

I'm in a bedroom but not my bedroom. It's small and simple, sparsely decorated. It smells like French roast and mothballs.

"Where am I?"

"Where are you? Don't you remember? You called me to come get you from some hippie commune in the mountains last night. Said you were being chased by a zom-bear."

Fucking punch.

I groan again and throw my elbow over my eyes.

"You were having a nightmare just now, weren't you?" I hear excitement in his voice.

"Yeah," I mutter. "I think it was about a creepy old man watching me while I slept."

"Deflection!" If I could see him right now, I'm sure he'd be pointing his little pen at me in accusation.

I gotta get out of here.

I sit up and rub my eyes, not even caring that they're probably still caked with yesterday's mascara. A brittle brown leaf falls out of my hair and lands in my lap.

Nice.

"Every minute you spend being defensive is another minute that your precious, subconscious cries for help are fading away."

Dr. Callahan is practically salivating over the chance to psychoanalyze my nightmare, but now that I'm sober and seeing him in broad daylight, I don't want to let him anywhere near my body *or* my mind.

"I'm sleeping with my former professor," I mumble. "I think that's a cry for help in and of itself."

"It is! I'm so happy you see that."

I roll my eyes as I crawl toward the other side of the bed. I'm still wearing my bra and panties—thank God. Maybe I didn't ... I don't even want to think about it.

As I look around for my shirt and pants, Dr. Callahan continues, "In fact, I think your attraction to older authority figures is directly related to—"

"Can we not do this right now?"

I spot some plaid fabric at the foot of the bed.

Ah, there they are.

"Your father's death."

Everybody has a button. That one round fire engine–red button that, when pressed, makes them go off like a volcano, spewing defensive, irrational outrage lava at anyone within range.

Bringing up my father when I'm hungover and un-caffeinated in a strange place is evidently mine.

I snatch my clothes off the floor and face Dr. Callahan—*Peter*—without a shred of former student politeness left. "I have a father," I snap. "His name is George."

"Luna, I read your entrance essay." His voice is so condescending that I can't even look at him.

Instead, I shove my jeans on one leg at a time while staring at a stain on his matted carpet.

"I know your father died by suicide when you were a kid. I know your mother remarried and then ran off to a hippie commune to avoid dealing with it. And I know you want to help other people with mental illness because of it."

"You got me all figured out, huh?" The words fly out of my mouth before my head has even emerged from the neck hole of my sweater. "Just another fatherless coed who might be needy enough to let you sleep with her."

"Luna ..."

"I bet you make all the girls with daddy issues feel special, so they'll spread their legs for you, don't you, *Doctor*?" I shove my feet into my unlaced Converse.

"Luna, don't you see what's going on here?" He shows his teeth in one of those patronizing smiles that adults give to kids when they think they're being overly dramatic. "It's not *me* you're angry with; it's your father."

"Oh my God. Just shut up." I stomp past him and out the door.

I don't know where the hell I am, so it takes me a second to figure out which way to go. I turn right, heading for the stairs, when Dr. Callahan emerges from his bedroom behind me.

"Running away is an ineffective coping strategy!" he calls out.

"So are those hair plugs!" I shout back, throwing my middle finger up as I jog down the stairs.

I'm really starting to regret this whole car-free lifestyle. Not that I can afford to change it anytime soon, but walking down Boulevard Avenue to the bus stop, wearing Friday night's clothes on a Saturday morning, is a look I thought I gave up back in undergrad.

I swipe a finger under my eye, and sure enough, it comes back smudged in mascara.

Great. I'm wearing Friday night's makeup too. All over my face.

I dig around in my slouchy, crocheted shoulder bag until I find a pair of drugstore sunglasses and a hair tie. As I attempt to fix my shit, a few drivers passing by honk or catcall me, and sadly, I'm flattered. I needed a nice, "Ow-ow! Lookin' good, mama!" this morning.

I know now why they call it a walk of shame. I was furious at Dr. Callahan when I first stomped away from his surprisingly cute little townhouse, but now that the October chill has sucked the fire out of me, all that's left is a deep, nauseating sense of shame. Not only because I let my wounded, bratty inner child off her leash back there, but also because, yet again, I put myself in a vulnerable position with an unavailable man.

After ten years of psychology courses, I pretty much know what all of my issues are. I know that I gravitate toward men who pose virtually no threat of trying to have a real adult relationship with me. My professor. Some douche bag at the bar who will be gone by morning. A famous author who lives in a foreign country and is now my client. I know that I'm afraid to get close because I don't want to form an attachment to another man who could leave me. I mean, *will* leave me. Psychology is a science. I study people and statistics, and the odds of losing any man that I fall in love with—either through a breakup, divorce, incarceration, or death—are simply too damn high to fuck with.

So, I hang out in the shallow end, where it's safe. Safe and sad and slowly killing me.

A teenager sits on a low wall next to the sidewalk up ahead. He looks like he can't be older than fourteen—baby fat clings to features that have sprouted at inconsistent rates—so I don't feel bad at all when I reach out and snatch the joint he just lit out of his mouth as I pass.

"Hey! What the fuck, man?"

I take a drag and keep walking.

I need it more than he does.

Even with my chill partially restored, I still palm the can of pepper spray in my purse as I approach the bus stop. The benches are enclosed in a large covered shelter that is wallpapered with posters and advertisements, so I can't see who's in there until I come around to the front. When I do, I almost scream. There, staring back at me, larger than life, is Kimberly "The Drama Llama" Kline. It takes me a minute to realize that she's on a tattered, old *Boss Wives of Atlanta* poster and isn't actually about to attack me with her inch-long acrylic nails.

But I mace her anyway, just to be sure.

By the time I finally get home, I'm starving, pissy, and in desperate need of a shower.

I live in a rented bungalow down by the old, abandoned Braves stadium. I don't really mind that there are bars on the windows or that instead of birds chirping, the background noise is mostly dogs barking and car alarms going off because the rent is cheap, the water is hot, my bedroom is an actual *room* with a *door* that *locks*, and it's a six-dollar Uber ride away from work.

As I drag myself up the driveway, someone shouts, "Sup, Lou!" from the house to my left.

Ugh.

I turn and give my neighbor Paul a two-fingered salute. He beams and waves at me with giant, enthusiastic motions from his own driveway ... where he appears to be washing an ambulance.

The fuck?

"Paul," I ask even though I really just want to go inside and pretend like this isn't happening, "why is there an ambulance in your driveway?"

"I just bought her for the Halloween parade, dude! I'm so winning first place this year. Check it out! The roof is gonna open, and a ten-foot-tall Grim Reaper is gonna rise up outta there with, like, smoke and lasers comin' outta its fuckin' eyeballs and shit. I got it all planned out, man. It's gonna be so rad."

I raise my eyebrows and nod. It's the most excitement I can muster in my current condition. "Cool, bro. Good luck with that."

"Oh, and I'm gonna have a bunch of zombie chicks walking behind it, like, doing the Thriller dance and whatnot. Hey, you wanna be one of my fly ghouls?"

"Oh, uh ... yeah, I think I'm gonna pass. Thanks though."

Paul grins, looking just like the Chewbacca on his *Star Wars* T-shirt. "Hey, no sweat, man. Lemme know if you change your mind."

I drag myself the rest of the way down the driveway and into the house, where I face-plant on the couch. My purse lands somewhere on the floor, and my Converse-covered feet dangle over the armrest.

I hear Mark approach before I see him because his silky American flag boxer shorts swish with every step.

"Somebody didn't come home last night. Haaaaay—oh my God." He gasps as he turns the corner and takes in my bedraggled appearance. "Christ on a cracker, honey. What happened? And what is that *smell?*" He wrinkles his nose.

"Old man," I croak.

"Yes"—he nods—"I am definitely pickin' up some notes of tweed."

"I broke up with Peter this morning."

"Who?"

"Dr. Callahan," I mutter. "The professor guy."

"Ohhh." Mark pulls his eyebrows together, as if he actually remembers who I'm talking about. "M'kay. And we're sad about that, why?"

"Because I'm gonna die alone with nothing to my name but student loan debt and a portrait of Ruth Bader Ginsburg." I gesture over to the sad gray half of the house—my half—where a painting of RBG flipping double middle fingers above the words *I DISSENT* hangs on the wall above the thermostat.

"Ugh," Mark groans. "Your energy is so nasty right now. And you're gettin' it on my side of the couch."

Mark shoves my legs off the sofa, and I let them fall without a fight. They pull his camouflage throw blanket down with them. Now, I'm only half on the couch, but somehow, I'm more comfortable.

"Good Lord. You need an intervention. I wasn't gonna do this till later, but … desperate times and all that."

Mark leaves the room.

I hear him banging around in his bedroom for a few minutes before the unmistakable twang of country music begins to play. The song sounds super familiar.

Wait, is that …

Suddenly, Mark leaps over the couch and lands between the coffee table and me. He's wearing head to toe leopard print—fuzzy leopard-print bathroom slippers, a leopard-print velour track suit with the hood pulled up over his head, and even leopard-print gloves—and when he grabs a remote control off the table and starts singing along, it all makes sense.

Yep, it's Shania.

Mark twirls and dances around the living room, singing in his Southern-fried accent about men who don't impress him much while expertly stripping off layers of animal print. The slippers go first, then the velour pants, which must have been Velcroed on because they disappear with a flick of his wrists. I cover my face and pray that he's wearing boxer shorts underneath, but God must hate me because I'm confronted with a bouncing leopard-print G-string as soon as I peek through my fingers.

Mark cackles like a witch as he dances away, wiggling his bare ass as he unzips his hoodie. He looks at me over his shoulder. Then, he turns and spreads the jacket wide open, revealing a leopard-print string bikini top underneath in addition to an obscene amount of body hair.

A shocked laugh bursts out of me and then another when Mark takes his hood off and three feet of Shania-esque auburn waves come tumbling out. He wiggles and body-rolls across the living room, where he flips a switch on the wall to turn on the ceiling fan, which has evidently been set to warp speed. Wind tears through our tiny living room as Mark belts out the final line, thrusts both hands into the crack between the cushions on our love seat, pulls out two fistfuls of confetti, and releases them into the air.

Little paper squares hit me like buckshot, landing in my eyes, my mouth, and probably leaving indentations in my skin.

When I finally unblind myself, I find Mark standing with one leg up on the coffee table, panting like a dog as he tries to get the last few strands of wig hair out of his mouth.

I sit up and laugh, forcing the words out despite the lump forming in my throat. "You did all this for me?"

"Well, duh." Mark huffs. "You're my best friend. Also … you're on Instagram Live right now."

Mark motions toward the counter that separates the kitchen from the living room, and sure enough, his phone is propped up against an empty can of Pabst Blue Ribbon, recording every cringey moment.

"Ugh!" I stand up and stomp off toward my bedroom.

"What?" Mark calls after me. "I wasn't gonna do all this twice in one day!"

I slam my door shut, but I can still hear him talking to his followers through the hollow slab of wood separating us.

"Sorry, guys! I have to cut this week's dance party short, but I'll see y'all again next Sunday at four! Stay sexy! Love and light!"

I roll my eyes and flop onto my bed like a miserable starfish.

The door bursts open, and Mark twirls in. He's still wearing his string bikini, but the Shania wig is gone. His shaggy dark brown hair is shoved under a nylon cap, but the hair on his chest and beer belly are out in full force.

"You are *not* in here pouting about Dr. Viagra and his liver-spotted balls, are you? Because …" Mark's voice trails off as his eyes land on my bookshelf. "Helloooo, sailor! Is this your new client?"

Mark picks up one of Thomas's books and lets out a loud, redneck whistle.

"If you so much as bend the spine, I swear to God—" I sit up and try to snatch the book out of Mark's hand, but he easily jerks it out of my reach.

"He looks like a sexy little Harry Potter, doesn't he?" Mark winks. "But, like, the daddy version. Like, if they had a Red Room of Pain up in Hogwarts."

"Put it back," I snap.

"Wait a minute." Mark's face swivels from the bookshelf, over to me, and then back to the bookshelf. "Why was this book turned around …"

I pick up a pillow and bury my face in it.

Mark gasps. "You dirty little slut! You make Daddy Harry Potter watch while you whack it, don't you?"

"Get. Out," I mumble into my pillow.

"So that's why it sounds like there's a lawnmower in here every night."

"Oh my God, get out!" I smack him with my pillow, but Mark's too busy smirking at Thomas's picture to notice.

Then, without warning, he grabs an armful of Thomas's books and takes off running, cackling like a hyena in a leopard-print G-string.

"I'm serious, Mark! Do not bend those fucking spines!" I shout after him. Dread slithers into my veins as I realize that the man making me irrationally angry right now is the same person I chose to lead my Anger Management group tomorrow.

Great job, Lou. This won't be a disaster at all.

Lou

MY EYES BEGIN TO water from the lemon-scented bleach
fumes radiating off the table. I chose the booth in the front right
corner of the bar because it's secluded but still has a direct view
of the door, but it must have taken fifteen Clorox wipes to get
the tacky, adhesive layer of French fry grease and spilled
appletinis off all that reclaimed barnwood. I assume that
millionaires do not appreciate being physically stuck to the
furniture they sit on, but that's just a hunch. Other than my
clients, I don't actually know any millionaires.

"Ooh, somebody just pulled up in a Mercedes!" Mark
whisper-shouts at me from his spot behind the host stand.

I sit up on my knees in the booth, peeking over the back so that I can watch the door. It has to be Thomas. Almost everybody else is here already.

I glance past Mark to the large, round table on the opposite side of the bar. Courtney is seated on one side of it with a poster board sign hanging over her head that says *ANXIETY* in big, sloppily written letters. Mark made it, bless his heart. Across from her, my four jitteriest clients sit, wringing their hands and shredding paper napkins.

Dee is standing behind the bar like she owns the place with another homemade poster board taped to the wall behind her. On the other side of the counter, my four saddest souls—plus Teen Angst Adelynn—sit with their backs hunched over from the weight of the world. Dee's face is about as enthusiastic as their posture, causing a knot to form in my stomach. I hope it wasn't a mistake, assigning her to the Depression group.

The sign affixed to the swinging door into the kitchen announces that Life Coaching is inside, which makes me want to take back my offer to let Beth bring her Twister mat. The floor in there is fucking disgusting. Luckily, when I checked on her a second ago, she and her four clients were all standing. Actually, she was marching back and forth in front of them like a drill sergeant while they stood at attention in a perfect line.

This was definitely a mistake.

The front door opens, and my heart leaps into my throat. My head swivels in that direction, but when a manicured hand holding a Chanel clutch comes into view, I exhale and slump over the back of the booth.

"Well, hello, gorgeous!" Mark beams. "Welcome to group therapy! We have five amazing healing experiences for you to choose from …"

Aggressive Celeste, the mug-thrower, stops in front of the host stand, eyeing Mark up and down, as if she's afraid that his country-chic wardrobe might actually be contagious.

"Anxiety is at the round table," he continues, and I swear he's ratcheting up his accent just because of the snarky-ass look on her face. "Depression is at the bar. Life Coaching is in the kitchen. Anger Management is in the back with yours truly. And Creativity is over there with Dr. Sterling, but it's totally full and you can't choose that one."

Celeste's eyes cut over to me and then to the all-caps, hand-scrawled sign taped to the wall behind me that reads *CREATIVITY CORNER*. I swallow and give her a little wave.

Celeste looks back at Mark with a scowl. "Why can't I see Dr. Sterling? There's literally nobody over—"

"Totally full! Right this way," Mark cries, steering her toward the back of the bar. "You look like you can do a mean down dog, am I right?" Mark tosses me a wink as he holds open a door marked *ANGER MANAGEMENT* and leads a volatile woman in a Gucci jumpsuit and red-bottomed heels into the stockroom of a dive bar, where a bed of used yoga mats awaits her.

Biggest. Mistake. Ever.

Before I can run to the stockroom to do damage control or at least find something that Mark can wear as protective headgear, I see—or rather, *feel*—the front door open.

My head turns, and I watch with nauseating anticipation as Thomas emerges from the night like a ghost or a vampire. Graceful. Timeless. Panic-inducing. With one sweep of his head from left to right, his eyes land on me, and I'm frozen. I should smile or wave him over, but I'm glued to the back of this booth, my forearms propped up on top, as I watch him approach in a state of paralysis.

Sit down, dumbass!

I slide down into a weird half-crouch just as Thomas appears at the end of the table. Thankfully, I wore Converse instead of heels tonight but only because I didn't think he'd be able to see my feet.

He doesn't sit.

Tell him to have a seat!

"When your secretary called and said we'd be meeting at The Yacht Club, I pictured something a little—"

"Less splintery?" I offer with a cringey smile.

"More maritime." He smirks.

83

"There is a boat." I point to the bar, where a seven-foot-long rowboat is suspended from the ceiling and a plastic skeleton—wearing a captain's hat and navy-blue blazer—is holding the oars.

"Ah, it all makes sense now," Thomas says dryly, glancing from me to the empty spot across from me.

"Please"—my hand shoots out—"have a seat."

While Thomas effortlessly slides into his side of the booth, I try to wriggle into a normal sitting position and adjust my shirt as inconspicuously as possible.

"With you being America's *premier creativity specialist*, I expected there to be a few more people in this group," he says, the corner of his narrow mouth curling on one side.

"Huh. I guess everybody must be sick." I shrug. "It is cold and flu season."

That smirk broadens into a knowing smile, and I hate the way it makes me squirm. He's looking at me like this is a date. Like he asked me out two days ago and I went and moved heaven and earth to make it happen. Like this is *not* a completely professional therapy group for one that just so happens to be in a cozy, secluded booth in the back of a bar at ten o'clock at night.

He is a human being. He needs your help. Sit up, lean forward, and for God's sake, stop looking at his mouth! You're his therapist!

I clear my throat. "Since you're new here, I'd like to begin with an icebreaker. This will get us up and moving around, so everybody can meet each other."

Thomas looks around at our invisible group members. "You can't be serious."

"I'm going to ask you some questions," I continue. "To answer them, you have to sit on one side of the booth or the other."

I motion to the wall next to us. Under Mark's beautiful *CREATIVITY CORNER* sign, I have two paper napkins taped to the wall. The one on Thomas's side of the booth says *NO*—I borrowed Mark's Magic Marker—and the one on my side says *YES*.

Thomas glances from the wall back to me. "I hardly see how this—"

"Have you ever...," I interrupt, "ridden an elephant?"

Thomas pauses, caught off guard by my question, and his gaze slides slowly back over to the napkins on the wall. I focus on breathing and pumping blood and thinking thoughts at a totally nonchalant, non-hysterical pace while I wait for his response. When he doesn't move, I scoot out of my side of the booth, casting my eyes down to avoid his skeptical stare, and slide over next to him, making sure to leave a solid, super-professional two feet of space between us.

"Me neither," I exhale, finally meeting Thomas's amused eyes.

Fuck. I can smell him again. That crisp, bright, oceanic scent that makes me feel like the sun is warming my sand-speckled skin. The urge to close my eyes, lean in, and sniff is almost as overwhelming as the particular smirk on his posh, pore-free face. You know the one ... from his book cover.

An alarm in my head goes off, blaring, *CLIENT, CLIENT, CLIENT*, and immediately douses my inappropriate thoughts with a bucket of ice water. I tear my eyes away from the face on my bookcase and glance across the room, hoping to find something distraction worthy.

I succeed.

On the other side of the bar, Courtney smiles sweetly at a group of my most anxious clients. Then, she reaches out and knocks over a salt shaker in the middle of the table. She must have pre-loosened the cap because salt pours out all over the table. All four group members gasp and recoil.

"Oopsie." Courtney's former cheerleader voice really projects. "I just made a big ol' mess, didn't I?"

Norman, my client who has to breathe into a paper bag in the lobby if his session doesn't start on time, makes a pained sound deep in his throat.

"I'll bet that's gon' drive y'all crazy, isn't it?" Courtney beams. "But you know what, guys? Life is messy ..."

Next, Courtney knocks over the pepper shaker. Black and gray granules spill out, mixing with the white salt on the table.

"...And your job is to learn how to be okay with that. So, if y'all can sit here and stare at this mess without tryin' to fix it for five whole minutes, you get a sucker."

I think Nervous Nicole is sweating. It's hard to tell from here, but I wouldn't be surprised. This has got to be the longest she's ever gone without talking.

"But if ya can't ..."

Courtney reaches for something under the table.

Oh no. No, no, no.

"You're gonna meet my little friends..."—Court pulls out two water guns, one pink and one yellow—"Taylor Soak and Reese Witherspray."

"Are those ... water pistols?" Thomas asks, leaning toward me so that he can get a better glimpse of the semiautomatic Super Soakers in Courtney's hands.

I blink and turn to face him again. "It's fine. Courtney's a behaviorist."

Thomas raises his eyebrows and nods once, obviously unconvinced that it is actually fine.

That makes two of us.

"What kind of therapist is *she*?" Thomas asks, nodding toward the bar.

I hold my breath as I follow his gaze.

Despite only being here for twenty minutes, Dee is standing behind the bar with the posture of a Waffle House waitress on the tail end of a double shift. Her voice doesn't project like Courtney's, but she's only about twenty feet away from my booth, and with Courtney's group engaged in a silent salt-and-pepper stare-off and Beth's and Mark's groups in other rooms, Dee is the only one talking at the moment.

"So, what are y'all hoping to get out of this group? For real."

Mack, the older gentleman who switched to my caseload after hearing Thomas accuse me of being a sadist, answers first. "Honestly, I just want to stop wishing I was dead."

"Me too, brother," Dan, the day trader sitting next to him, replies. He has three different cell phones scattered in front of him on the wooden bar.

"I want to stop crying in the shower every day," Winnie the Wine Mom responds. She still comes to see me every week even though she thinks all of my holistic recommendations are an attempt to convert her to "the Nation of Islam."

"You shower every day?" The woman to her right coughs out. Depressed Dixie. She smells like cigarette smoke and looks like she might have been an extra on *The Dukes of Hazzard*. "Hell, yesterday, I found a caterpillar in my hair. In the cocoon."

I love her.

"Chrysalis," Teen Angst Adelynn drones. "They call it a chrysalis now."

Dee gives Adelynn *the look* until she answers the original question.

Adelynn sighs. "I just want my parents to think I'm getting better so they'll let me see my boyfriend again, okay?"

Dee nods. "So, don't kill yourself …" She sweeps a finger from Mack over to Winnie.

"Wash ya ass …" That was definitely directed at Dixie.

"And fake it till you get some booty." Dee points at Adelynn.

"I can work with that." She shrugs. Then, rummaging around under the bar, she asks, "Okay, next question: is everybody here an alcoholic?"

"Hmm?" I turn back toward Thomas. Which was a bad decision. He's still far too pretty and pleasant-smelling to look at. "What was the question again?"

"Never mind." He frowns, glancing over my shoulder at the bar, where I really hope Dee isn't lining up tequila shots for everybody.

I shift in my seat to block his view. "Where were we? Oh yeah. Have you ever been arrested?"

Thomas thinks for a moment. Then, he scoots toward me, like he needs me to get up and let him move to the *YES* side of the booth, but as soon as he sees my eyes go wide, he smiles and returns to his spot.

I cough out a laugh. "I knew it."

"I did get a parking ticket once," Thomas says. "And I didn't even pay it until the fourteenth day."

"What happens on the fourteenth day?"

"In England, if you pay a parking ticket within the first two weeks, your fine is half the price."

I snort out a laugh before quickly regaining my composure. I have got to steer this ship back toward creativity. Thomas is way too fucking charming for casual banter.

"Okay, let's talk about art," I say. "Have you ever created something that made you question your mental health?"

Even though it pains me, I slide out of Thomas's side of the booth and head back over to the *YES* side.

A second later, Thomas follows. He sits on the end of my bench, leaving our unspoken two feet of space intact. His face is cautiously curious. Mine curves into a smile.

"Was it *Nightmare Falls*?" I whisper. It's as if Fangirl Me thought Psychologist Me wouldn't notice that she snuck in a question as long as she did it really quietly.

Thomas smiles and points to something over my shoulder. I turn and see the napkin taped to the wall next to our side of the booth.

"Yes," he whispers back. His voice sounds so close.

I close my eyes and smile, picturing him leaning toward me while my head is turned.

A loud *whack* rings out from the direction of the kitchen, and my eyes immediately pop open again. I can only imagine what Beth is doing in there. I told her that the clients I was giving her are insecure and indecisive and need somebody to whip them into shape, but that sounded like an actual whip.

"Would you …" I turn back around to find Thomas already sliding out of the booth.

He sweeps a polite hand out, motioning for me to exit.

"Thanks."

I run over to the kitchen door and push it open a few inches, just enough to peek inside and make sure that Beth is not in fact flogging my clients.

All four of the Life Coaching members are lined up against the stainless steel counter, eyes wide in terror, as Beth paces in front of them. Her back is to me, so I can't see what's in her hand until …

Whack!

The end of a rubber spatula comes down on the stainless steel counter next to sweet little Leonard, making him jump.

"Stand up straight!" Beth barks.

All four wallflowers snap to attention. Leonard's glasses slide down his nose, but he waits to fix them until Beth's back is turned again.

"I know your type," she says, resuming her pacing. "You're here because you're sick and tired of life making you its bitch, am I right?"

No one answers.

Beth stops and slaps her palm with the spatula. "Am I right?"

"Yes, Coach Beth," they mumble in fear.

"Course I'm right!" She continues marching. "Life is the bruiser in the prison showers with the teardrop tattoo, serving a double life sentence for straight murder, and you're just the little asthmatic accountant who got locked up for tax fraud and keeps dropping the goddamn soap! Well, I'm here to give you the tools you need to make life *your* bitch once and for all. What do you say, team? Are you ready to give life a stick to bite down on and a safe word?"

Oh, Jesus Christ.

"Yes, Coach Beth."

Beth hones in on Leonard, who didn't answer out loud.

"What's that, Four Eyes?" she barks. "I couldn't hear you. Drop and give me twenty!"

I'm just about to run in and tell Leonard that he does not have to drop and give her anything, especially not on a floor covered in three decades' worth of salmonella and roach poison, when I hear something—or a lot of somethings—crash in the storage room next door.

Shit.

I sprint around to the other side of the bar, giving Dee a warning look as I pass, and barge straight through the Employees Only door and into the stockroom, where the Anger Management folks are gathered.

It's surprisingly Zen inside—other than the two-hundred-and-fifty-pound man lying on his side against a shelf covered in knocked-over cans.

The storage room is tiny—fifteen, maybe twenty feet long at the most. A third of that is sectioned off by a floor-to-ceiling chain-link fence and padlocked gate to store the extra alcohol, and the rest serves triple-duty as an office, dry and canned goods storage, and a locker room/place where the employees go to make out and/or cry. What little open space there is has been carpeted with five overlapping yoga mats upon which Mark and four very irritable yuppies are bent into inverted Vs.

Well, three yuppies. Angry Bill must have lost his balance and fallen into the shelf next to him.

Mark is positioned at the front of the group, wearing a bandanna around his head, bicycle shorts, and a Garth Brooks T-shirt with the sleeves cut off. His downward-facing dog pose is so perfect that his face is almost touching his mat.

"Now, slowly swoop your booty down and bring that chest up into a big ol' cobra pose," Mark says as his hips meet the mat and he lifts his head with a snakelike hiss.

Angry Bill curses while he stacks the cans back on the shelf, but then he begrudgingly rolls over and shoves himself into something resembling Mark's pose.

"Okay, now, bring it on back into child's pose." Mark drops his chest to the mat before pushing back into a fetal position with his arms outstretched over his head.

I can't believe it, but the privileged rageaholics I entrusted him with are actually doing it. Even Celeste.

Mark sits up and gives me a little wink. "Good, y'all. Now, listen. We are here to perform a stress séance. An anger exorcism. We're sweatin' it out through our pores, and now, we're gonna cast it out through a nice, cleansing, primal scream. Here we go …"

Thomas

Meanwhile...

IN THE FIVE MINUTES since Lou got up from the table, I heard what sounded like someone being slapped repeatedly in the kitchen, felt the building shake when something—or someone—fell into what must have been a vat full of scrap metal and tin cans in the room Lou had just run into, saw a woman get assaulted with a pump-action water pistol at the Anxiety table, and now, I'm watching the "therapist" behind the bar pass a stack of papers out to her clients.

"Y'all are gon' do some autonomous art therapy real quick while I go under this bar and have myself a little nightcap," she says, slapping a handful of crayons down on the counter.

"But these are just kids' menus," the bloke in the Polo shirt declares.

"Exactly," the therapist snaps, pointing a finger at him. "That's some nostalgic, feel-good shit right there. Go on; express y'alls' selves."

Then, she grabs a bottle of Patrón off the counter and ducks beneath the bar just before Lou comes barreling out of the Employees Only door.

No sooner does it swing shut behind her than a chorus of synchronized screams erupts on the other side. She doesn't even flinch.

What the fuck is this place?

"Everything okay?" I ask as she slides into the booth across from me, looking a bit frazzled.

"Primal scream therapy," she says with a smile, as if five full-grown adults screaming bloody murder is absolutely nothing to be concerned about.

"Primal scream therapy," I repeat, letting my skeptical tone speak for me.

"Mmhmm." Lou nods. "It's great for releasing repressed anger from childhood trauma."

"In that case, perhaps we should give it a try," I tease.

Then, I do the second-stupidest thing I've done since I met Dr. Luna Sterling—asking her out taking the number one spot. I reach out and wrap my hand around her wrist.

My intention was to pretend as though I were getting up from the table and taking her with me, but the moment my skin touches hers, a bolt of electricity courses through my body, rooting me to the spot.

Lou's eyes go wide, and her lips part as she slowly looks down, as if needing visual confirmation of the fact that her client had the audacity to actually touch her.

No, grabbed. You bloody grabbed her, you daft prat.

I release Lou's arm immediately and run that same hand through my hair, needing something else to do with it. I open my mouth to apologize but stop when Lou reaches down to the end of the table and picks up a stack of large white cards that I didn't notice was sitting there.

"Primal screaming won't help you write books," she says, glancing back at me with a tense smile.

She shakes her head a little, encouraging her hair to fall around her face, and I wonder if it's an attempt to hide the pink flush now staining her cheeks.

Well done, arsehole.

"What's on the cards?" I ask Lou, eternally grateful for the change of subject.

"Inkblots," she says, clutching the stack to her chest like a shield. "I'm going to place one down in front of you, and I want you to tell me what you see."

I see a bat.

I can't tell her it looks like a bat. Everybody probably says that.

"Just say the first thing that comes to mind. Don't overthink it."

I shrug in defeat. "A bat."

She cocks her head to the side and raises her eyebrows. "Okay, maybe overthink it a little."

I huff and stare down at the symmetrical black design again. "Fine. I see … a sandwich. Somebody cut it diagonally and left space in the middle for a bowl of soup, but then they tripped and spilled the soup all over the plate."

"Better … but you write psychological thrillers, not cookbooks," she says, using the same tone she used the last time I was being an uncooperative prick. "Try to make it scary this time."

"Right. Okay."

I prop my elbows on either side of the card and rub my temples as I consider the black splash of ink in front of me. It reminds me of blood, honestly. A lot of it. At night. The bat is gone now, but I still see the sandwich, which gives me an idea.

"So, whoever made this sandwich didn't trip. They served it … to their captive, a man called Julius, who'd been chained to a pillar in the basement for weeks. After finally torturing the information they wanted out of him, they asked him what he'd like his last meal to be. He said a cheese toastie. He didn't even know why. Perhaps it'd reminded him of his mum. But he never got to eat it because as soon as they returned with his request, he stabbed his captor in the eye with his own sharpened finger bone, which they'd severed the day before and left lying on the ground."

Without reacting, Lou points to the card. "So, all this splattery stuff around the sandwich is …"

"Blood. From his captor's eye socket, yes."

She nods, obviously unimpressed. "B-minus."

"B-minus?" I frown.

"You are a *New York Times* best-selling author. Think outside the box."

Ugh.

I clench my teeth and stare at the card again.

Clang-clang-clang!

A sweaty man with a bandanna tied around his head rings a large bell behind the bar. The therapist from that group emerges from under the counter right next to him, holding a bottle of tequila in one hand and covering her ear with the other.

"Gotdamn. Warn a bitch next time," she sneers.

"Dry your eyes and pack up those daddy issues!" the man calls out. "Y'all don't have to go home, but ya sure as hell can't stay here!"

While Lou is distracted, I reach to the end of the table and grab a plastic bottle of ketchup.

B-minus, my arse.

"And remember," the man adds, "what happens at group therapy stays at group therapy!"

Once his speech is over, Lou turns back to face me, and her mouth instantly falls open. I want to beat my chest with pride, but instead, I lean back in my seat, cross my arms nonchalantly, and wait to receive my new grade.

"A-plus," she whispers, admiring the blood-like spatter I added to the inkblot for emphasis. "A-plus-plus."

As Lou and I make our way to the exit, we pass the therapist at the bar, collecting her clients' children's menus.

"Good job. Good job. Ooh, you are in a dark place. Good job …"

The man who rang the bell holds the door as everyone flows out. He winks at me as I pass. Americans in Atlanta seem to be a completely different species than in New York, where my publisher is based. There, people are more likely to push you into oncoming traffic than hold a door open for you.

And winking is out of the question.

In the car park, the other clients gather in loose circles, laughing and processing whatever just occurred in their respective groups. Some are teary-eyed. Some are tense. A few have lollipops. One is soaking wet and talking incessantly. But they all have one thing in common.

None of their therapists walked them out.

As we approach my rental car, the lights inside illuminate, and a blue trident logo shines on the ground like a welcome mat. I hear Lou gasp quietly next to me.

"What kind of car is that?"

"A Maserati." I shove my hands into my pockets to keep them warm. "In my defense, I didn't know it did that when I rented it. A bit ostentatious, isn't it?"

"It's beautiful." I love the way she looks at it. Like it's a work of art instead of a symbol of wealth. "Your publisher must really like you."

"They're not *that* accommodating." I laugh. "I rented it. I don't really need it—my flat is just round the corner from your office—but there's so much open space here. It reminds me of the roads back in Oxford."

"Oh yeah. I guess you can't really drive around in London, can you?" she asks. "It's probably like New York."

"But with less public nudity," I quip, regretting my choice of words immediately.

"That's … unfortunate." Lou looks down as she smiles at her own inappropriate joke.

We've stopped walking, and for the first time in a very long time, I have no idea what this woman wants from me. Why did she walk all the way out here in the cold when she could have easily said good night in the building? Why did she react to my touch like it pained her, yet now, she's standing so close that her elbow is nearly grazing my arm? Did I misread the situation? Does she want me to take her home? No, she wouldn't even agree to have a drink with me.

Perhaps she just wants a nice, private place to tell you to bugger off.

I turn to face her, propping my hip against the driver's side door, which I will never get used to being on the left side of the car. "Well, that was … an experience," I say with a smirk.

"Yeah." Lou glances from the inky-black paint, back to me, and then to the ground as she pulls her blazer closed over her chest with a shiver.

The silence stretches on between us as a parade of BMWs, Porches, and Teslas file past. These people are her clients as well, I assume, yet she doesn't even wave at them. She just stares at her trainers, waiting for … for what?

"Do I get homework after group therapy as well, or do you save that particular punishment for in-office sessions only?"

Lou lifts her head with a small smile. "Inkblots," she says. "You can make them at home to help get your creative juices flowing. Just use whatever you have—ketchup, coffee … tea. You probably drink tea …"

She's stalling. It's like she doesn't want to leave or …

I scan the car park again now that the other clients have gone and realize that the car-to-therapist ratio is off. *That* must be what she wants. Of course.

"Do you … need a lift?" I ask, hearing a tinge of hope in my voice that should definitely not be there. "If so, I should warn you. I have very little practice driving on the right side of the road. You'd be taking your life into your own hands."

Lou lets out a polite laugh and takes a step backward, away from me.

"Oh, wow, um … thanks for the offer, but"—she glances over her shoulder in the direction of the man in the bandanna, who is swearing under his breath as he tries to shove five yoga mats and five rolled-up posters into the back of a Smart car— "Mark is my roommate, so … I'll just ride with him."

"Right." I force a tight smile. "So …"

"So, um … good night." She takes another step backward, stumbling on an errant pine cone before righting her posture. "Try the inkblots." Another step. "And the treadmill …" Step, step. "And, you know …"

"Keep it in my pants?" I say with a teasing smirk.

Lou's eyes widen before she turns and speed-walks over to her waiting roommate. *Mark.* He watches her approach with a look that tells me I should definitely wait to leave until I hear whatever it is he's about to say.

"Ooooooh-wee!" he howls as Lou hustles over to her side of the car with her head down. "Looks like somebody's in a hurry to get home and diddle her Skittle."

He winks at me again, and I have to physically bite my tongue to keep from laughing out loud.

Thankfully, the roads are mostly empty as I drive home because the image of Lou *diddling her Skittle* makes remembering which side of the street to stay on damn near impossible.

Lou

Monday, 10:00 a.m.: Shy Sheryl

SHERYL SEEMS DIFFERENT THIS week. Her posture is straighter. Her eyes are brighter. And her voice is actually at an audible human volume.

"What did you think about the Life Coaching group?" I ask, almost afraid to hear her answer.

"It was great." Sheryl beams. "Last night, I told my husband that if he wanted another helping of mashed potatoes"—she looks down and smiles to herself—"he could get it himself."

She does a tiny little head waggle to show her pride, but her eyes are still trained on the floor.

"That was very assertive of you."

Sheryl finally looks up, still smiling. "Coach Beth walked me through the whole thing before I did it. She even held her finger over her lip like it was a mustache and pretended to be Mr. Grayson, so I could role-play it with her."

Sheryl actually refers to her husband as Mr. Grayson. Every. Single. Time.

"Can you maybe ... share with me what that experience looked like?" I ask, hoping she can't hear the underlying fear in my voice. "I haven't gotten a chance to observe Coach Beth's role-playing technique just yet."

"Um, sure. I guess. Do I ..." Sheryl looks around, obviously flustered at being put on the spot. "Do I need to stand up?"

"Oh, no. Whatever you're comfortable with."

Sheryl's shoulders relax. "Okay. Well, she was like ..." She holds her finger above her upper lip and scowls. Then, in a comically deep voice, she says, " 'Yo, Sheryl. Where's my fuckin' dinner?' "

I have to bite my lip to keep a straight face.

"So, then I said, 'I'm sorry, Mr. Grayson. I just had a really long day.' And then Coach Beth was like ..." She furrows her brow and lifts a finger to her lip again. " 'Doing what? Spending my money and growing that fuckin' lady beard?' "

My eyes go wide.

"I didn't know what to say to that—"

Uh, yeah. Me neither.

"But then Coach Beth told me to 'woman up,' so I pulled my shoulders back, and I said, 'I don't need to justify myself to you.' "

"What did Coach Beth say?" I realize that I'm leaning forward, not because I was trained to, but because I'm hanging on her every word.

"She said"—Sheryl puts her finger above her lip again and frowns—" 'Then, I don't need to justify puttin' my foot in your ass if you don't fix my plate in T-minus—' But she never got to do her countdown because"—Sheryl grimaces and puts her hand next to her mouth, like she's about to tell me a secret—"I slapped her."

She covers her mouth with that hand in shame as mine falls wide open.

"You slapped Coach Beth?"

"I didn't mean to!" she whispers. "It just … happened. I felt so bad."

"What did she do?"

"Well"—Sheryl smiles wistfully as she looks down at the massive rock on her left hand—"she said that if I ever have to do that to Mr. Grayson … that I should turn my ring around."

She holds up her left hand to show me the substantial diamond that is now twisted around to the palm side. "Are we meeting again this Sunday?" she asks. "I can't wait to tell her how it went."

Tuesday, 11:00 a.m.: Day Trading Dan

The man sitting across from me in a five-thousand-dollar suit has made—and recently lost—more money than I will ever see in a lifetime. He's legitimately addicted to stock trading, and he's been pretty depressed ever since losing his ass on a series of bad picks a few months ago. His wife wants to leave him over it, but the irony is that they can't even afford to get divorced now. Needless to say, things have been better for Dan, but today, he greets me with a smile.

"How was your week?" I ask.

"Good actually."

"I can tell. You look … refreshed. Have you been sleeping better lately?"

"I have … thanks to Dr. Dawson." He drops his eyes, and I swear I see his cheeks redden. "It sounds silly, but … she had us color these kids' menus on Sunday, and I swear I can't remember the last time I felt that relaxed. I came home and slept like a baby."

He pulls out his phone and taps on the screen before turning toward me. It's a black-and-white outline drawing of a bouquet of flowers in a vase, and all the segments have been filled in with bright, solid colors. "I've started coloring on my phone before bed every night."

I smile, resisting the urge to reach out and pinch his cheek for being so adorably embarrassed about his new hobby. "That's fantastic, Dan."

"Thanks," he says, closing his floral still-life coloring app and pocketing his phone. "That Dr. Dawson is a miracle worker."

Wednesday, 8:00 a.m.: Perspectively Challenged Penelope

"… and then she was like, 'No hablo Ingles,' and I was all, 'If you no hablo Ingles, then why did I see you watching *The Kelly Clarkson Show* on the nanny cam yesterday, Maria?'"

Penelope has never lived anywhere that didn't have a heated pool *and* a helipad. She's what I like to call *perspectively challenged*. Unfortunately, as someone who currently lives on the south side of town in a bungalow with bars on the windows that I need a roommate to help me pay for, I'm a little perspectively challenged myself.

I am also *not* a morning person. If I'm going to have to deal with this level of entitlement on a weekly basis, I should really do it once I've at least finished my coffee.

I write, *Move appt to afternoon?* on my notepad. Then, on the bottom corner of the page, I scribble the name of a restaurant and tear it off.

"So, remember how we identified empathy as an area to work on?" I ask, handing her the triangle of paper. "Your homework is to go to this restaurant for lunch or dinner one day this week. The employees only speak Vietnamese, and the menus are in Vietnamese as well. I want you to go there by yourself and try to figure out what and how to order *without* using Google Translate. Then, take a few moments to consider how hard it must be for Maria to live in a country where she doesn't speak the language."

Penelope scowls at the piece of paper. "Are we doing group therapy again this weekend? Because that primal-scream thingy was way better than this."

Thursday, 1:00 p.m.: Anxious Andy

Anxious Andy's knee is bouncing at a rate of thirty-two beats per second.

"I only locked the door once this morning. Once. I only locked it once."

"Really?" I lean in. "How many times are you up to now?"

"Five. Five times."

"And you only locked it once this morning?"

Andy stares intently at his thumbnail as he picks at the cuticle with his index finger. "I locked the car five times though."

"That's okay." I smile. "Let's focus on your victory. How did you do that?"

"At group therapy, Dr. Baker showed us how to wait five minutes for an urge to pass."

I remember watching him gnaw his nails down to nubs over at Courtney's table while he stared at that spilled salt and pepper.

"So, after I locked the door, I set a timer on my phone and promised myself that I wouldn't lock it again until the five minutes were up."

"And it worked?"

Andy nods, rubbing his palms up and down the thighs of his jeans. "The whole way here, I wanted to turn around so bad though."

"But you didn't! Andy, that's great!"

He looks at me with exhausted, desperate eyes. "Are we having group therapy again this Sunday? I really need it."

Friday, 3:00 p.m.: Thomas Keep-It-In-Your-Pants O'Reardon

"So, Sunday was interesting," Thomas says, pretending to pick a piece of fuzz off his fitted, caramel-colored cashmere sweater.

My heart, which has been in my throat all damn day, slithers down my esophagus into my ulcer-filled stomach. All my other clients described their group experiences as *amazing, life-changing, miraculous* but not my group member. No, *my* group member thought his experience was *interesting*.

God, I suck at this.

I nod in fake agreement. "Do you ... feel like it was helpful at all?"

"I don't know about the therapy part," Thomas says, glancing up at me in amusement, "but I'm pretty sure at least one person there is going to turn out to be an alien or a serial killer, so ... I should probably keep going. Might be good material."

"Hey, whatever it takes." I cringe. Inwardly. At least, I hope it was inward. "Any progress so far?"

Thomas shakes his head, biting the inside corner of his mouth as his eyes drift toward the bookshelves.

"Oh. Well, did you get a treadmill?"

"Hasn't been delivered yet," he says to the wall.

"And the inkblots?"

"Bats. All of them." Thomas shifts in his seat.

You suck, you suck, you suck ...

"What about a muse?" I ask, bracing myself for his response. "Have you found one?"

Thomas's steely gaze slides back over to me. I swear I hear a click the moment his eyes lock on to mine, like the cocking of a gun.

"Unfortunately."

And there's the bullet.

Pain, searing and acute, rips through my chest as the faces of a thousand supermodels, reality stars, heiresses, and pop icons flash like a strobe light behind my eyes.

"But ... you're not ... you haven't ..." I stutter, needing to know if he's sleeping with this starlet but terrified to find out.

"No"—he arches a brow—"I haven't. And it's killing me— thanks for asking."

"Okay, so ..." I try to exhale the breath I was holding as inconspicuously as possible. "Good job." I smile—I think. "You're doing your homework. That's important. Now, while we wait for the effects of those strategies to kick in, I think this week, we should focus on something a little bit more immediate." I ready the clipboard in my lap and sit up straighter. "I want to identify and challenge some cognitive distortions that might be reinforcing your writer's block."

"Cognitive distortions?" Thomas looks suspicious, as usual. And possibly offended.

We're off to a great start today.

"We all have them." I smile. "Cognitive distortions are inaccurate thoughts—things that you might overgeneralize, catastrophize, minimalize, deny—or sometimes, they're straight-up lies that you believe and tell yourself on a regular basis."

"And how exactly are we supposed to identify these?" Thomas crosses his arms, as if he's trying to shield himself from my invasive, mind-reading powers.

"I think you already have."

Lean forward.

Make eye contact.

Don't be intimidated.

"Last week, more than once, you referred to yourself as being 'empty' or out of ideas."

Thomas's eyes widen and his lips part, as if I'd just guessed the number he was thinking of on the first try.

"Now, that's an easy one to challenge." I soften my voice. "Based on what we know about the nature of the mind, do you think it's logical to conclude that an intelligent, creative, healthy person with fifty or sixty years of life left will never, in those fifty or sixty years, have another original idea?"

Thomas thinks for a moment. His jaw muscles clench and relax. "Based on how I feel right now? Yes."

The hopelessness in that single syllable echoes through the room and settles into my chest, making it ache. I want to tell him that he has so much greatness left in him. I want to tell him that his stories are my most-prized possessions, that my favorite place to be is lost inside his head. I want to tell him that the change he longs for is coming even though I don't know what that looks like yet. But the longer I hold Thomas's defiant stare, the less my heart aches, and the more it begins to pound. Looking away, I take a breath and force myself to challenge the false belief I just heard.

"I want you to repeat after me," I say. *"Feelings are not facts."*
Thomas glares at me.

I tilt my head to the side and raise my eyebrows. "Say it."

He sighs heavily. "Fine. Feelings are not facts."

"Good. This is your new mantra. Whenever you sit down to write or can't even bring yourself to try, I want you to repeat that phrase as a reminder that your belief is scientifically false. It's a feeling, not a fact."

Thomas pulls the corner of his mouth between his teeth, literally chewing on what I just said. Then, he nods. "Okay."

"Okay."

Now what? Oh yeah …

"The second false belief I picked up on last week, which doesn't pertain to writing but does pertain to your feelings of stagnation and emptiness, is that serious romantic relationships only cause pain and should be avoided at all costs."

Thomas leans forward, propping his elbows on his knees. "If you mean that love is an escapable pit of despair that leaves you in a suspended state of misery from the moment you say *I do* until you finally lose the will to live, then yeah, I do believe that. And good fucking luck in convincing me otherwise."

So, that hit a little too close to home. I try not to react to his statement, but I must have flinched or something because Thomas's face softens almost instantly.

"Oh fuck, Lou. I'm sorry. I didn't mean …"

"It's okay." I smile a little too big. "Actually"—I swallow—"let's pretend like maybe I also have that same irrational belief."

Thomas's forehead wrinkles as he nods in understanding.

"What evidence could you provide me with to change my mind?"

"Why would I want to do that?" He looks genuinely concerned. Like changing my mind would actually hurt me.

And maybe it would. In fact, I'm positive that it would. But this isn't about me.

"Because it's a false belief. Because you want me to be happy."

"You're not happy?"

Thomas goes from looking at me to looking through me, and I have the sudden, overwhelming urge to cross my arms too.

"Hypothetically," I say, crossing my legs instead, "no."

"Well then, *hypothetically*, I'd tell you to get a puppy."

"Thomas," I snap. "I want you to think of an example of a healthy, long-term relationship that would disprove my false belief."

Please?

"Sorry, but *healthy, long-term relationship* is an oxymoron," he scoffs, finding another invisible piece of fuzz to remove from his sleeve.

I sigh. I was hoping that he'd come up with this example on his own, but it looks like Thomas is going to make me challenge him every step of the way.

Sitting up straighter, I play my ace in the hole. "What about Stephen and Tabitha?"

Thomas freezes. Then, his eyes slide back up to mine like a chess player who knows he's been bested but refuses to concede the game.

"I did some research." I shrug. "Your favorite author is still Stephen King, I assume."

"Isn't everyone's?"

Nope. I'm looking at mine.

"Did you know that Stephen King didn't publish a single novel until after he was married?"

Thomas shrugs. "I suppose."

"And how many books has Mr. King published to date?"

His shoulders slump. "Maybe fifty?"

"Plus all the ones he wrote under the name Richard Bachman." I smile. "And his nonfiction books. And his short story collections."

"Right." Thomas glares at me. "So, eighty?"

"Almost a hundred," I correct. "And he's been married for how many years now?" I cock my head to one side, as if I didn't already know the answer.

"I see what you're doing."

I lean in, going for the kill. "Despite years of tireless trying, mountains of rejection letters, Stephen King didn't publish a single novel until *after* he got married. Everything you've ever read of his was written within the context of a loving, committed relationship."

Thomas's shoulders slump.

"Stephen King is living proof that your belief about relationships is not only false, but might even be holding you back as a writer."

Thomas shoots to his feet, running a hand through his hair as he paces over to the bookshelf. Propping an elbow on it, he turns to face me.

"So what?" he barks. "So what if I admit that perhaps not *all* relationships end in disaster? Even if I can convince myself of that, which is doubtful, how is that going to help me now? I have four weeks left to write this book. I can't just fall in love and get married tomorrow."

"You don't have to." I smile. "All you have to do is admit that maybe it's not your mind that's empty; it's your heart. That longing is where your creative voice lives. You've just been silencing it for too long with meaningless"—*sex*—"relationships."

Thomas folds his arms over his chest again. "So, admit that I'm lonely and lying to myself? Anything else? Do I need to take a vow of silence or rent a rowing machine?"

"No." I shake my head, trying to pretend like his tone doesn't make me want to cry. "That's all for this week."

I stand.

Thomas's face falls. His arms drop. And if there were a rock on my floor, I'm pretty sure he would kick it. I wait for him to leave, but he doesn't. He just stands there, silently apologizing with those impossibly blue eyes before a crooked smile begins to tug at the corner of his mouth.

"How do you know about all my *meaningless relationships* anyway?"

I walk over to the door, hoping he'll follow my lead. "The tabloids love you here," I say with my back to him. "I can't buy a pack of gum without getting an update on your love life."

Thomas's crisp, clean scent announces that he did in fact follow me, so I stand to one side of the doorway, holding my breath as he breezes past. I notice that he's tapping on his phone as he enters the hallway. Then, he stops and turns to face me.

"Did you see this one?" He smirks, handing me his phone.

Accepting the slim black device, I see that there's a TMZ.com article pulled up on the screen. The headline reads, "Thomas O'Reardon Gets Cozy with Georgia Peach." Below it is a picture of the two of us at The Yacht Club. We're sitting in the corner booth. Thomas is smiling at me, and I'm staring down at the place where his hand is wrapped around my wrist. My skin tingles from the memory of that touch.

The angle of the photo looks like it was taken from the bar area.

Adelynn, you little shit.

"You might want to collect everyone's mobiles from now on." Thomas's voice pulls me out of my head and back into the hallway.

I exhale as I glance back up at him. "Thomas, I am so sorry about this."

"I don't give a toss." He chuckles, taking his phone back. "But that lady looks like she might."

Thomas tips his head toward the end of the hallway, where the Notorious E.I.C. is glaring at me from the doorway of her office.

"Dr. Sterling," she barks the second I make eye contact. "A word, please."

Fuck, fuck, fuck, fuck, fuck.

I sit bolt upright in the chair across from Dr. Ito-Cohen, wondering if I'll even be able to hear her over the sound of all that adrenaline pumping through my veins.

Lacing her bony fingers together, E.I.C. leans back in her chair the way a cobra leans backward before it strikes.

"Luna ... will you please explain to me why there is a Rorschach test checked out in your name? I hired you to do therapy, not psychological evaluations. We have psychometrists for that."

The Rorschach!

My shoulders slump in relief.

"Oh." I smile. "I wasn't giving an evaluation. I was just using the inkblot cards with my author client. I thought they might help with his writer's block."

Dr. Ito-Cohen's eyes narrow.

"I see." She tilts her head to one side. "You *thought* it would be a good idea to break testing standardization while simultaneously using some *non*evidence-based technique on our most important client."

Thumpa-thumpa-thumpa-thumpa ...

"What did I say about fucking this case up?"

I swallow. "That I should not... ... do that."

"Exactly. So, stop it. And also, why have four new clients called, requesting appointments with you this week? No one ever asks for you."

I shrug, looking about as innocent as a four-year-old with her hand in the cookie jar.

E.I.C. points one long red talon directly at my face. "You're up to something."

Thumpa-thumpa-thumpa-thumpa... ...

I do a weird, simultaneous shrug/head-shake thing while desperately trying to suppress the nervous laughter percolating in my throat. "I'm not up to anything," I squeak. "Hey, do you hear that?" I angle my body toward her open door. "I think that's my desk phone."

Hopping up, I jerk my thumb in the direction of the door as I walk backward toward it. "I'd better get that. My four o'clock's probably here, so …"

Without waiting to be excused, I turn and bolt, thankful that Atlanta Psychology Associates has carpeted hallways, so Dr. Ito-Cohen can't hear the rapid clickety-clack of my heels as I literally run away from her office.

Lou

"I DON'T UNDERSTAND WHY she hates me so much. I mean, I know I'm not the most experienced psychologist on staff or the best dressed, and I am kind of running an unsupervised therapy group out of a bar behind her back ..." I ramble as I add another layer of dried blood to Fly Ghoul Number Eight's mouth. I've never painted actual faces to look like zombies before, but so far, so good. It's actually way easier than drawing them from scratch.

We're standing in the middle of Euclid Avenue, behind my neighbor Paul's ambulance, waiting for the annual Little 5 Points Halloween Parade to begin. A group of grown-ass men, dressed like bearded Disney princesses, walks by as a contortionist in a unitard limbers up on the creepy carnival-themed float next to us.

Behind me, fly ghouls one through seven are practicing a twerky version of the Thriller dance in bikinis that look like triangular flaps of rotting flesh.

"I know how you feel," Fly Ghoul Number Eight says as I dab a few more grayish-green splotches onto her forehead with a makeup sponge. "My boss treats me like a child too. I mean, just yesterday, he told me to call him Papa Bear."

I stop dabbing. "And where exactly do you work?"

"The Frisky Pony." She shrugs. "I'm just a server right now, but I'm on the wait list for a pole position."

"I might need you to put me on that wait list," I say, only half-joking. "Okay, I think you're done."

FG8 checks her reflection in the blacked-out back window of the ambulance and skips off. I'm just about to pack up all my makeup and art supplies, which are lined up across the rear bumper, when the door swings open and knocks most of it onto the pavement.

"Thirty seconds till go time!" Paul yells a foot away from my ear before he notices me standing there. "Dude, killer job!" He beams, dressed in a blood-spattered doctor costume. "The fly ghouls look sick as fuck!"

We both turn and watch The Frisky Pony's finest laughing with their cheeks laid open and their eyes hollowed out as they take turns, recording each other doing this week's viral TikTok dance.

"You should come with us, man," Paul says, giving my shoulder a friendly shove.

"Nah, I'm good here." I gesture to my ripped jeans, cowboy boots, Decemberists T-shirt, and floor-length cardigan with one sweep of my hand. "I don't really think I fit your aesthetic."

"You could ride shotgun! Come on. It'll be fun!"

A parade official walks by with a bullhorn and yells in my other ear, "Positions, everyone! The parade is starting in one minute!"

"First place, here I come!" Paul shouts, thrusting his fist into the air. "Woohoo!"

He disappears inside the ambulance, and I head toward the sidewalk. It's not that I don't want to share a confined space with Paul for forty-five minutes—he's ... nice enough; it's that I genuinely love watching this parade. The number of truly talented people out there astounds me.

I watch them ride by on floats that must have taken the entire year since last Halloween to design, wearing costumes and makeup and prosthetics that rival some of the best horror movies, acting like the actual undead, or singing and playing instruments, or contorting and tumbling like Olympians, and I think, *These people probably all have day jobs that they suck at too.*

And then I take a little notebook out of my big, slouchy purse, sketch a few zombified versions of my favorite characters, and wish I felt as happy as they looked.

A whistle signals that the parade has begun, and the marching band at the front of the group stomps into action.

Paul's ambulance pulls away a minute later. The fly ghouls all give me a wave as they zombie-shuffle by. I watch them go as smoke and loud demonic laughter pour out of some unseen opening in the roof, followed by a ten-foot-tall Grim Reaper. It is mostly made out of black fabric, but there must be some kind of telescoping structure inside of it because it wobbles and sways like a radio antenna.

The crowd's eyes go wide as they smile and point and snap photos of Paul's creation, and for a moment, I feel really happy for him. Happy and, if I'm being honest, a little jealous.

That is, until the screaming starts.

I jerk my head in the direction of Paul's ambulance just in time to see it take out some low-hanging power lines about a block away. Sparks rain down on the crowd as they shriek and run for their lives. Screaming bystanders, terrified fly ghouls, and hysterical carnies stampede past me, filling the street with the sounds of terror.

I take off running in the opposite direction, fighting my way through the crowd to check on Paul, when I see someone in an inflatable T. rex costume go down like a bowling pin in front of me. I stop to help the big fella up, trying not to get stomped on in the process, and feel a sudden, renewed commitment to my career choice.

Psychology = Helps people.

Art = Borderline homelessness, chlamydia, and evidently, stampedes.

I definitely made the right choice.

Right?

Lou

LUCKILY, NO ONE WAS injured during the Halloween Parade from hell yesterday, but I can't shake the feeling that it was some kind of omen. If something as innocent and low stakes as the annual Little 5 Points Halloween Parade can go sideways that fast, then it's just a matter of time before this thing with Thomas explodes in my face too. He's not making progress, I have no idea what I'm doing, and this entire group feels like a ticking time bomb.

Not to mention the fact that he looks like *that*.

From my spot in the corner booth, I watch as Thomas enters the bar. He never fails to take my breath away. Tall and graceful and effortlessly cool. The garish overhead lights only accentuate his cheekbones as he greets Mark with a polite smile.

Mark extends a basket full of cell phones toward Thomas, and his smile widens. He drops his in and makes his way across the bar. He eyes the clients at the Anxiety table, who are snapping themselves on the wrist with a rubber band every time they have an intrusive thought—which, from the look of it, is pretty damn often—and he raises an eyebrow as he passes Dee, who is coloring a yacht-themed kids' menu along with her depressed group members. By the time his gaze falls on me, I've already begun to sweat through my clinical-strength deodorant.

"So, what exactly is the definition of group therapy?" he asks, one side of his perfectly sculpted mouth curving up in amusement.

I sit up straighter and clear my throat. "Uh, well, according to the Georgia licensing exam study guide, group therapy is defined as, *One or more practitioners engaging in psychotherapy with multiple clients at the same time.*"

Nailed it.

Thomas's smirk disappears. "Study guide?"

Ohhhhh … fuck.

"You're not licensed." He doesn't even raise his voice at the end to pretend like it might be a question.

He knows. He knows I'm a fraud, and he has since the moment he stepped into my office.

I wipe my sweaty palms on my thighs and cringe. "I will be. Soon."

"Soon." Thomas's lips press into a hard line as my stomach tries to fold in on itself. "Are you even a doctor?"

"Yes, I am. I swear. I just … can't practice without supervision yet." I find the braid tucked behind my ear and twist it around my index finger.

Please don't fire me … please don't fire me …

"So, all that about you being a *specialist* …"

I frown through my tight, terrified features. "I'm so sorry, Thomas. My boss lied to your editor, and … I went along with it."

Thomas leans back in his seat and crosses his arms. "I have four weeks to come up with a book idea or give back a million-dollar advance, and they sent me to an amateur. Perfect."

His comment lands like a fist in my gut.

Amateur.

I can't even argue with him. I am an amateur, and I have no defense. Nothing I say will justify uprooting this man's life for six weeks under false pretenses. All I can do at this point is beg. So, I do. Shamelessly.

"Thomas, please. I know I don't deserve it, but ... please give me a chance. I might not be a specialist, but I promise you will never find another person on this planet who is more invested in helping you than I am. Not only because I'm your biggest fan, but also because if I *can't* help you write this book, my entire career will be over before it even begins. My job's on the line here too."

Thomas chews the inside corner of his mouth as he studies me through narrowed eyes. Then, he shakes his head. "Fuck. Now, I'm the one who's sorry."

"Why?"

His eyebrows pull together as he holds my stare. "Because there is no way I'm going to write this book in time."

"Yes, you are." I grin.

Thomas shrugs in defeat and lets out a heavy sigh. "So, what now? More inkblots? Tea leaves perhaps?"

"Even better." My smile widens as I pick up the stack of *Mad Libs* booklets sitting next to me and hold them up for him to see.

Thomas's head falls back against the wooden bench with a thud.

I laugh, partially at his dramatics and partially out of relief over not being fired *yet*, when a noise I've never heard before comes from the direction of the storage room.

"Primal scream?" Thomas asks, locking eyes with me.

"I know all of Mark's screams, and that was *not* primal."

I bolt out of the booth and take off running toward the shrill, high-pitched sound as a dozen concerned faces look on.

Well, a dozen, minus Dee. Instead of concerned, she's going for more of a nonchalant, *nothing to see here* look while she tries to hide a row of shot glasses brimming with brown liquor behind her forearms.

I'll deal with her later.

I push through the Employees Only door and find Mark practically pressed up against one of the shelves, blocking himself with his arms. Celeste grabs a can off the shelf next to her yoga mat and chucks it at him, hitting him on the elbow.

He shrieks again.

"Celeste!" I shout. "What are you doing?"

"He said my proud pigeon pose wasn't proud enough! Who's proud now?" she growls, reaching for another projectile.

"No!" I launch myself across the tiny space and grab her arm before she can throw anything else.

With a very unladylike growl, Celeste wraps her free arm around my neck and begins spinning me in a circle. I flail and reach for anything that might help me regain control of my body, but my fingers only graze metal shelving and the clothes of the other group members as they stumble away from my grasp … and directly into each other. I can't see them, but I hear their bickering.

"Ow! My foot!"

"Hey! Get off my mat, asshole!"

"None of these are your mat, asshole. They're his!"

"You guys! Stop fighting! Mountain pose! Come on, y'all! Mountain pose!"

I catch a glimpse of Mark, backed into a corner with his arms up over his head.

On my next rotation, I see a pair of dark gray slacks silhouetted in the doorway.

Then, a white button-up shirt, cuffed at the elbows, stretched over a V-shaped torso.

On the rotation after that, I see a blur of enviable cheekbones and jawbones and chiseled lips parted in shock.

I open my mouth to tell him to leave, but Celeste has my larynx in a death grip. I wave Thomas away instead, hoping he understands the universal sign for *I have everything under control. Please return to your seat until the pilot has turned off the Fasten Your Seat Belt sign*, but my flailing only knocks an industrial-sized plastic jar of mustard off the shelf.

The yoga mats cushion its fall.

From the chaos and clattering and grunting I hear nearby, it sounds like Angry Bill and Angrier Anton are in a full-on fistfight. They slam into the shelf next to Mark.

"Ah!" he shouts. "Toxic masculinity!"

A comically large tub of mayonnaise falls off the shelf next to him.

It bounces.

I dig my heels in and finally get the spinning to stop just as Perspectively Challenged Penelope picks up a giant cardboard box and brings it down on Anton's head. The bottom folds in, and at least fifty plastic spoons fly out the top.

I exhale in relief, but before I can recover, Celeste slams my body into the shelves beside us.

Thomas darts forward, and I watch in slow motion as his arms reach out and catch a thirty-pound glass jar of pickles as it falls off the top shelf and careens toward the ground.

Wow.

Anton shoves Bill into the shelf across from us, causing it to teeter and wobble. I shout Thomas's name, and before the second syllable can escape my lips, he sticks a foot out to stabilize it.

Celeste slams me against the shelf again, and Mark makes that same high-pitched shrieking noise I heard earlier. Unscrewing the lid from the jar Thomas is holding, he begins pelting us with wet, briny pickles.

"Stop it! Stop it! Stop it!" he yells as slimy, astringent cucumbers bounce off of Celeste's ear, her shoulder, my head.

"Oh, sorry, hon." Mark grimaces at me.

With Celeste distracted, I blindly pat the items on the shelf behind me until my hand closes around a plastic squirt bottle.

I shove it in Celeste's face without warning, and her eyes go crossed as they focus on the bright red nozzle. Her hands immediately shoot up in surrender as she takes a step back, staring down the barrel of a bottle of sriracha.

The other group members stop fighting and watch.

Thomas sets the pickle jar down and glares at Celeste with nostrils flared.

"Celeste …" I pant. "Your behavior"—*gasp*—"is unacceptable. And from now on"—*gasp*—"there will be consequences."

Taking a page from Courtney's behaviorism playbook, I squeeze the bottle in my fist with all my might. A laser-like beam of red hot sauce shoots straight out, hitting Celeste right between the boobs.

"My sweater!" she shrieks in the exact same pitch and tone as the *I'm melting!* death rattle of the Wicked Witch of the West.

Then, her face contorts into a snarl so ferocious that I consider offering to buy her a new sweater. And a new condo to match.

Celeste shoves a manicured finger in my face and shouts, "You'll be hearing from my lawyer!" before shoving her bare feet into her stilettos, stomping toward the door, slipping on a pickle, and landing ass over tit on a bed of yoga mats.

Bill and Anton help her up as Thomas rushes over to me.

"Are you okay?" he asks, searching me with his eyes for any signs of injury.

I have no idea if I'm hurt or not because my entire awareness is focused on the shiny lock of chestnut-brown hair that has fallen over Thomas's forehead.

Don't you dare touch it.

"I'm fine," I say, forcing myself to look away as I straighten my posture. "Come on. Let's …"

I take one step forward, but instead of stepping onto a yoga mat, my foot glides across something slippery and round. I squeal and grab Thomas's arm as I go down, but unfortunately, I squeeze the bottle in my other hand at the same time.

Two splats follow—me landing on the pickle brine–splattered yoga mats and a volcanic squirt of sriracha landing on me.

They say club soda will take out any stain.

They lied.

The Yacht Club is now empty as I stand behind the bar in my camisole, scrubbing a massive red stain out of my favorite striped sweater while Thomas O'Reardon holds an ice-cold can of Miller High Life against the knot on the back of my head.

"Welp," I sigh. "Looks like you aren't going to be the reason I get fired after all."

Thomas scoffs behind me, "Fired? For that? No way. That's what they came here for, you know? A release."

I turn sideways and cast a doubtful look at him over my shoulder, my arms still elbow deep in wet polyester.

"It's true." Thomas gives me a sheepish half-smile. "In fact, I'm a bit jealous. I've never been in a fight."

His admission is adorable.

"Really?" I smile. "Not even as a kid?"

Thomas shakes his head, and before I can stop myself, I reach out and play-slap him across the face, leaving a smear of spicy red sauce on his cheek.

Thomas grimaces in disgust and touches the spot I left behind.

Looking at his fingertips, he asks, "What *is* that?"

"Sriracha." I smirk. "The hipsters put it on everything."

"You say that like you're not one." Thomas sets down the beer and grabs a napkin.

"I prefer the term *emo-lectual*, thank you very much."

Thomas wipes his cheek with the napkin but doesn't get the whole streak.

"Here." I laugh.

Wetting a bar towel, I reach up and wipe the spot he left behind. The moment my terry cloth–covered fingers graze his skin—the second time I've touched his face in as many minutes—Thomas's jaw clenches beneath my palm, and my smile dies. His casual, friendly posture goes tense, his breathing stops altogether, and I am reminded that I SHOULD NOT BE TOUCHING MY FUCKING CLIENT. Especially while we're alone, in a bar, at almost midnight, and I'm missing, like, a quarter of my outfit.

A spot on the side of his stupidly perfect neck pulses at the same speed as the blood rushing in my ears.

You're freaking him out!

With a nervous laugh, I turn back toward the sink and wring the towel out so hard that I'm surprised it doesn't rip in half. "So, you've never been in a fight, huh? Even I've been in a fight."

Thomas laughs behind me, soothing my nerves. "Really?"

"Mmhmm." Next, I wring the club soda out of my sweater. "Catherine Pessavento. Ninth grade. I found out she'd kissed my boyfriend on the bus, so I slapped her."

"I'm picking up on a pattern."

I peek at him over my shoulder, and he points to his cheek.

I smile and look away. "What was your childhood like? Besides, you know, your parents' issues."

"Fine, I suppose. My sisters never let me out of their sight, so I rarely got in trouble. My mum treated me like a human security blanket, as you know. And my father's a professor at Oxford, so he made sure we attended all the best schools."

"Really? What subject does he teach?" I give up and drop my sopping wet sweater into the trash can. It lands on the pile of beer bottles inside with a surprisingly loud crash.

"Economics—something boring." Thomas glances into the trash can at my ruined sweater and arches an eyebrow. "It was all so beautifully boring."

The Employees Only door swings open, and Mark pushes his way through, carrying all five rolled-up yoga mats.

He gives me a pointed look. "You're helpin' me hose the pickle juice offa these when we get home, just so you know."

Mark holds the mats with one arm as he flips all the lights off on the breaker box next to the bar.

The three of us walk outside, and the cold November air steals my breath. My arms break out in goose bumps as they wrap around my chest, both to keep me warm and to keep Thomas from seeing how hard my nipples are in this camisole.

Thomas's Batmobile and Mark's little roller skate are the only two vehicles left in the parking lot. Even the street is empty at this time of night.

"If it makes you feel any better, out of all my clients, I think you win the Least Dysfunctional Childhood award," I joke, trying to break the silence as we walk toward Thomas's car.

"It was functional but ... empty."

There's that word again. It makes my heart ache.

"No one truly expresses themselves where I'm from. They just ... do what's expected. Go through the motions. It's nothing like it is here." Thomas jerks his head in the direction of the building we just exited.

"What, *that*? That was not normal." I laugh, but then I remember how many times I've had to duck flying objects in my office or call maintenance to come patch holes in my drywall and think again. "Actually, you're right. Americans are animals."

Thomas laughs—like a head-back, eyes-closed, full-bodied laugh—as he comes to a stop next to his car. A warm, tingly sensation floods my body as I enjoy a rare glimpse of Thomas, unrestrained. He is beautiful in his broody, cynical, self-composed state, but Joyful Thomas is breathtaking.

It doesn't last though. When his chuckles die down and he turns to face me, what he sees steals the light from his eyes.

"Bloody hell. You're freezing." Thomas pats his chest like a jacket is going to magically appear on his body before peering into the car's window. The interior lights are already on, thanks to some kind of Bruce Wayne technology, but they don't reveal what Thomas is looking for. Turning back toward me, he says, "Here."

My eyes go wide in horror as Thomas begins unbuttoning his shirt.

"No! Oh my God. I'm fine. I swear." I hold my hands out like a Stop sign.

He ignores me and continues unbuttoning, revealing a crisp white tee stretched across a body that looks like it belongs to an action hero, not an author.

"Thomas, really, I'm ..."

Warm, ocean-scented oxford cloth wraps around my shoulders, and for some strange reason, my eyes begin to burn. I blink the stinging sensation away and focus on my breathing as my fingers instinctively curl around the open material and cinch it tighter around my body.

It feels like a hug.

A hug that I didn't realize I'd needed so badly.

"Thanks," I whisper, swallowing the emotion lodged in my throat.

Thomas folds his arms across his chest and shrugs, his shoulders already tense from the cold.

Say something!

"So, you weren't freaked out by what happened in there?"

Please say no. Please say you'll come back next week.

"Actually"—Thomas gives me a crooked smile—"it was kind of fun." The corners of his mouth drop along with his gaze as it drifts slowly to the ground. "I wonder what it's like to feel that free."

"You only say that because you weren't the one in a headlock."

He laughs silently, and it's the perfect example of the self-control he wishes he could let go of.

"Maybe that's why you write about psychopaths," I say, missing the weight of his eyes on me. "So you can experience what it's like to be that … uninhibited."

A crease forms between his eyebrows. "Wrote," he says, his eyes darkening as they travel to a place even farther away from me. "Past tense."

With that, Thomas turns to open his car door, and I panic. I panic, and I do the dumbest thing I've done yet, which is saying a lot.

I reach out and grab his hand.

Thomas goes completely still.

I go completely still.

Even the wind, which had been swirling brittle orange leaves around our feet, goes completely still as the words, "Will write," leave me on a shaky breath.

I try to let go of Thomas's hand, but he laces his fingers through mine, holding me captive. Then, he turns and captures me with his eyes as well.

"Future tense," I add, unable to look away from the restraint and madness I see warring in his eyes.

Thomas's gaze drops to my lips, and when I run my tongue along the seam instead of screaming or slapping him or prying my fingers loose, he begins to lean forward. No. He is being *pulled* forward. By me. By *my* actions. By my confusing fucking mixed signals. I invited this. And I have to stop it.

Now.

Riiiight ... now.

Now, bitch!

But I can't. My brain is barking commands that my body is no longer listening to. Dee and Courtney were right. I've denied my own needs for way too long. And now, I'm starving.

I watch helplessly from inside my traitorous body as Thomas lifts his other hand, slides it beneath my curtain of hair, which is still tucked inside his shirt, and cups the side of my neck.

His thumb caresses the ridge of my jaw, and like the strike of a match, my neglected husk of a body goes up in flames. The heat engulfs me, spreading like a forest fire as it burns away the fingerprints of every man who's ever touched me before. It ignites something deep inside of me—an inextinguishable need. An excruciating singular desire.

I close my eyes and lean into his touch. And I hate myself for it.

I can't do this. I can't kill my career. I can't sabotage his treatment. But as I stand here, rooted to the spot, with Thomas's fingers laced in mine and his hand splayed across my skin, I can't even make myself exhale, let alone walk away.

Just as Thomas's breath, warm and sweet, dances over my parted lips, as my body tenses and braces for the impact of this wrecking ball of a man, it is the voice of another man that finally breaks the spell.

"I smell like brine, bitch. Let's go."

My eyes pop open, landing first on Thomas before darting over to a six-foot-tall redneck standing next to a three-foot-tall car.

Thomas lets out a frustrated laugh and gently presses his forehead to mine instead of his lips. "Pickle juice waits for no man."

With one final squeeze of Thomas's hand, I force myself to do the hardest thing I've ever done. I let go, and I take a step back.

When Thomas's palm falls away from my neck and his fingers slide out from between mine, the loss I feel is sharp and swift, like an amputation. Like something that should be there but isn't anymore and never will be again. I stumble backward another step or two before realizing that the extraction isn't over yet.

"Oh, here," I say, trying to keep the anguish out of my voice as I shrug off his warmth and his scent as well.

"Keep it," Thomas says, holding up a hand to stop me from returning his shirt. "It looks better on you anyway."

Despite my best efforts, I can't suppress the smile that spreads across my face as I clutch a piece of Thomas O'Reardon to my chest and skip backward a few more steps. "Uh … thanks …"

"Ahem!" Mark clears his throat loud enough for the entire neighborhood to hear. "Tonight, please."

"I better … you know." I jerk a thumb over my shoulder in the direction of my ornery-ass roommate. "Good night, Thomas."

It's hard to tell in the dark, but I swear I see a whisper of a smile belie his infuriatingly unreadable, perfectly poised face before he nods once. "Good night, Dr. Sterling."

God, I am so fucked.

Lou

IT'S BEEN A LITTLE over seven hours since I forcibly extracted myself from the clutches of Thomas O'Reardon. I slept for three of those; stared at the ceiling, overanalyzing, for four; and spent the last ten minutes or so waiting in line to order a latte from some fancy Midtown coffee shop with one of those names that has a plus sign in the middle of it. Cradle + Ox or some shit like that. They probably got it off one of those hipster business-name generators online.

This hole in the wall is so small that we have to wait in line outside, which Mark seems to find invigorating. Inhaling the crisp air through his nose, he sweeps his hands up over his head, practically showing his nipples in that camouflage midriff sweater, before lowering them back down to his sides with an appreciative exhale.

"I just love sweater weather," he sighs, twisting left and right as he checks out the other twelve-dollar coffee consumers in line.

I hardly notice the spectacle he's making of his calisthenics, not only because *everyone* in line is stretching and praising the autumnal gods while wearing athleisure and waiting half an hour for a pumpkin-spice-cinnamon-chai whatever, but also because I'm still very much back in The Yacht Club parking lot, reliving every single second that I spent alone with Thomas.

Did you notice that he called you Dr. Sterling?

So? That doesn't mean anything.

He called you Doctor because he likes that you're off-limits. That's all you are to him now. A challenge. Some unavailable piece of ass for him to chase while he's in town with zero risk of commitment. God, you are such an idiot.

God, he's so perfect.

I can't believe you almost let him kiss you!

I can't believe he almost kissed me!

Why don't you just roll your degree up and flush it down the toilet when you get to work?

Why don't I just Google him a few thousand more times to see if it makes me feel better?

A sudden hip bump disrupts my game of emotional ping-pong, but luckily, I've been keeping score.

Self-loathing: 3,000,582

Heart-wrenching angst: 3,000,583

"Looks like Daddy Harry Potter cast a loooove spell on somebody last night," Mark teases, twiddling his fingers at me while he holds the door open.

I shoot him a murderous glare as I pass, but my mortified magenta cheeks really take the edge off my malice.

Mark steps up to the counter. "Good morning! I'll have a grande nonfat, one-pump mocha, and she'll have a tall vanilla Englishman. I mean, latte. With extra whip."

Mark cracks an invisible whip.

"That'll be eighteen forty-seven," the apathetic, purple-haired barista drones.

"It's on her." Mark grins. "You owe me for savin' your ass last night."

I hand over my nearly maxed-out credit card with a sigh. "Thanks for that, by the way. I just ... froze."

"Oh, I did that for me, not you. I can't have you losin' your job. Believe it or not, findin' a roommate who's okay with weekly Shania karaoke isn't as easy as you'd think."

We head over to the napkin/condiment counter to wait for our drinks. Mark goes down the line, grabbing both of our cup sleeves and napkins and whatever else because it's obvious that I'm too frazzled to function right now.

"Why does God hate me?" I ask out loud, more to myself than anyone. "I finally meet the actual, literal man of my dreams, and if I sleep with him, my career is over."

Mark smirks at me over his shoulder. "Only if you sleep with him *now*."

"Elaborate, please."

Mark turns toward me with an annoyed eye roll. "Think about it. If you can get *that* man ... to write *that* book ... on time—"

"I'll get licensed. Yeah, I know."

"No, dummy. Then, he won't be your client anymore. And *then* you can bump uglies with him all you want." Mark thrusts his hips a few times for dramatic effect, completely unconcerned about the crush of people surrounding us. "Fix him, and *then* you can fuck him."

I nod slowly, his words bouncing around in my sleep-deprived brain until they finally hit their mark. Somewhere deep inside, a tiny kernel of hope begins to bloom.

What if I don't have to choose between my career and my crush?

What if I can have them *both* ... just not right now?

It's a long shot—one that would require Thomas to not only write a damn book, but also decide that he actually wants to date me once he's done with it, never mind the whole we live on two different continents thing—but it's still a shot.

Fix him. Then, fuck him.

My eyes flick back to my roommate's beautiful, bearded face. "Mark, you're a genius."

"You just now figurin' that out?" Mark rolls his eyes like he can't believe I'm the one with the PhD in this equation, and honestly, I can't either.

I've been so focused on the fact that I can't have Thomas *now* that I never stopped to consider that maybe ... just maybe ...

As a smile gradually spreads across my face and my heartrate increases to a level that probably makes caffeine consumption a bad idea, a pierced, pouty barista approaches the counter and calls out the names on our cups. "Lou and ... Markle? Meghan Markle?"

I glare at Mark.

"What?" He shrugs, turning his face sideways to show off his profile. "The resemblance is uncanny."

Thomas

I'VE SPENT THE LAST five days in a state of self-flagellation. When I wasn't beating my head against a wall for nearly kissing my therapist, I was forcing myself to write in order to atone for nearly kissing my therapist.

What is wrong with me?

I've always put my career above everything else. No, not my career—my work. My writing. I love it more than anything. There's nothing I wouldn't do to get it back. So, why am I spending what little time I have left of this more than generous extension with an inexperienced, unlicensed therapist who—

I walk into Lou's office and find the answer to that question before I can even finish asking it.

Pacing the floor in black high heels and black leather leggings, Lou has her long, dark hair pulled up off her neck with one hand and is flapping the bottom of her white button-up shirt with the other. She looks like she's having a hot flash or a panic attack or both, but all I can focus on is that shirt in her fist.

I'm transported back to the car park Sunday night when Lou had a very different crisp white shirt draped over her shoulders. When, instead of a degree on the wall behind her, it was a pub. When her cheeks were flushed pink, not from heat, but from the cold November air. When the scent of my cologne on her skin sparked something primal in me.

Something I vowed not to let happen again.

I can't be the reason Lou loses her job. I won't be. Not because I can't write and definitely not because I can't, as she says, *keep it in my pants*. I can, and I bloody fucking will. I've achieved everything I've ever set my mind to, and making sure I don't ruin this woman's life became my primary goal the moment she walked away from me last weekend.

"Rough client?" I ask, leaning against the doorframe.

Lou drops her hair and shirt at the same time and spins around to face me. "Thomas! Hi!" Her face brightens, and the joy she expresses over seeing me feels ... real.

"Please, have a seat." She gestures to the chair closest to me as she grabs a clipboard and pencil off her desk.

I do as I'm told. When Lou joins me, I watch her transform into Dr. Sterling before my eyes. Her back straightens, her knees pull together, her chin lifts, and her pencil goes still. Her eyes, always the last to assume their position, lock on to mine, and when they do, I feel as though time is standing still, waiting to see how I'll bugger things up this time.

Lou clutches her clipboard to her chest, using it like a shield. Like I'm someone she needs protection from. I hate that my actions made her feel that way.

I don't even know what came over me. When she touched my hand, it just ... it felt different. Most women ... *all women* ... want something from me. Even my own mother. But when Lou touched me, it wasn't because she wanted something from me; it was because she wanted something *for* me. She wants me to succeed. She wants me to believe in myself. But most of all, she wants me to know that she believes in me enough for the both of us.

But that's her job, isn't it? This woman is literally being paid by my publisher to try to get me to write. She's figured out that I respond creatively to this feeling of longing, so she's trying to simulate that. For money. That's all this is—a transaction, just like every other relationship I've ever had. I'm just so fucked in the head right now that I mistook her professional attention for a genuine connection.

Lou leans forward slightly. "How was your week? Have you ... made any progress?"

I shrug. "Wrote a few chapters."

"Really?" she exclaims, a grin erasing the tension from her features. "Thomas, that's fantastic."

The hope on her face guts me, so I stare at her bookshelf instead. "It's rubbish though. All of it."

"I seriously doubt that," Lou says, a teasing lilt to her voice. When I don't reply, her shoulders slump.

"I mean ... I'm sorry you feel that way. You sound really ... frustrated."

I cut her a glance out of the corner of my eye. "You have no idea."

I didn't intend for that statement to have so much sexual innuendo, nor for the hostility I feel toward myself to be directed at her, but then again, maybe I did.

"Thomas ..." Lou's perfect posture returns. "You have every right to be upset with me. I lied to you about my credentials, I guilt-tripped you into not firing me, and I've been sending very mixed signals, which led to what happened in the parking lot. But from now on, I assure you—"

As Lou rambles on in her professional demeanor, it becomes more and more obvious to me that I was right. This whole psychologist persona is an act. A lie. And if this is a lie, then what I feel when I'm around her might be a lie too. A clever manipulation. Nothing more.

"Can I ask you something?" I interrupt.

Lou pauses for a moment and then nods.

"At the end of *Ruby Lies*, what did you think about the double meaning of the title?"

Lou's entire demeanor shifts as a smile spreads across her face. "I loved it," she says, pulling her legs up underneath her like a child. "It was one of my all-time favorite plot twists. Seriously. When he finds that tombstone and it says—"

"*Here lies Ruby Donovan*," I recite along with her.

"Yes! Oh my God. I screamed when I read it. You can ask Mark. The way those four words made every single clue click into place at the exact same moment"—she shakes her head, still beaming with excitement—"it was perfection."

"My publisher hated it. They said it was too 'on the nose.' "

"On the nose? That's bullshit. Calling it *Here Lies Ruby Donovan* would have been on the nose. *Ruby Lies* is brilliant, especially because it sets up the expectation for her to be untrustworthy, so readers don't realize that the clues she's dropping are actually true."

"What about the end of *Hope Hollow*?" I ask, keeping my expression as neutral as possible.

Lou presses her lips together. "Um …"

I watch as her eyes dart around the room, and I know that I've got her.

"It was …" She presses her fist to her lips, tapping them a few times with her knuckle.

Which lie will she go with? It was great. Awesome. Sooo good.

"Unsatisfying."

Fuck.

My face must broadcast my dismay because Lou frowns and begins to backtrack.

"Don't get me wrong. I still love that book—"

"No." I shake my head. "You're right. The ending is completely and utterly unsatisfying. It feels rushed, and anyone who tells me different is lying."

Lou waits for me to make my point, but I don't know if I can.

"You wanted to see if I would lie to you?"

"I didn't want to *see* if you would lie to me. I wanted you to lie to me," I correct.

Lou's eyebrows pull together. "Why?"

Because if you're just some puppet my publisher hired, I can tell myself this isn't real.

If this is all some contrived manipulation, then what happened between us wasn't real.

Because if you're real and I can't have you ...

My eyes drift to the framed degree on the wall behind Lou's head as a bitter laugh rumbles through my chest.

"Thomas?" Lou sets her feet back on the ground, knees together, and begins the Dr. Sterling ritual all over again.

"Don't," I snap.

She locks eyes with me and freezes just before the transformation is complete.

"Not with me. Okay? Just ... be real."

Lou smiles, but there's a sadness behind it that mirrors what's swirling inside my empty chest. Kicking off her heels, she pulls her feet up under her in her chair again and lays her clipboard on her lap.

"Better?"

I nod. "So, what'll it be today? Hypnotism? Past-life regression?"

Lou laughs, graciously allowing me to change the subject.

"Well ... on Sunday, our discussion about your childhood got me thinking... ..."

I cross my arms.

This should be delightful.

"I work with some of the most successful people in this city," Lou says, tapping her pencil on her clipboard. It seems absentminded, and I can't help but smile at the fact that she's allowing herself to do it. "And they all have one thing in common. No matter how mature or confident or glamorous they seem, when I peel back the layers, they are *exactly* who they were when they were eight years old. Or twelve. Or fifteen. On the inside, we're all just wounded children, pretending to be grown-ups."

I don't like where this is going.

"I want you to take out your phone and find a picture of someone who looks the way you see yourself on the inside."

"My inner child?" I scoff. "You're serious?"

Lou nods.

I lean back in my chair and point my chin at her. "You go first."

Lou smiles. "We'll go at the same time, okay?"

I sigh in defeat and pull out my mobile.

Lou retrieves hers from somewhere between her armrest and seat cushion. "Ready?"

I nod rather unhappily.

"Aaaaand ... go."

A simple Google search pulls up the exact image I have in mind. Lou must have known what she was going for as well because our eyes lock again within five seconds flat.

"All right." I extend my hand and flick my fingers at her. "Let's see it."

She hands it over, and there on the screen is a GIF of Jonah Hill from the film *21 Jump Street*. He's dressed like some kind of goth teenager, brushing a curtain of black hair out of his eyeliner-rimmed eyes as he walks down the hallway of his high school.

I can't help but laugh.

"What?" Lou shrugs. "That's actual footage of me in tenth grade."

I hand her mobile back with a smirk. "I would have killed for your five o'clock shadow."

Lou rolls her eyes. "Okay, your turn."

With a huff, I place the glowing device in Lou's outstretched hand. The moment she sees the image on the screen, a very unladylike snort bursts out of her, followed by a series of unrestrained giggles.

I snatch the mobile back and pocket it immediately.

"Harry Potter?" Lou says, pressing her lips together to keep from laughing again.

"That was me," I admit with a frown, "right down to the bowl cut and glasses. Always got good marks in school, never got in trouble, and was completely invisible to everyone, except the other brainy boys with bowl cuts."

Lou gazes at me with pure, unbridled joy on her face. I have no idea why she's so delighted, but it does make her reaction to seeing my inner child sting a little less.

"What?" I ask, cutting her a sideways glance.

Lou points at my pocket with her pencil. "That's *Sorcerer's Stone* Harry Potter. That Harry had no confidence, no friends, no idea that he was destined to be the most powerful wizard in the entire world."

I raise an eyebrow. "I believe you mean, *Philosopher's Stone*."

Lou doesn't appreciate my literary humor.

"You know what I mean. You're a *New York Times* best-selling author now. You just got a million-dollar advance for a book you haven't even written yet. And I saw you catch a thirty-pound jar of pickles like a freaking ninja. You are *not* eleven-year-old Harry anymore."

"Okay." I shrug. "Then, which Harry am I?"

Lou's smile spreads into a maniacal grin. "You're *Deathly Hallows* Harry now, bitch!"

I'm a bit taken aback by my therapist calling me a bitch, but I did ask her to be real, and there's nothing more real than Lou in this moment, barefoot and grinning like a loon as her fingers tap away at her mobile.

"Look!" She turns the screen toward me to reveal an image of a much older, more competent Harry.

His face is streaked with soot, his lip is cut, and he's shielding his friends with his body while shooting a bold red laser out of his trusty magic wand.

"*This* Harry was straight murdering Voldemort one Horcrux at a time and making out with Ginny Weasley, like, every chance he got."

A pang of guilt cuts through me at the term *making out*, but luckily, Lou doesn't seem fazed by it at all.

"*This* is your new inner child," she says, shoving the device even closer to my face.

I take it out of her hand and hold it while she speaks. She's so much more animated than I've ever seen her. Gesturing with her arms and emoting with her entire face. I thought giving her permission to be "real" would make this easier on me, but seeing her like this only makes me want her more.

I flip her mobile over, wanting to see what kind of case she chose, wanting to know everything about her. The case is simple and black, obviously not sturdy enough to keep the screen from shattering, as evidenced by the spiderweb-like cracks in the upper-left corner of her screen.

"I want you to find this picture and put it everywhere," she continues. "Make it your lock screen, your screen saver, your—"

Before she can finish that thought and certainly before I can think better of it, I copy the image, navigate to her home screen, open her messaging app, and text the photo to myself.

When the mobile in my pocket vibrates, Lou stops talking, and her eyes go wide.

"Now I don't have to Google it," I say, handing her cracked iPhone back with a shrug.

Real smooth, arsehole.

Lou's mouth falls open as she accepts the still-glowing device.

I gesture to the clock, barely visible beneath the shattered glass. "Looks like our time is up."

It's not. We have five minutes left. But after what I just did, leaving with my dignity intact is getting harder and harder to do by the second.

Lou

Did he just …

I glance down at the phone in my hand and see my messaging app open with a text to a very unknown, very international phone number still glowing on my screen.

Thomas stands abruptly and strides over to the door, pretending like he didn't just commit yet another cardinal client-therapist sin, and I follow like a dog on a leash, clutching my phone with both hands.

"See you Sunday," he says from the doorway.

There's a promise in his voice, a challenge in his eyes, and I don't like it. I can't have another Sunday like the last one. My heart won't survive it. My job won't survive it. And my panties definitely won't survive it. I'm supposed to be in charge here. I'm supposed to enforce the rules, but all I can do is nod mechanically as Thomas disappears from view, taking one more of my broken boundaries with him as a souvenir.

I stand in the doorway and watch him go while I wait for my brain and my heart to finish duking it out. I don't know how to feel or what to think or whether I'm elated or mad or guilt-ridden or simply riddled with anxiety.

But then something buzzes in my hand, and when I look down, any question I had about how I feel is immediately answered. Adrenaline and dopamine and oxytocin flood my bloodstream as I look at the new text that just came in.

I have a teenage boy on my lock screen. This feels wrong.

A smile splits my face in two as another text pops up with a screenshot as proof. I lean against the open door and text back.

If it makes you feel any better, Daniel Radcliffe was 20 when he filmed that movie.

I barely finish pressing the Send arrow when my phone vibrates again.

It doesn't.

Stifling a giggle, I fire back.

Stop texting your therapist. You shouldn't even have this number.

My smile fades with every passing second that a response doesn't come. Dropping my phone to my side, I let my head fall back against the door with a sigh.

"Any progress with the author?"

"Ahh!" I shriek, clutching my phone to my chest as I look into the beady little eyes of Dr. Ito-Cohen, who's standing just a few feet away.

"Sorry," I pant, trying to catch my breath. "Yes, actually. He's writing again." I stand up a little straighter. "I think I finally got his number."

I cringe at my own Freudian slip, but E.I.C. doesn't seem to notice.

"I hope so," she snaps. "His editor's been breathing down my neck." Her eyes drift off to the side as she mutters under her breath, "Boyfriend-stealing bitch."

My eyebrows shoot up.

Refocusing on my stunned face, she barks, "I already started writing your letter of recommendation. And by started, I mean, I told April to do it. As soon as Thomas submits that manuscript, it's yours."

"Yes, ma'am." I nod, hiding my phone behind my body with a tense smile.

Then, I shriek again when E.I.C. reaches out and yanks on my feather extension. Hard.

"Ow!"

Her pencil-thin eyebrows pull together. "Oh … sorry. Thought you had a …" She gestures at the side of my head in disgust before turning and walking away.

Lou

WALKING BAREFOOT THROUGH THE Indigo Hills orchard while wearing a flowing tie-dye broom skirt and holding a basket of apples on her hip, my mother is the epitome of hippie-commune coolness. Wrinkles kiss the corners of her eyes and mouth, and her dreadlocks are a little grayer than they used to be, but she's still an ethereal beauty. It makes me so mad. She looks like the kind of mom who would braid your hair while you talked about boys and give you a hit off her bong when you were stressed about work, and she would, but ... then she'd tell you that the answer to all your problems was to bury a piece of rose quartz under a maple tree during the first full moon in Aquarius or some shit like that.

I just … wish she could actually help me with something for once.

With a soft smile, Crystal reaches out and runs a finger down the length of my nose. "I'm so happy you came, Lou Bear."

"Why wouldn't I come?" I ask, dropping an apple into the basket on my own hip. "It's free food."

My mother's smile morphs into a frown. "Sweetie, your energy feels like microwaved Styrofoam right now."

"Well, your energy feels like a stoned Care Bear, so …"

"Thank you." She smiles. "Now, tell me what's on your heart."

I sigh. "Mom, I love you, but I can't talk to you about this stuff."

I walk over to the next tree in the row and pluck an obviously bruised apple off the nearest branch, just to have something to do with my hands.

"What stuff?" Crystal asks, joining me.

"You know, real-world stuff."

"Excuse me, but I have more years of 'real-world' experience than you do, young lady." Crystal tries to sound sassy, but her half-smile betrays her.

"Well, it's a work problem, so …" I snatch another organic hunk of fruit off another low-hanging branch and feel my thumb sink into a mushy spot. I drop it into my basket anyway.

"I see." Crystal furrows her brow as she gazes at her upside-down reflection in the perfectly non-rotten apple she just picked. "Have you stopped to ask yourself *why* you're having this problem?"

I roll my eyes. "Uh … because my boss hates me? Or God. Or both."

"Honey"—I can already hear the patronizing sweetness in her voice—"the goddess doesn't hate you. She's doing all of this *for* you. Stress is her way of telling you that you're on the wrong path."

"How am I on the wrong path?" I snap, turning to face her. "I'm trying to help people."

"You're not using your gift."

Ugh. That look. That's her *I'm so much more enlightened than you* look. Like she wants to pat me on the head and laugh at my non-transcendental energy field.

"What gift? *Art?*" I spread my arms, gesturing at the expanse of woods and spray-painted recreational vehicles a few hundred feet away. "So I can live in an RV on a mountain, eating apples and squirrel meat for the rest of my life? No, thanks, Mom."

"That's nonsense," Crystal corrects me, using an authoritative tone that I haven't heard in years. "You know we're vegan." She chuckles to herself as she saunters over to the next tree, shaking her head. "Squirrel meat."

I drop the rotten apple into her basket when she's not looking.

Lou

WHILE I SIT IN the Creativity Corner and wait for Thomas to arrive, I use the time—and all of my nervous energy—to build a two-story card house out of beer coasters. It only falls down, like, three times.

How's that for using my gift, Mom?

As easy as it is for me to dismiss her advice due to her being off the grid and completely out of touch with modern civilization, I can't stop thinking about what she said yesterday.

I mean, I know she was wrong. *Obviously.* If everyone were to quit their stressful jobs, there would be no teachers, no emergency room doctors, no celebrity wedding planners. The goddess didn't drop Thomas O'Reardon into my life to destroy everything I'd worked for just because she'd rather see me become a penniless artist, selling zombie caricatures for five bucks a pop at the Indigo Hills farmers market every Sunday.

Right?

A shadow falls over my cardboard condominium. I look up to find Thomas standing at the end of the table, more dressed down than I've ever seen him. He's wearing a black T-shirt and an old pair of threadbare jeans—both of which fit him like a second skin. No belt. No watch. No jacket.

"Uh … hey," I greet him, trying not to act too confused by his appearance. "Have a seat." I gesture toward the booth across from me, but Thomas ignores my invitation.

"I've been thinking a lot about our last session." He nods a little too fast. "About how I need to internalize a manlier, more confident version of my inner child."

"I didn't say *manlier* but … okay."

"So, I've decided that this week, I'm joining that group." He points over his shoulder to the Employees Only door. "The fight club."

"Thomas—"

He slaps his hands down on the table with a manic grin. "Wish me luck!" Then, he turns on his heel and takes off toward the storage room.

Fuck.

"Wait!"

I hustle after him, feeling everyone's eyes on us as I call out, "Thomas! Stop! It is *not* a fight club. It's an Anger Management group. They're probably in there, listening to Enya—"

Thomas pushes open the door, and inside the tiny space, Mark and all four of my angriest clients are barefoot and shirtless, bouncing on their toes and cracking their knuckles. Celeste and Penelope still have on their bras—thank God. Mark is wearing a red bandanna around his head as he paces back and forth in front of them in a pair of cutoff jean shorts. He's holding seven fingers up as he recites some kind of a list.

"… no belts, shoes, or jewelry! Rule number eight"—he raises another finger—"if this is your first time at Anger Management, you have to fight!"

Thomas turns to me with a very *I told you so* smirk on his face.

"Mark!" I shout. "I need to speak to you. *Now*."

I pull my deranged roommate out the door and into an alcove by the bar.

"What the hell are you doing?" I whisper-shout. "Have you lost your mind?"

Mark's brown eyes are wide and glassy as he bounces from foot to foot. "That fight last week really opened my eyes, Lou. *This* is what people need. A true release!"

"Are you high right now?" My head bobs from side to side as I try to maintain eye contact.

"I been tryin' to help people dance the rage away, stretch the rage away, fuckin' vision-board the rage away, but this is what I should have been doin' the whole time! Helpin' people purge that anger the way God intended, Lou—through the long-lost art of hand-to-hand combat!"

"Okay, Tyler Durden, put your shirt back on. I'm shutting this shit down." I grab him by his furry forearm, but before we make it two steps toward the storage room door, it swings open, and a tall brunette Englishman comes flying out.

Thomas lands on his ass and slides backward about six feet into the side of a booth.

"Oh my God! Thomas!" I shriek, but before I can run over to him, the door swings open again, and Angry Bill comes charging through, headed straight toward him with smoke practically billowing out of his nostrils.

"Oh no. No, no, no ..."

Mark grabs my arm to hold me back just as Thomas rolls to the side and sweeps Bill's legs out from under him. Bill goes down hard, and the two men start wrestling on the dirty-ass floor.

"Let 'em work it out," Mark says, a look of sheer delight on his Rambo-looking face.

"Are you fucking crazy?" I twist my wrist out of his grip and run over to the fight, but I have no idea how to separate two full-grown men who are twisted in a thrashing, grunting testosterone pretzel.

The other groups form a crowd around them.

"Fight! Fight! Fight!" the other shirtless Anger Management group members chant.

"Stop! Stop! Stop!" I chant louder.

"Let allllll that toxic energy out," Mark yells over my shoulder.

"No! Do not let it out!" I yell louder.

Thomas bites Bill's arm, and he screams out in pain.

Oh my fucking God. I want to cover my eyes.

"Thomas!" Mark shouts. "Rule number six! Come on, man!"

Perspectively Challenged Penelope leans over to him, her double-Ds spilling out of what looks like a C-cup bra, and in a rare showing of, well, *perspective*, she says, "I don't think he was here when you told us rule number six."

"Oh shit. You're right." Mark turns back toward Thomas. "Sorry, hon!"

I run over to the breaker box next to the bar and flip the lights on and off like a first-grade teacher trying to regain control of a rowdy classroom.

Nobody even notices.

"You should stay back here, so you don't get any DNA on ya." Dee chuckles from her vantage point behind the bar. She twists the cap off a beer bottle and points the neck toward the fight. "This shit's about to turn into a crime scene."

"Real helpful." I glare at her before running back over to the crowd.

Thomas is on his ass again, but Beth is standing behind him, rubbing his now-shirtless shoulders like Rocky's coach.

I'm momentarily distracted by the sight of Thomas's glistening, heaving, naked chest and abs, which gives Beth just enough time to finish her pep talk.

"Come on, champ. You got 'im up against the ropes. You just gotta dig a little deeper."

Thomas pulls himself up with a determined nod and begins shadow-boxing with Bill.

For fuck's sake!

"Beth!" I shout, raising my arms in her direction from the other side of the crowd.

"What?" She shrugs. "I'm a coach!"

"A life coach!"

"This *is* life, Sterling. Life or death!" She turns from me to Thomas and yells, "Uppercut, Tommy Boy! Get him!"

Thomas takes a hit so hard that his head jerks to the side. I gasp as his eyes open, landing on me. Then, a wide, maniacal smile spreads across his face before he cocks his fist back, twists forward, and clocks Bill right on the chin.

I scream.

Bill reels from the hit, almost falling over, but then he lurches forward and tackles Thomas. They stumble backward until they crash into the empty table next to Courtney's group, knocking it over and falling to the ground along with it.

I hadn't realized it before, but Courtney's group is the only one still seated. Her group members are twitchy-eyed and sweating profusely as they stare intently at the middle of the table. There, Courtney has about twenty straws lined up in a perfectly spaced row with one straw slightly askew.

In a moment of weakness, Nervous Nicole glances down at the men fighting next to her. A water balloon immediately explodes in her face.

Courtney smiles, holding up another water-filled orb as a warning to the rest of the group. "Life is chaos, y'all. All you can do is breathe and ignore that which you cannot control. Say it with me: breathe ... and ignore."

I race around to the other side of the fallen table and find Bill squeezing Thomas's neck in a sleeper hold.

"Bill, if you don't let go in three seconds, I'm calling the police!" I yell. "One, two... ..."

Before I get to three, Thomas's eyes close, and his head rolls forward. Bill lets go of his unconscious body as Mark yanks him up by the arm, congratulating the victor.

With a scream lodged in my throat, I drop to my knees beside Thomas. Lifting his head with both hands, I place it in my lap and begin rapidly patting his cheek.

"Thomas!" Tap, tap, tap. "Thomas, wake up!"

His eyelids begin to flutter, and I exhale in relief as they slowly open and focus on me. Despite his split lip—or perhaps because of it—Thomas's mouth widens into a heart-stopping grin. For someone who was going for a "manlier, more confident" vibe tonight, Thomas looks about as boyish and vulnerable as he's capable of being. Boyish, vulnerable, and really fucking happy.

"Did I win?" he asks with a sleepy grin.

My eyebrows practically hit the roof. "Seriously? Do you *feel* like you won?"

"I feel bloody amazing." He beams. Then, without warning, he lifts his head and presses those battered lips to mine, stopping more than just my heart.

Time dissolves along with the entire outside world as all five of my senses narrow their focus to the tiny spot in the universe where Thomas's lips are touching my lips.

I see nothing.

I hear nothing.

I taste mint, laced with the faintest metallic tang of blood.

I smell the ocean, if the ocean smelled the way it felt. Bright and cool, like the color aqua.

And I feel ... *everything*. I feel fizzy, candy-colored bubbles shooting through my bloodstream as a Molotov cocktail of hormones and pheromones and excited, adrenaline-laced *yes* signals explode in my brain. I feel the curvature of Thomas's smile against my lips. I feel the warmth of his breath and the weight of his body in my arms. I feel the space in my heart where he lived before he entered my life stretching to accommodate the enormity of my feelings for him now. And as my awareness slowly begins to retract ...

I also feel as though I'm being watched.

I crack open one eye, just a sliver, but it's enough for me to see that all four groups—even Courtney's—are staring at us with their mouths hanging open.

Panic hijacks all control of my extremities, causing me to scoot away from Thomas faster than you can say *ethics violation.*

Thomas props himself up on one elbow and blinks at me, as if awoken from a dream.

"You need to leave," I announce, loud enough for everyone to hear. My voice is angry and authoritative, but my eyes plead with him to go along with it.

If Thomas gets the memo, he's way too convincing for me to tell. With his eyebrows pulled together and his bottom lip beginning to swell, he runs a bloody-knuckled hand through his hair and nods his head.

"Lou, I'm so sorry—"

"You too, Bill," I shout, cutting Thomas off before he has a chance to make this any harder than it already is. "I want both of you out—now. Everybody else, back to your groups!"

Hauling himself off the ground, Thomas gives me one last remorseful glance before turning to grab his T-shirt off the floor.

I pin the rest of my shirtless clients with a sobering stare as I pull myself to my feet. "Anger Management, y'all are with me."

I continue barking orders as my clients scatter, but my eyes are on Thomas as he pushes his way through the crowd and out the door.

I want to run after him. I want to tell him to wait for me.

But what I want doesn't matter.

It never has, and it never will.

Thomas

"ANOTHER, MR. O'REARDON?"

I shrug and slide my nearly empty highball glass across the bar to the bloke waiting to refill it for the fourth or fifth or seventh time.

"Smooth, isn't it?" he asks, as if I'm drinking them at this rate because I give a toss about the flavor. "Lagavulin, from your side of the pond."

All scotch is from my side of the pond. I wish I could roll my eyes, but my proper English manners are even harder to shake than the memory of what happened tonight. Hence all the drinking.

"Aged sixteen years." He swirls my glass under his nose. "Strong, smoky notes of peat … sherry … and a sweet vanilla finish." He sets the glass down in front of me, a proud smile lifting the curled points of his fluffy mustache.

I swallow it with zero appreciation for the peat or the bloody fucking sherry.

I've been avoiding this pub since the first time I came here, right after I moved in. I thought it would be so convenient to have a pub in the lobby of my building, a place to get away from the deafening silence of that soundproof box upstairs, but unfortunately, one of the other patrons recognized me immediately and proceeded to spend the next hour and a half talking my ear off about the psychological thriller he was going to write and asking for my advice on every ill-conceived plot point and half-cocked red herring he'd ever thought up.

But tonight, I was desperate enough to try again. I got nervous when the barman knew my name as soon as I walked in, but at least he hasn't asked me to read his manuscript. *Yet*.

"It's none of my business, but ... I hope you kicked his ass," he says, blessedly pouring another round.

"Hmm?" I raise an eyebrow as I swirl the amber liquid in a lazy circle around the sides of the glass. It's the same color as Lou's eyes. *Goddamn it.*

"The fella who busted your lip there." He points to my face, which I can no longer access through my nerve endings so I reach up and touch the spot with my hand. I can't feel that either, but my eyes still work well enough to register a faint smear of red on my index finger, which I now have three of, apparently.

"I believe I gave the gentleman a black eye," I announce before returning my gaze to Lou's unblinking, liquid iris.

I don't think there's enough scotch on this entire cursed continent to make me forget the way she looked at me when I kissed her tonight. Like I was a monster. And she was right. What I did was ... inexcusable. Reprehensible. Unforgivable. Tomorrow, she'll be fired, and the only thing I will have succeeded in doing by coming to America is destroying the future of a brilliant, beautiful, blindingly sexy young woman ... right along with my own.

I ball up a black serviette and drop it into the glass so that I won't have to look at that color anymore.

"I know it's not my place, but whatever's going on that's got you down, it'll change. Just give it time."

"That's just it," I say, clutching the edges of the bar to keep it from tilting. "There is no more time. I've wasted all my time." I shake my head with a bitter, humorless laugh, causing the room to spin. "And now, I'm wasting yours. Good night, sir."

I stand up and steady myself before making my way toward the door.

"Mr. O'Reardon, your tab!"

"Whatever it is," I mumble without turning around, "double it as a token of my appreciation for not asking me to read your manuscript."

"How do you know I have a manuscript?"

I stumble across the empty marble lobby, thankful that no other sad sacks are milling about at two a.m. on a Monday morning, and board one of the dozen or so shiny lifts waiting to deliver me back to my prison. It only takes three tries for my finger to finally connect with the correct button.

Inside, the walls are made of mirrors, but for some reason, they're crisscrossed with golden streaks, as if an army of slugs, drunker than me, slithered through metallic paint and then wandered aimlessly inside this box until the toxic chemicals eventually seeped into their tiny, porous bodies and killed them all.

The motion of the lift causes my stomach to lurch, so I try to focus on my own reflection—or one of them at least. That's when I notice the bloody gash on my lip that the barman pointed out. It looks familiar. Like something from an action movie. A Jason Statham film perhaps. Or Liam Neeson.

No.

Goddamn it.

I pull out my phone and illuminate the screen. There, staring back at me, are two Harry Potters with identical cuts on their determined bottom lips. I close my right eye to reduce the number down to one, and then I unlock my phone and delete the photo entirely.

"Sod off, Harry."

As soon as his image disappears from my screen, I feel a sense of relief. Control.

And I want more.

When the door finally opens on the nineteenth floor, I stumble down the carpeted hallway on a mission.

I drop my keys on the table just inside the door without pausing to remove my shoes.

I stomp through the sitting room without opening the balcony door.

I don't turn on the lights.

I don't stop to take a piss.

I keep going until I'm hovering over a glowing laptop on the desk in the office.

I highlight everything I've written since I got here. Every trite, predictable, disposable word.

And then …

I press Delete.

Lou

TODAY WAS BASICALLY JUST one long panic attack. Every time someone appeared in my office doorway, I had to stifle the urge to scream. I knew Dr. E.I.C. was going to waltz through that door any second and tell me that I was being sued or physically escorted from the building or both. And every time my phone vibrated, my heart rate would skyrocket hoping it was a text from Thomas. Or a call from Thomas. Or an email from Thomas. But mostly, it was just Dee, asking if I'd been fired yet.

When I told her *no* for the hundredth time, I guess she sensed that I wasn't in a great place and volunteered to give me a ride home. Which only made me feel worse.

If Dee Dawson is taking pity on you, you're in bad fucking shape.

"Thanks for the ride," I say as I flip on the lights and drop my bag on the counter separating the kitchen from the living room. When I notice my roommate lounging on the couch in his shiny nylon American flag track suit, I raise my voice and add, "Mark and I AREN'T EXACTLY ON SPEAKING TERMS RIGHT NOW."

Mark ignores my comment but switches to his middle finger as he continues scrolling on his phone.

"He's not happy that I shut down his fight club last night," I explain as I head over to the fridge and pull out a five-dollar white wine blend that was probably made from fruit fermented in a tenement bathtub in New Jersey, "and *I'm* not happy that HE STARTED A FUCKING FIGHT CLUB LAST NIGHT."

"Well, I ain't mad about it." Dee chuckles as I pull a giant plastic souvenir cup out of the giant plastic souvenir cup cabinet and set it on the counter. "I haven't seen a fight that good since *Boss Wives of Atlanta* got canceled."

"What am I gonna do, Dee?" I ask, twisting the cap off the bottle of piss-colored alcohol. "Thomas punched my client—"

"Bit him too." She smirks.

"Thomas punched *and bit* my client and then kissed me in front of everybody! He's out of control."

"Looked to me like he was havin' a good-ass time. Matter fact, I think everybody there had a good-ass time, except for you."

"Exactly." I concentrate on pouring as I try to make sense of my racing thoughts. "Because I'm the one taking all the risk. Nobody cares if I lose my job. Thomas obviously doesn't care. This is one big vacation to him. And at the end of it, when his deadline's up, he's gonna get on a plane and fly back to his penthouse in London and land right between the legs of another supermodel."

Glug, glug, glug.

"And where will I be? Unemployed, unlicensed, and living in an RV on the side of a mountain. This has gone way too far. I mean, Angry Bill had a black eye today."

"My boy Bill?" Mark calls out. "How's he doin'?"

I think back over our session this morning.

Bill actually seemed ... great. He was calmer, less agitated, and for once, he didn't punch a single thing in my office. And also, he literally said, "I feel better than ever."

Of course, I'm not going to tell Mark that.

"Dee, will you please remind Mark that I'm not speaking to him right now?"

Dee rolls her eyes. "This is why you gotta work with kids. I keep tellin' you, adults are not right. You gotta get 'em while they're young. By the time they come to you, they're too far gone."

"They are. They really are." I shake my head sadly as the last few drops of wine roll out of the bottle and into my dangerously full cup. "Oh shit. Did you want some?" I lean over and take a noisy sip from the rim to keep it from overflowing.

"Nah. I'm fuckin' pregnant."

Aaaaand I spit it right back out.

"What?" I cough. "How? With Vasectomy Mike?"

"Turns out, those bitches are only, like, ninety-nine percent effective." Dee lifts an apathetic shoulder, but the slight tilt of her usually pursed lips tells me she's happier about her situation than she's letting on.

"Deeeeee!" I squeal. "You're gonna be a mommy!"

"Yeah, yeah."

"Oh my God. Can I... ..." I reach out to touch her belly, and Dee smacks me on the head.

"What are you doin'? Stop it."

"Congratulations, breeder!" Mark calls from the living room.

Dee's self-contained pout slips even further, revealing a wide, uncomfortable smile. "Jesus, can we talk about something else? I'm tryin' to be in denial over here."

I press my grinning lips together and nod.

"So ... back to *your* drama." Dee rummages through her purse and pulls out a tube of lip balm. It's like that single smile was so taxing that she has to slather her lips in moisturizer to make them feel better about what just happened.

I take another sip from my wine and wait for her to drop the hammer.

"Listen," she says, tossing the ChapStick back into her bag, "I'm wrong all the time, but in my experience, the best way to get over one dick is to get on a different dick."

I swallow with an audible gulp. "A different dick?"

Dee nods. "If you wanna stop obsessing about Thomas, you're gonna need some vitamin D." With a wink, she turns toward the living room and shouts, "Mark, get yo fine ass in here and help ya girl out."

I glance into the living room just in time to see a red, white, and blue blur disappear from the couch. Half a second later, Mark has me bent over the counter, dry-humping the side of my ass with one foot propped up on the peeling laminate surface. I have to grab the edge of the sink just to stay upright.

"Get off of me!"

"Ooh, she's talkin' to me now!" Mark tosses his head back to look at my BFF. "The make-up sex is workin' already."

"Not helping!" I squeal, holding on for dear life.

Dee cackles. "Okay, so maybe a *different*, different dick."

Two hours later, I'm standing on the porch of a townhouse that I literally ran away from three weeks ago, trying to figure out what to say to its owner.

Excuse me, sir, I hope you're not busy, but may I borrow your dick real quick?

Hello. Sorry to bother you, but is your dick home?

Hi. I'm here for my dick appointment. I hope walk-ins are welcome.

When Dr. Callahan finally opens the door, he's wearing nothing but a bathrobe the same color as the fluffy white chest hair poking out of it … and a smile.

"Luna, to what do I owe the—"

"Nope." That's all I manage to say before I turn and bolt off that porch for the second time in less than a month.

Sprinting down the driveway, I wave my arms and shout at my Uber driver, who is just starting to pull away from the curb. The brake lights of her Honda Pilot light up, and I dive into the pine-scented backseat like a bank robber after a botched heist.

"Go, go, go!"

The driver—a woman with short gray hair, wearing leather driving gloves and sunglasses at night—chuckles as she pulls away from the curb.

"They never look as good as their profile pictures, do they?"

I lie sideways across the backseat, picturing the headshot on Thomas's book cover, and shake my head. "No," I say, pushing the syllable past the lump forming in my throat.

Sometimes, they look better.

Lou

Tuesday, 1:00 p.m.: Nervous Nicole

"*I THOUGHT I WAS mental.*" Thomas turned his cell phone screen toward me with an amused smirk, revealing a zombified portrait I drew a few years ago. "*Is that George Washington? Bloody brilliant.*"

"*No.*" My face reddened as I snatched the phone out of his hand and slapped it facedown on the desk behind me. "*It's Alexander Hamilton.*"

A grin spread across his face, warming his hard, cold features. "Forgive me." Thomas chuckled, placing a hand over his heart. "I didn't recognize him without his ... nose."

"It's an honest mistake." I took a breath to calm my nerves. It didn't work. *"Shall we begin?"*

"Yes. Please." Thomas leaned forward, resting his elbows on his knees. *"You can start by telling me where you come up with those gloriously morbid images."*

My breath hitched, and my heart skipped one, three, maybe ten beats as I found myself assaulted by Thomas O'Reardon's wide-eyed singular interest. I swallowed and said, *"We're not here to talk about me,"* but there was absolutely zero authority behind my words.

"We might not be"—Thomas smirked—*"but I am."*

"Dr. Sterling?"

"Hmm?" I blink, and the mirage of Thomas disappears, revealing my actual client, Nervous Nicole, who hasn't stopped rambling about some drama on her kids' school's PTA board since she got here.

I sit up and blink again, clutching my clipboard and pencil like I'm confident that whatever she's about to say will be profound and noteworthy.

"And how did that make you feel?" I ask, realizing as soon as the words are out that it's the first time Nicole has let me ask an entire question without cutting me off since she was assigned to me.

She stops and thinks before responding, which is another first. Then, she beams with pride. "Fine," she says, her eyes brightening. "I didn't even have a panic attack. Normally, I would, but this time, I was like, 'Breathe and ignore that which you cannot control,' and it totally worked, just like Dr. Baker said."

"That's great, Nicole." I smile back. "I'm so happy to hear that the group is working for you." Then, dropping my eyes to my legal pad, I write a quick summary of today's session.

You suck.

Courtney is sooo much better at this than you.

Call The Frisky Pony this afternoon to check on that pole wait list.

Wednesday, 11:00 a.m.: Lost Leonard

"Thomas O'Reardon Gets Cozy with Georgia Peach," the headline on my phone reads.

Georgia Peach. More like Georgia Fangirl Who Needs to Face Reality and Stop Pretending Like She Has a Chance with This Guy Because It's Pathetic and Potentially Destroying Her Life.

"... and then Coach Beth pretended to be my dead dad so that I could finally say everything I ever wanted to say to him. It was liberating."

I glance up from my clipboard—where I was staring at TMZ.com and pretending to take notes for the last three minutes—and give Leonard my full attention.

"Really?" I ask, leaning forward to block the glow from my still-illuminated phone screen. "What did you say?"

"Um ..." Leonard drops his eyes and picks at his thumbnail. "Mostly just, 'Fuck you,' and, 'I'm glad you're dead,' and, 'Mom's a lesbian now, you abusive asshole.' Stuff like that."

"Wow. That sounds really ... cathartic."

Leonard pushes his glasses up his nose and makes direct, sustained eye contact with me. "I've never felt so heard."

In the margins of my legal pad, I write:

Beth: 4

Lou: -18

Thursday, 4:00 p.m.: Depressed Dixie

Hey, Thomas. It's Lou.

I delete *Lou* and type *Dr. Sterling*, but that just reminds me that I'm his doctor and I shouldn't be texting him at all. I frown and delete the entire message.

"... and that's when I realized, I haven't thought about dyin' all week."

Depressed Dixie is in my chair. She looks better than usual. Her hair isn't just clean; it's *styled*. My hair isn't even styled—unless you count three ratty braids and a feather extension that will probably have to be cut out of my hair because it's gotten twisted so many times that it's forming a dreadlock at the roots.

Look who needs therapy now, Doctor.

"I think it was something Dr. Dawson said last weekend," Dixie continues.

I think we should talk about what happened.

I delete that text immediately. I'd rather poke my eye out with this pencil than talk about the shitshow that took place last Sunday.

"... Dr. Dawson said, 'Aren't y'all glad you didn't kill yourselves?' and for the first time since I can remember, my answer was yes."

Dee said what?!

My eyes snap up from my clipboard. "Dixie, please tell me *exactly* what Dr. Dawson said."

Dixie smiles, bringing my attention to the fact that she's wearing lipstick today too. "As soon as that crazy fight was over, Dr. Dawson said, 'Congratulations. Because y'all decided to come to therapy instead of killin' yourselves, y'all got to see a couple of fine-ass men rolling around with their shirts off.'"

I raise my eyebrows. "And that made you feel better?"

She nods, still beaming. "It changed my whole outlook on life. Now, instead of dreading getting out of bed every day, I can't wait to leave the house and see what'll happen next!"

I blink, taking in her surprising new attitude, when Dixie abruptly stands up.

"Speaking of leaving the house, I gotta go. I signed up for book club, and I promised the girls I'd bring a big ol' seven-layer dip tonight."

My mouth falls open as Dixie turns and heads toward the door with a straight back and a swish of her hips.

"See you Sunday!"

I don't understand what's happening. It has been four days since the group therapy session from hell—four days of walking on eggshells, waiting for the guillotine blade to drop—and not only have I *not* been fired yet, but also my clients actually seem to be doing better.

No, not my clients. My friends' clients. I had nothing to do with any of their progress, and the one client whose progress I am solely responsible for has actually regressed from a proper English gentleman into some kind of physically and sexually aggressive frat boy who hasn't even texted me, which I shouldn't be expecting anyway because HE SHOULDN'T EVEN HAVE MY NUMBER, and—

Riiiing!

With a hopeful gasp, I snatch my cell phone out of my lap, but the screen is black.

Riiiing!

That's when I realize that the noise is coming from the desk behind me.

Dammit.

I twist around backward in my seat and grab the receiver, making sure to sigh *before* I lift it to my face. "Dr. Sterling."

Five seconds later, I'm marching down the hallway, through the doorway into the lobby, and over to the check-in desk, where April watches me approach with big, wide eyes.

"What do you mean, he canceled?" I hiss through the little speaker holes in the Plexiglas window. "What did he say?"

"Nothing." April shrugs, looking slightly terrified. "Just that he needed to cancel his appointment tomorrow."

"Well, did he give an excuse? Did he say where he's going? Is he going somewhere?"

"I don't know." April glances past me to the two clients sitting in the waiting room.

"Call him back. No, fuck that. What's his address?"

"You can't just go to your client's house," April whispers. "Are you crazy?"

"What if he's firing me?" I snap. "What if I'm not his therapist anymore? Then, it won't matter."

"Uh, then you're just a stalker."

"April …" I look around, making sure there aren't any other employees within earshot. Then, I level with her. Cupping my hands around my mouth just in case there are video cameras recording my confession, I mouth the words, *Thomas kissed me.*

"No!" April gasps.

"Shh … *yes.* And now, he's canceling his appointment. Please, you have to help me fix this."

"Oh my God, he kissed you," April whispers back. "Was it just like Harry Styles?"

While I try to figure out how to respond to that, April busies herself, flitting around the front desk.

"Oh my God, oh my God, oh my God!" she squeals to herself, tapping on her keyboard as the printer behind her lights up and coughs something out.

She rolls her chair over to it and snatches a piece of paper from the tray, hugging it to her chest before passing it to me through the slot at the bottom of the window.

"Here!" She beams. "That's his address, his birthday, his blood type, everything."

"April"—I jam my finger against the glass, pointing at her perfectly contoured little face—"thank you."

Clutching the paper in my fist, I turn and head for the door as April calls out behind me, "Tell him I said 'Watermelon Sugar' is my favorite song!"

Lou

I CAN'T EVEN AFFORD to get a haircut in this neighborhood, and Thomas is living on the nineteenth floor of a building that looks like it was dipped in gold and rolled in opulence.

As my Uber drives away, the doorman—yes, there's an actual doorman—opens one of the twelve-foot-tall glass doors for me with a smile. "Good afternoon."

I nod weakly as two wobbly legs carry me inside what can only be described as *Southern Living*'s version of Oz. The front desk is located on the opposite end of a huge two-story rotunda with a polished marble floor; white columns as big around as my coffee table; fat, ornate crown moldings; and a crystal chandelier the size of a hot air balloon suspended in the center.

My burgundy Converse squeak as I walk across the pristine floor, and that squeak has an echo.

My house has bars on the windows.

Thomas's apartment has someone playing a grand piano in the lobby.

No big deal.

As I approach the man at the front desk, I try to remember to hold my chin up and pull my shoulders back, but his disapproving stare already has me ready to hyperventilate. I get halfway to him before I freak out, hook a left, and head straight for the bar in the back corner of the expanse.

Inside, it's all carved mahogany and leather wingback chairs and men in suits, sipping brandy. So, not much better.

"Shot of Jameson, please," I tell the bartender, who is sporting a pin-striped vest and a non-ironic handlebar mustache.

While he pours my liquid courage, I glance around the masculine space and notice a certain painting displayed prominently behind the bar.

"Fuck. Is that an original Picasso?" I cringe. "You better make that a double."

Tingly warmth spreads from my stomach out to my extremities as I exit the bar, shaking my hands and cracking my neck.

This time, I make it all the way to the front desk.

"Good afternoon," the man with the judgy face says. "How may I—"

"I'm here to see Thomas O'Reardon," I blurt out, feeling my armpits begin to sweat, even through my new goblin-strength deodorant. "Apartment number..."—I pull the piece of paper that April printed for me out of my pocket and unfold it with shaky hands—"nineteen twenty-eight."

Mr. Sourpuss looks down the length of his nose at me. "Your name, please."

"Lou. I mean, Dr. Lou ... na. Sterling."

He picks up the receiver on his desk phone, and I add, "I'm his therapist."

Fuck! I'm not supposed to tell you that.

Tapping four buttons, Concierge Man covers his mouth as he murmurs into the handset, glancing at me repeatedly before hanging up.

I'm ninety-nine percent sure he's actually calling security on me until he hangs up and says, "Mr. O'Reardon will see you now, *Doctor*. Take the elevator on your right to the nineteenth floor and have a marvelous day."

The elevator is just as opulent as the rest of this damn place. Even the mirrored walls are covered in sparkly golden flecks and streaks. It reminds me of the Japanese kintsugi pottery I learned about in art history class years ago. But instead of admiring its beauty, I'm admiring my every flaw, which are conveniently on display in three hundred sixty degrees. With a shaky sigh, I fluff my hair and tell myself not to be weird before the doors open again, revealing a sultry hallway wallpapered in dark filigrees and lit at even intervals by glowing brass wall sconces.

I check the number on every door as I pass.

Nineteen twenty-four, nineteen twenty-five …

Up ahead, a beautiful blonde woman leaves one of the apartments and walks past me with a knowing smile. She looks too old to be living here with her parents and too young to be able to afford it herself.

Maybe she's a trophy wife, I think … until I see the number on the door she just came out of.

Nineteen twenty-eight.

My blood turns to napalm, and all thought abandons me as I watch my hand reach out and catch the door just before it clicks shut. With a shove, I slam it back open, harder than I intended, and find a very dressed-down Thomas O'Reardon standing in the foyer, almost close enough to touch. He glances at me over his shoulder as he reaches into an open coat closet.

My heart climbs into my throat along with the words, "Who the fuck was that?" which tumble out of my mouth all shrill and screechy.

"That," Thomas replies with a bored expression, "was Kyla. Or is it Kylie? I can never remember. Sweet girl. She drops off my dry cleaning."

He then pulls his arm out of the closet to show me the plastic-wrapped jacket on a hanger in his hand.

Oh my fucking God.

My face flushes as burgundy as my stupid choice in footwear.

Thomas closes the closet door and turns to face me, crossing his arms over his broad chest. He's wearing nothing but a tight white T-shirt and a pair of gray sweatpants, which is a real problem for my cognitive recovery time.

"If I didn't know better, I'd think you were jealous." A ghost of a smirk appears and then vanishes just as quickly. "But I do know better."

"I am ... *so* sorry, Thomas. I just ... I thought you were"— *fucking that blonde*—"going against your treatment plan."

Thomas purses his lips, chewing on the inside corner. "So, definitely not jealous then."

The door feels heavier with every crawling second.

"Are you gonna invite me in or ..."

"No."

"No?"

Thomas shakes his head slowly. "I owe you an apology, Lou. What I did ..." His eyes drift to the floor. "I don't know what came over me, but I assure you, it won't happen again."

My heart, still lodged firmly in my throat, suddenly feels like it's breaking. "What are you saying?"

"I'm saying, I can't do this anymore. Whatever this is. You make me ... crazy. Crazier than I already am. I fought a man, Lou. I bit a perfect stranger. *Sober.* Have you ever done that?"

I shake my head.

"Exactly. 'Cause it's fucked." Thomas points to his temple before running that same hand through his disheveled hair. It doesn't fall back into place like it usually does. It stays back, as if he'd run his hands through it so many times in exasperation over the last four days that it was permanently stuck that way.

"I thought I wanted to ... let go," he says, "lose control, but when I did ..."

I take a step toward him, not even realizing it until I hear the door close behind me. "You liked it."

Thomas licks his lips, his steely-blue gaze boring a hole through any hesitation I might have had.

"Between you, me, and this giant bowl of citrus fruits ..." I drop my eyes to the round table beside me, where an elegant silver hammer-finished bowl is overflowing with painted wooden lemons and limes.

"They came with the flat," Thomas says, flicking his chin toward the fake fruit.

"I liked it too." My voice is barely above a whisper as I risk another step in his direction.

My ribs probably look as hammered as that bowl from the way my heart is pounding against them right now. But the way Thomas is looking at me, with the inside of his bottom lip between his teeth, spurs me on.

"Yeah?" he asks, narrowing those skeptical eyes at me.

"Yeah," I answer, sliding my fingertips along the edge of the table as I take another tentative step toward him.

Thomas turns his head, watching me through the corner of his eye. "Why are you here, Dr. Sterling?" His use of my formal name isn't lost on me.

"Because you canceled your appointment."

Step.

"So, now you make house calls?"

"I guess so." The intensity of his stare makes me drop my eyes. I pluck a lemon out of the bowl and study it as an excuse to catch my breath.

"And what do you do ... at these house calls?" Thomas asks, his voice taking on a husky quality that has me asking myself the same question.

I am completely out of my league here. In this building, with this man. Hell, this lemon is probably more worldly and experienced than I am. This is not a *fake it till you make it* situation. Because I can't even *pretend* like I belong here. So, I decide to go with honesty. Thomas is always asking me to share first, to be "real," so here goes nothing.

"I was hoping you would help me figure that out." I set the lemon down and meet his curious stare, gripping the edge of the bowl for support. "In case you haven't noticed … I don't actually know what I'm doing."

With one stride, Thomas closes the distance between us completely. I have to tilt my head back to make eye contact as I will my lungs to keep expanding and contracting.

"I think you know exactly what you're doing," he says, his jaw clenched and muscles taut.

"And what's that?" I breathe.

"Making me do this …"

One heartbeat. That's all it takes to go from wishing Thomas would kiss me to being engulfed by him. When he kissed me in the bar, it was fleeting, jovial, a burst of adrenaline seeking an outlet. But *this* kiss is anything but impulsive. This kiss is intentional and powerful and feels like a promise.

I wrap my hand around the back of Thomas's neck, sighing inwardly as my fingertips glide over the short, downy soft hair that I never thought I'd get the chance to feel. Lifting up onto my tiptoes, I unknowingly press down on the edge of the hammered bowl and cringe as the deafening clatter of two-dozen wooden lemons and limes bouncing off the marble floor fills the foyer. The sound brings a smile to Thomas's hungry mouth as warmth blooms in my chest and across my cheeks.

"Would you like a tour?" those smiling lips murmur against mine.

"Now?"

"Mmhmm," Thomas growls as he slides his hands over my ass and lifts me off the ground.

I squeal and wrap my legs around his waist as he chuckles and gives my plump backside a squeeze. His lips never leave mine as he carries me down the hallway. I shed my purse, my oversize cardigan, and my Chuck Taylors along the way, adding them to the pile of things that don't belong on the floor.

"Kitchen," The word vibrates against my lips as we pass a well-lit, ultra-modern space that looks like a team of astronauts could pilot it to Mars.

Swiveling toward the cozy expanse just off the kitchen, Thomas breaks our kiss long enough to whisper, "Sitting room."

My mouth falls open in disbelief.

It looks like something off of one of my secret Pinterest boards. Swaths of grays and midnight blues and tufted ottomans and fuzzy throw pillows surround a fireplace, flanked by a wall of floor-to-ceiling windows facing downtown Atlanta. The setting sun bathes the west side of the skyscrapers in one last splash of light, and the low-hanging clouds above soak it up like pink cotton balls.

My kiss-swollen lips fall open as I take in the splendor that Thomas gets to enjoy for free. "I think I can see my office from here," I marvel before pulling his T-shirt off over his head.

Next, Thomas carries me past a small room attached to the living room. It is filled by a massive wooden table with a surface so shiny I can see the clouds floating by upside down on it. The chairs that surround it are overstuffed and regal. And there, in the center, is yet another bowl of expertly carved wooden fruit.

"Dining," Thomas mutters, claiming my mouth again as he continues past.

But then he stops.

"Actually …" With a spin and a few steps, Thomas walks over to the dining table and sets me down on the edge. He leans forward until I'm flat on my back and he's hovering over me. "I've never eaten in this room before," Thomas teases as his mouth begins to roam leisurely down the side of my neck.

My jugular pounds against his lips. My fingers find their way into his hair just so that I have something to hold on to. I am completely untethered from reality, literally floating nineteen stories above the city in some fantasy world where Thomas O'Reardon is peeling my plaid work pants off and the chandeliers have little baby chandeliers hanging off of them. I suddenly have to fight the urge to laugh.

Of course! I'm dreaming! It all makes sense now. Too bad though. I was really starting to—

A gasp bursts from my body as Thomas grabs my bare thighs and slides me toward him. Then, with a wicked smile that touches his eyes more than his swollen lips, he sinks down into the chair at the head of the table. The one right between my legs.

I hold my breath as Thomas's warm hands wrap around my ankles, placing them on his shirtless shoulders before gliding their way back up to my thighs. My knees fall open with a gentle push, and I stare up at the crystal raindrops suspended in mid-downpour over my head to hide the flush creeping into my cheeks.

Sweet, hot breath and featherlight kisses trail down my inner thigh as two expert fingers glide over the satin of my panties. It's too gentle—it's all too gentle—serving as a cruel reminder that none of this is real. It's like when you try to punch someone in a dream, but it feels like you're hitting a pillow. Thomas's touch, his caress, is just a simulation in my subconscious mind, a hollow echo of a memory. The thought sits heavily on my heart until his fingers are joined by a thumb. Until his lips give way to the grazing of teeth. Until that black strip of satin is pulled to the side and my aching is answered with one long swipe of his tongue.

It's impossible to count the number of times I've fantasized about seeing that guarded blue gaze peering up at me from between my legs, but as I glance down the length of my body, I'm treated to that exact view. As if he can sense that I'm watching, Thomas's stormy eyes connect with mine, gleaming under dark brows, as he drags his tongue over my flesh again.

Holy shit.

My head falls back against the table with a *thunk*.

I feel Thomas's smile against my inner thigh. And then he goes to work.

I bite my lip and arch my back and close my thighs around his head as I struggle to cope with the immaculate sensations flooding my body. Swirling and sucking in a rhythm that matches the involuntary rise and fall of my hips, Thomas ruins me for all other mouths in a matter of seconds. When your only sexual experiences are a couple of clueless boys in high school, the handful of drunk guys you brought home from the bar, and your geriatric psychology professor, you don't get … *this.*

Which means that *this* is definitely *not* a dream because how could my mind possibly conjure a feeling that it didn't even know existed?

But figuring out how I conjured Thomas in the flesh? That's even harder to fathom.

I peek down at the man assaulting me with pleasure again, searching for more validation that he's not a figment of my imagination. Warm brown hair juts out from between my fingers. I run a thumb over the strands and marvel at the silky texture.

That feels real.

Thick, dark lashes spread out across enviously high cheekbones, which are the tiniest bit scratchy against my inner thighs.

Also real.

And his broad, bare shoulders are covered with not only my lower legs, but also a smattering of freckles the same color as his chestnut hair. Every detail is a living, breathing, tangible work of art, as is every flick and swirl of his expert tongue.

My breaths turn to pants, and my pants turn to moans as my back arches higher and higher off the table. Thomas waits until I'm as close to the edge as I can get, and then, with a single finger, he pushes me over.

My orgasm feels like a free fall into a pool full of static-charged cotton candy. Terrifying, and then tingly, and then fuzzy and sweet. When I open my eyes, I find Thomas braced over me on his forearms, and my heart swells. His hair is a tangled riot. His lips are fat and slick and curled up on one side. His eyes are hooded and dark. And his manhood, I realize, is pressed against the throbbing parts of me through the thick gray fabric of his sweatpants.

Thomas's blown-out pupils bounce back and forth between my own before he finally speaks. "I would take you right here ..." His voice is husky and low as he flexes his hips, applying the perfect amount of pressure to my oversensitized flesh.

"But?" I breathe, wishing he would do exactly that.

Thomas drops his forehead to mine and kisses me with that sex-smeared mouth. My heart twists as I prepare for him to let me down. *Tell me we can't do this. That I should go.*

Thomas slides his hands under my shoulder blades and lifts me into a sitting position.

Here we go. He's going to take a step back, hand me my pants, and tell me that he got his "inspiration" for the weekend.

But he doesn't. With another soft kiss and his dick still nestled firmly between my legs, Thomas smiles … sweetly. "But … I haven't finished my tour."

With a grin that I feel all the way to my toes, I sweep a hand out toward the living room, now cloaked in darkness. I open my mouth to say, *By all means*, but something occurs to me just before he scoops me back up into his arms. "Wait!"

Thomas arches a brow as I twist away from him, reaching toward the center of the table until my fingertips graze the edge of the metal bowl. Then, with one final push, I press down, letting two-dozen wooden citrus fruits spill out. I turn back around to find Thomas with his eyes shut and head tilted back in laughter as the now-familiar clatter of wood hitting marble echoes all around us.

I drink in the sight of him poised between my bare legs— happy, shirtless, hard, *real*—and feel a smile bloom across my own face. "It's like applause, only louder."

Thomas lifts me up off the table—his hands cupping my ass as my legs wrap around his waist—and kisses me again. "I've never gotten applause for *that* before. I quite like it."

I'm about to make a joke about psychologists and positive reinforcement when Thomas trips on a runaway lemon. I squeal and cling to his shoulders for dear life as he stumbles forward, catching his balance as we enter the darkness of the back hallway. We laugh in relief until Thomas claims my mouth again. With our heart rates elevated and his cock between my legs, our kiss becomes deeper, needier. We pass a door, but Thomas doesn't bother to stop and tell me what room it is. Then another. Then another. His hands are guiding me up and down his length as his tongue does things that I recently experienced somewhere else.

Kicking the final door open wider, Thomas crosses the threshold with purpose before depositing me on the edge of a bed as big as my entire backyard. The last few rays of sunlight stream in through a wall of windows, illuminating every sparkly, shiny, reflective surface in the room. The beveled, mirrored headboard; the glass coffee table and framed art; the copper lamps and wall sconces; yet another crystal chandelier …

"Bedroom," Thomas growls, pulling my shirt off over my head in one fluid motion. The deep vibration in his voice sends a shiver of anticipation through my body.

As Thomas reaches behind me to unclasp my bra, his situation is suddenly staring me in the face. Licking my lips, I grasp the waistband of his sweatpants and boxer briefs with both hands and slowly shimmy them down over his firm ass. His length falls forward, thick and heavy, and I'm overcome with the need to touch it. To taste it.

As I drag the flat of my tongue up and around his crown, my eyes flutter closed as I relish the whispered, "Fuck," he releases in response to my touch.

My hands slide over his hard thighs and up the rolling ridges of his abdomen as I take him deeper. I've never been one of those girls who loves to suck a guy off. It always felt awkward to me and, if I'm being honest, kind of demeaning. But something about Thomas is different. Hell, everything about Thomas is different. I want to worship every square inch of his body and every dark corner of his mind. I want to *feel* him in every sense of the word. I want to tell him things with my touch that I can't express to him any other way.

Things like, *I'm in love with you.*

And, *I always have been.*

Things like, *I don't want you to leave.*

And, *I wish I could have helped you.*

As I wrap a hand around his velvety length, I feel as though another is being wrapped around my throat. I'm overcome with emotion as I begin to pump him faster, suck him harder.

Stay. Please stay. Please stay.
I'm sorry. I failed you. I'm sorry.

"Lou," Thomas chokes out, threading a hand into my hair and gripping it tightly. "Lou, fuck, come here."

Pulling me to stand, Thomas scoops me up, and once again, I'm in his arms with my legs around his waist, only this feels different too. Thomas's heart is pounding against my bare breast. His face is buried in the crook of my neck. And his hands are clutching me to his body, like he's afraid I'm the one who's going to leave.

I feel the tip of him press against my entrance, penetrating me ever so slightly through the damp fabric of my satin thong, and an electric current of desire courses over my skin. Without questions or doubts or anything other than blind trust and blinding need, I slide my panties to the side, Thomas looks into my eyes, and together, we sink.

I press my forehead against his and dig my nails into the back of his neck as he fills me, inch by agonizing inch. Our breaths weave together, creating a ragged tapestry of understanding as we share a moment that feels bigger than any that have come before it. Bigger than this ridiculous apartment. Bigger than the ocean that separates our homes.

"I am so giving this tour five stars on Yelp tomorrow," I whisper, earning me one of Thomas's elusive silent laughs.

My heart is full to bursting when he presses that grinning mouth to mine again. I hold on tight as he turns around and sits on the edge of the bed, the motion causing him to fill me even deeper. I gasp around his tongue, and his hands begin to roam. He guides my hips up and down, setting the pace. He cups and caresses my full, needy breasts. And when he breaks our kiss to lavish my tender nipples with the same attention, when I look down at his beautiful face—eyelashes fanned out over chiseled cheekbones—and clutch it to my breast, I fall apart.

Thomas holds me tight as I whimper and pant and detonate around him. But he doesn't let me fall back to earth. Instead, he grabs my hips and thrusts into me harder, prolonging my almost-painful ecstasy as he swells inside of me.

"Thomas ..." It's a desperate plea, one that I've uttered a thousand times in the throes of pleasure but one that has always fallen on deaf ears ... until now. With those two syllables, the face I've stared at on the back of a book cover for so long crumples.

No longer steely or guarded or cold or calculating, Thomas's features twist into a raw, soul-bearing expression of pleasure and pain. But as soon as I see it, it disappears from view as Thomas rolls me onto my back, buries that face in the crook of my neck, and surges into me with a desperation all his own. I catch him as he follows me over the edge, squeezing his taut, shuddering body with my thighs, my arms, my hands. Thomas's fingers dig into my shoulders as he pours himself into me, his teeth graze my collarbone, and I know he's found a taste of the madness he's been chasing.

But all too soon, his muscles relax, his grip loosens, and I feel him returning to reality. I hold my breath as his eyelashes blink open against the side of my neck, wishing I could stop time. Three words sit on both of our tongues, but they're not the same ones.

His will be, *Good-bye, Dr. Sterling.*

And mine will go with me to my grave.

Pressing up onto his forearms, Thomas plants a sweet, lingering kiss on my worried mouth before sliding the tip of his nose down the bridge of mine. "Stay the night," he whispers, kissing me again.

All I can do is kiss him back and hope he tastes my answer.

Lou

MY EYES FLY OPEN in a panic as I register the sound of my alarm going off somewhere far, far away. They dart around the room, taking in my surroundings as the events of last night come crashing back into focus.

I'm on the floor, sandwiched between a fluffy white shag rug and the down comforter that Thomas must have yanked off the bed in the middle of the night. His chest rises and falls slowly beneath my cheek, and his body is hard and warm and perfectly entwined with mine. Blue flames dance along a strip of crystal rocks in the fireplace near our feet, and two still-full wineglasses sit on the hearth, where we abandoned them in favor of other activities.

The sky is dark beyond the wall of windows, but there is enough ambient light in the room that I can tell the sun is rising out there somewhere.

The sound of digital wind chimes in the distance stops, meaning that my cell phone alarm has given up on me and shut itself off.

As quickly and quietly as possible, I slip out from under Thomas's arm and crawl over to my discarded bra and silky T-shirt. I leave my ruined panties on the floor and tiptoe out the door, clutching my clothes to my bare chest. The hardwood is cold under my feet. I didn't notice yesterday, probably because Thomas carried me everywhere.

The thought makes me smile until I pass an open door that catches my attention. There is an office inside, sleek and modern. An L-shaped desk brackets another large window, and behind it stands a wall of floating glass shelves, dotted with creamy porcelain pottery and black-and-white photos of places where you can actually see the horizon.

A black laptop sits closed on the desk, and the sight erases the smile from my face. There are no empty coffee cups or wadded-up napkins lying around, no notebooks or chewed-up pen caps. The trash can is empty, and so is this room. Devoid of all life and activity.

Nothing is being created here.

I pad the rest of the way down the hall and into the main living area. Yellow lemons and bright green limes are the only pop of color in this otherwise cool, neutral cage—unless you count my plaid pants. I step over a few wooden fruits and snatch them up off the ground too.

I wriggle into my clothes in the kitchen while I wait for my coffee to brew. This place came equipped with a Keurig machine and a discreet basket full of those "little plastic cups that you drop in" that my stepdad hates so much. I open the cabinets until I find a nice, big mug to steal and stick it under the spout.

As I check my reflection in the microwave door, wiping mascara out from under my eyes and finger-combing my ratty hair, I notice a book on the counter behind me.

A very. Familiar. Book.

Guilt settles on my sternum like a cinder block as I turn and face the textbook. Maslow's *Hierarchy of Needs*, the same exact edition as the one on my shelf, stares back.

"Morning, sunshine."

Warm hands wrap around my waist from behind as Thomas leans down and plants a kiss on the curve of my neck. I freeze, both startled and shamed by his touch, before Thomas lazily pads to the other side of the kitchen.

I turn to face him, hiding the book behind my back, and am confronted with yet another thing to feel guilty about. Thomas's hair is still tousled from my fingers. His eyelids are heavy, his features slack and sated. His sweatpants sit low on his shirtless torso, and his back—dotted with a dozen fading pink crescents from my fingernails—rises and falls at an unhurried pace as he fills a teakettle at the sink.

This is not a motivated man.

"Off to work?" Thomas asks, placing the kettle on the stove and turning to face me with a sleepy smile. His ab muscles contract as he leans against the counter, and then they relax, like the rest of him.

"It *is* Friday." I look around, needing something to do with my hands.

"Come back after." He shrugs. "Stay the weekend."

"Thomas ... I ..." I'm sweltering, so I sprint over to the refrigerator and yank it open, hiding my face behind the door as I drink in the cold air.

"You what?"

I grab a carton of milk and close the fridge, but I still can't bring myself to face him. I just stand there, staring at the closed stainless-steel door while I concentrate on breathing normally.

"Hey ..." His voice is soft. Concerned. "Talk to me."

Thomas's hands glide over my shoulders before gripping my upper arms and turning me to face him. With one glance, his content, lopsided smile morphs into a frown as he registers the gut-wrenching remorse etched into my features.

A deep V forms between his analytical eyes as they flick back and forth between mine. "What happened?"

"What happened?" I almost scoff. "I was supposed to fix you, and instead, I fucked you. That's what happened."

Relief brightens his worried face. "And you did a bloody amazing job." He smirks.

"It's not funny, Thomas." I push the words out around the painful lump forming in my throat. "You came to me for help. You came all the way here for help, and I ... I failed you." I shake my head as Thomas's frown returns. "And now, you're gonna lose a million-dollar book deal because of it."

I drop my gaze to the floor and swallow, trying to keep the emotion out of my voice when I tell him, "I'm so sorry."

With his finger and thumb, Thomas lifts my chin, forcing me to look at him through my stinging eyes.

"I'm not." The corner of his mouth lifts as he tucks a strand of hair behind my ear and slides his fingers down the length of the old, tattered feather he finds there. "I was going to lose that book deal anyway. At least, this way, I got to meet you."

"Stop it." I tear my eyes away, staring at the teakettle over his shoulder. "Why are you being so nice?"

"Because I spent last night with the most brilliant..."—Thomas leans forward and kisses my forehead. His tenderness only makes me feel worse—"beautiful"—his lips brush across my temple and land on my cheek, leaving a trail of fire in their wake—"talented"—warm, minty breath sweeps over my jawline before Thomas's lips connect with the place on my throat that is pounding and flushed—"...terrifying woman I've ever met."

When my frozen body doesn't respond to his touch, Thomas drops his hands and returns to his full height. "Forgive me if it put me in a good mood." With a scowl, he turns and pads back over to the sink, gripping the edge with both hands. "It obviously had the opposite effect on you."

His words burn even more than his touch. All I want to do is wrap my arms around his waist, press my cheek between his hunched shoulders, and accept the affection he's offering, but I've taken enough from this man for one lifetime. His trust, his time, his last chance at redemption, his body—I took as much as he would give me, and when he leaves, all he'll have to show for it is a cut on his lip and a hole in his bank account.

The sound of muffled digital wind chimes drifts in from somewhere beyond the kitchen, and I bolt into the main hallway, never more relieved to hear my alarm.

I pick up my cardigan and Converse along the way to my purse, which I find lying sideways in the foyer with half of its contents spilled out among the fruit. The words *Get up, bitch* illuminate the screen on my phone, which I silence with a tap.

I shove my feet into my busted canvas shoes and know without looking up that Thomas is watching me from the kitchen doorway. I can feel him.

"So, that's it then?" His voice is calm and cool. Guarded as usual.

"I don't know what else to say."

He shrugs, crossing his arms over his bare chest. "Say you'll stay."

"Thomas, this"—I gesture between us with two fingers— "is toxic. Don't you see that? It's going to cost us our jobs."

He lifts a shoulder. "We could get new jobs."

"I don't want a new job! I want the one I just spent ten years learning how to do! I'm not gonna throw all that away, so I can spend two more weeks with a guy whose relationships are usually over before the ink is even dry on the tabloid photos."

Thomas chews on the inside corner of his mouth as his head rises and falls in a slow, bitter nod. "Security."

"What?" I squat and begin shoving everything back into my purse.

"That's your motivation. Safety and Security Needs. Maslow. Level two."

I freeze, feeling completely and utterly exposed. It's shameful and embarrassing, but he's right. I have ten years' worth of student loans and can barely make ends meet. I can't risk my only source of income, the very roof over my head, on something that probably won't work out.

Definitely won't work out.

Standing to face him, I let my silence verify his assumption.

"And which of his levels did you say you wanted me to be on again?"

He's fucking with me now. Twisting the knife. But I'll play along because I know I deserve it.

"Level three," I say. "Social Needs. Acceptance, sex—"

"Love?"

I press my lips together and nod. "Yeah. Love is on that level."

"Well, congratulations, Doctor." Thomas's eyes turn to steel, cutting me down where I stand. "Turns out, you're better at your job than you thought."

He disappears into the kitchen, leaving my emotions as scattered as the fruit on the floor.

Love.

Did he just say that he loves me?

No. That's insane. Thomas doesn't love me. He can't.

He's just saying that to make me feel bad for leaving—that's all.

We both know that if I stay, he'll be the one leaving me in two weeks. And then where will I be?

No, this is what's best for both of us.

Thomas needs to go back to London and write more books. I need to figure out how to salvage what's left of my career. And we need to end this fatal attraction before it completely destroys both of our lives.

An image of my mother floats to the surface of my mind. One that hasn't haunted me in a long, long time. Her grief-stricken, emaciated body is curled around mine like a thorny vine, clutching me with desperate, knobby fingers as she cries uncontrollably in my twin-size bed.

That's what love does, a voice deep inside of me whispers. *Get out while you still can.*

When Thomas reappears from the kitchen, he marches up to me, holding the mug from the coffee machine and wearing a scowl. "Wouldn't want you to be late for *work*."

He says the word *work* like it's the name of my secret lover.

His eyes are hurricanes—an angry, stormy blue swirling around a central point of darkness—and I know what that darkness is. Because it's the same as mine.

"I'm sorry," I whisper, accepting the steaming hot mug with both hands.

Thomas opens the door with bitter resignation on his face, and I walk through, dropping my eyes to the light-brown contents of my cup.

He even put milk in it.

"Hey, Lou?" Thomas calls from behind me, causing my feet to stop in the middle of the nineteenth-floor hallway.

I turn to face him, hope stirring in my empty belly.

"Ring me when you get on my level."

With those words, door number nineteen twenty-eight closes in my face. I stare at the smooth surface for what feels like minutes, knowing that when I turn to leave, my heart won't be coming with me.

And neither will the coffee that I just spilled all over the carpet.

Lou

KIMBERLY IS A RECORD thirty-five minutes late, and I'm not even mad about it.

Because my ass was fifteen minutes late.

She looks worse than me too, which is quite a feat. She's managed to lose a couple of extensions, so there are some obvious gaps in her usually curled but currently limp blonde hair. Her dark roots are about an inch too long to be considered stylish. She's missing two fake nails on one hand, and the ones that remain have lost most of their glued-on crystals. And her false eyelashes are shockingly absent, replaced by too much eyeliner, which has already begun to settle under her eyes.

I swipe my fingers under my own eyes, remembering how my reflection looked in Thomas's microwave door this morning.

Thomas.

I shake my head, as if not thinking about him could ever be that easy, and force myself to sit up straighter.

"So, how did the audition go?" I ask with only a slight tremor in my voice.

This is going to be a long fucking day.

Kimberly takes a sip from her ten-dollar coffee, and I extend my hand, flicking my fingers toward myself.

"Ugh," she scoffs, handing the beverage over with a scowl. At least, I think she's scowling. Her unfortunate Botox paralysis hasn't worn off yet.

Crossing her arms over her ample chest proves difficult, so Kimberly crosses them under her chest, heaving her boobs up with her forearms. "I didn't go."

I set her drink down on my desk and turn to face her. "Why not?"

"What's the point?" she cries, throwing her hands in the air. "It's not like they were actually going to hire me. I'm never gonna be anything other than Drama Llama Kim for the rest of my life!" She jacks her boobs back up with her folded arms and crosses her legs to match.

Xs everywhere.

"Remember how we talked about false beliefs?" I ask. "This idea that you will never become a serious actress because you got your start on a reality show is not only holding you back, but it's also untrue."

Kimberly rolls her eyes.

"Okay, let's try something. I want you to name one reality star who went on to become an actor."

She purses her overfilled lips and turns her head away from me defiantly.

"I'll wait," I snap.

I'm in a shitty mood too, honey. Let's go.

"Fine," she huffs. "Snooki."

"Okay, that's a good start. I think I saw her in a Super Bowl commercial last year." *Playing herself.* "Who else?"

Kimberly shrugs and pouts and glances longingly at her beverage sitting on the corner of my desk.

"I'll give you your coffee back if you can tell me five more," I say.

With the nasty, exaggerated sigh that helped her earn the title of Drama Llama in the first place, Kimberly pulls a pink crystal-encrusted cell phone out of her Gucci bag. "Fine." A few taps of acrylic on glass, and she starts reading what she finds. "Emma Stone, Jennifer Hudson …"

"Emma Stone?" I interject. "Really?"

Kim looks up. "Yeah." Her voice sounds surprised, but her poor frozen forehead doesn't show it. "They both have Oscars too." She keeps reading. "Jon Hamm was on a dating show. Oh my God, his catch phrase was, 'Fabulosity.' How cringey!" She smiles. "Laverne Cox. I love her. Kelly Clarkson, Lucy Hale, Beyoncé …"

I hand over her cinnamon/cardamom/pumpkin/chai precious without a word.

Kimberly stops reading and snatches it out of my hand. Taking a long swig, she keeps one eye on me the entire time. I feel her defensiveness beginning to thaw as she lowers the mug to her lap and stares at the lid.

"So …" She shrugs. "How do I get past this false … whatever?"

"You do exactly what we just did. Every time you hear that limiting thought—the one that says you can't become a serious actor—you present yourself with evidence that proves it wrong. Maybe choose one of those actors you just listed, the one you identify with the most, and say their name over and over in your mind."

Stephen and Tabitha, a voice whispers inside of me.

"Or tape a picture of them to your bathroom mirror," I continue. "Or make it your"—I force the words out before my rapidly closing throat squeezes them off—"lock screen photo."

Unwelcome memories of giddy, forbidden text messages push their way in as Kimberly begins to tap on her phone again.

I have a teenage boy on my lock screen. This feels wrong.

"I'm gonna go with Jon Hamm," she says. "He's fine as hell."

I will my stinging eyes to dry the fuck up as I glance down at my own phone. "I'm afraid our time is up."

After Kimberly leaves, I make a few notes on my legal pad about her session, but my scribbles soon turn to sad, swirly doodles as my mind pores over every second, every word, every sharp glance and bitter regret from my morning with Thomas. I know my heart is broken because it hasn't beaten normally since I left his apartment. It's been pounding, seizing, aching, sputtering, and reminding me with sharp, stabbing acuity why my false belief isn't false at all. I was right. And so was Thomas.

Love will destroy your life if you let it, and the only way I can repair what's left of mine is to cancel the group, tell Dr. Ito-Cohen that Thomas quit therapy, and beg her to give me another chance.

A shadow falls across my lap, but when I look up, it isn't Winnie the Wine Mom I see scowling down at me. It's The Notorious E.I.C.

I clutch my clipboard to my chest and sit up straight.

"This look has walk of shame all over it," she sneers, waving a blood-red fingertip at the same outfit I was wearing yesterday. "Very on-brand for you."

I clamp my teeth together and focus on breathing as all the words I rehearsed abandon me like rats from a sinking ship.

Those long, crimson-tipped fingers lace together as Dr. E.I.C.'s eyebrows lift dramatically. "Would you care to explain to me why Celeste Casablancas is suing us in small claims court over a sriracha stain on a Burberry sweater?"

No words come to mind. No thoughts at all. The only thing I register between my ears is the *thumpa-thumpa-thumpa-thumpa* sound of blood being pumped out to my extremities.

"Or why Michelle Livingston wants us to reimburse her for X-rays due to a potential concussion she sustained during a trust fall?"

What? Goddamn it, Beth!

"Or perhaps why Bill Thurman's wife called, upset over the black eye he received at *group therapy*?"

The words *group therapy* are a death blow. She might as well have said, *The black eye he sustained at YOU'RE FIRED*. I was prepared to fight for my job, to do everything in my power to convince E.I.C. that I deserved another chance, but I don't deserve it. And now, she knows it too.

"I'm sorry," I whisper, forcing myself to meet her wrathful stare. "I'll just … pack up my things."

"You do that. Security will be here to escort you out in..."— E.I.C. flicks her wrist to illuminate her Apple watch—"four minutes."

With a bowling ball of remorse in my gut, I walk around to the other side of my desk as Dr. Ito-Cohen slithers over to the door.

"Unless, of course," she calls from the doorway, "Thomas O'Reardon has a manuscript ready."

I pull my framed degree off the wall and turn to face her. "He still has two weeks," I say, hope lifting my features fractionally.

"To write an entire book?" She laughs. No, she *cackles*. "God, you public school graduates get dumber every year. Tell Dr. Callahan I'm done taking on his charity cases."

Tears blur my vision as I clutch my degree to my chest. "Please don't do this," I beg. "Please. If you fire me, I won't be able to get licensed."

Her pointy features sharpen further as she curls her lips back and hisses, "You should have thought about that before you invited all of your clients to an *unsupervised therapy group*."

"I know, but they made progress!" I blurt out in desperation. "Bill said he's never felt better. Dixie isn't suicidal anymore. And Celeste, she didn't throw a single thing at me this—"

Before I can react, an Apple watch sails across the room and hits me right in the face.

"Two minutes," E.I.C. snaps before stomping out of my office.

With my cheekbone throbbing almost as painfully as the ache in my chest, I pick the watch up off the floor and hold it out over my desk. Half a second later, E.I.C. comes tearing back into my office and snatches the device out of my hand. With a final soul-withering glare, she marches back out the door, narrowly missing Steve, our plump security guard.

"Hey, Dr. Sterling," he greets me with a smile. "Do you think you could look at this for me?" He begins rolling up his sleeve.

"For the hundredth time, Steve, I'm not that kind of doctor!" I bark.

His face falls as he tugs the polyester material back down.

Thirty minutes and a six-dollar Uber ride later, I stand in my driveway, clutching a box full of my things from work under one arm, my worthless degree under the other, and I admire the rest of my meager possessions, which have been tossed in a heap on my front lawn.

Mark doesn't even acknowledge me as he plucks his Shania wig off the grass and crams it into his already-overflowing car.

"What the fuck happened?" I'm too stunned and despondent to even yell. I'm just … numb.

"The rapture," Mark snaps, turning toward me with his hands on his hips. "What does it look like?"

"I don't understand." I can't stop shaking my head. "How are we getting evicted when we pay the rent every month? Or at least, most of it." My voice trails off.

"Oh, grow up, Lou. I've been spendin' our rent money on coke and black-market Adderall for *months*. Honestly, I'm surprised it took this long." Mark trudges back across the lawn, picking up his scattered collection of beer koozies like it's redneck Easter.

"That explains the fight club," I mutter, my eyes landing on a precious collection of my own. Setting my box and framed degree down in the driveway, I let my legs carry me across the yard, delivering me to the spot where a familiar, guarded gaze stares back, upside down in the dewy grass.

I kneel beside the pile of books and pick up *Ruby Lies* off the top of the stack. The cover is dirty, and the corners are now bent, but Thomas's chiseled features and crooked smile are more heartbreaking than ever. I brush a smattering of dirt off his cheek, resisting the urge to kiss it.

Mark sits down next to me with a huff. "Well, you don't have to act so damn sad about it. Gah. Now you're makin' me feel bad."

"Where are you gonna go?" I ask without looking up from Thomas's smirk.

"Where all the fabulous people go when they fuck up their lives and don't wanna deal with it … rehab, honey."

I nod. "Good. That's good, Mark."

"Oh shit," he says, placing a hand over his heart as realization strikes. "Where are *you* gonna go?"

Lou

"THANKS, COURT. I OWE you one."

Courtney's eyes go wide as the gravel road we're bouncing over gives way to a clearing filled with RVs and shacks and a bonfire ten feet tall, surrounded by gyrating bodies. "What is this place?"

"You should probably let me out here," I say, unbuckling my seat belt. "If they see this gas-guzzler on their property, they'll chase you down the mountain with citronella torches. I've seen it happen."

Courtney comes to a stop on the edge of the clearing, but it's too late. The rumble of a Birkenstock stampede pounding the earth and faraway shouts perk my ears just before a half-dozen middle-aged hippies come into view, running toward us with their environmental protest signs raised and their teeth bared.

"Shit." I jump out of the SUV and throw open the back passenger door, unloading my stuff as fast as I can.

"Lou?" Courtney asks in her pageant-queen voice. "Um …"

"Earth killer!"

"Pollution Nazi!"

"Make love, not carbon emissions!"

The commune members' voices grow louder and louder as I yank my belongings out faster and faster.

"Loooou?" Courtney's voice takes on a shrill, panicked tone before she suddenly throws the Suburban in reverse and stomps on the gas.

I get out of the way before the door takes me out, but I can't say the same for my boxes and suitcase, which are knocked over, smashed, and/or dragged by Courtney's still-open back door.

Until, of course, it hits a tree trunk and gets ripped clean off.

Courtney's three-doored SUV disappears backward down the steep gravel drive—along with her screams—as Leif and five of Indigo Hills' finest go sprinting after her, half-naked and shouting about climate change and trees being people too.

God, I hate this place.

"Hey, Lou Bear."

The voice behind me is sweet and comforting. I hate that too.

I muster a fake smile and turn to face my mother. Her eyes are kind and crinkled at the corners, and her bangles jingle like wind chimes as she lifts her arms for a hug.

George is by her side, a faded Mets cap covering his balding head and a warm smile at the ready. "Hiya, kid."

The pity on their faces is more than I can bear. My chin buckles, and I dive into my mother's arms, if only to keep them from seeing me break.

"Shh …" she coos, smoothing a hand over my hair as tears that are fifteen hours in the making finally start to fall. "Shhhhhh …"

George pats me on the back, unsure of what to do with all this emotion. "Uh … come on, kiddo," he finally says, giving my shoulder a gentle squeeze. "Let's get you settled in."

George hadn't lied—my bunk/coffin is exactly the way I left it. I decline an invite to mingle with the burnouts around the bonfire and instead retreat to the psychedelic tin can that I swore I'd never step foot in again. The tie-dyed graveyard of my failed adulthood.

Outside, people are singing and chanting and speaking in joyous tongues, but in here, it feels like a funeral that nobody came to. Just me, in my casket, leaking silent tears while I wait for someone to remember I'm here and cover my miserable ass in dirt.

I stare up at the My Chemical Romance poster taped to the ceiling, eighteen inches above my head. It's an illustration of a blood-spattered boy and girl on the verge of a kiss, gazing into one another's eyes. I rip it down in a fit of rage and wad it into a spiky ball, but instead of throwing it across the RV, my body betrays me. It curls around that fucking poster like it's a teddy bear and sobs even harder.

I thought leaving Thomas would save me from suffering the same fate as my mother.

Turns out, it only sped up the process.

Lou

TIME EXISTS IN A vacuum in this place. I feel like I just got here, but at the same time, I feel like I never really left. That decade I spent in the real world disappeared in the blink of an eye, and all I have to show for it is a framed piece of paper with my name on it, a pile of student loan debt, and some shiny, new emotional baggage for my collection.

I sit in a bed of rust-colored leaves under the oak tree where I used to draw, flipping through one of my old sketchpads. There's a pencil tucked in the spiral binding, but I don't feel like using it. I don't feel like breathing either, but since when has what I wanted mattered?

There's a zombified portrait of everyone at the commune inside this relic, plus a few celebrities and boys that I fooled around with in high school. I can see how much time and attention went into each and every drawing. I forgot that Bianca, the former beekeeper here, had an asymmetrical nose. And that Kevin Watersby from my honors English class had his ears pierced. I also forgot how many different styles of shading I tried before I settled on crosshatch.

All of them. I tried all of them.

The sound of approaching footsteps causes me to slam my notebook shut and flip the hood of my black sweatshirt up over my head. I don't look up to see who's coming. Eye contact, even accidental, is an invitation for a thirty-minute conversation about composting techniques around here. But the feet that come to a stop in front of me aren't covered in vegan moccasins. In fact, they're not feet at all.

They're hooves.

Tilting my head back, I follow a pair of furry white legs up to a broad, muscular body, which is draped with a colorful, hand-dyed broomstick skirt that I would recognize anywhere. I release a sigh and glance the rest of the way up at my mother's glowing face, backlit by the autumn sun, like some kind of ethereal, bohemian angel who travels the cosmos on her trusty white steed.

A white steed that just chuffed at me in disapproval.

"Lou Bear, you've been in this same spot all weekend." Her voice is soft, concerned, as she strokes a hand down the horse's silvery mane. "Come with me. I know what'll make you feel better."

"Alcohol that wasn't made from distilled corn?"

"Don't be so dramatic," Crystal says with a hint of parental sternness. "You know Jethro makes muscadine wine too."

I grimace, picturing Jethro—an old, pantsless, gap-toothed man with a long white beard—grinning as he mashes muscadines in a barrel with his feet.

"Nah, I'm good."

"You are not. Come." She extends her hand, forcefully enough to let me know she's serious. "It'll be wonderful, I promise."

Five minutes later, I'm sitting on the back of a horse, straddling my mother as she trots up to a wooden pavilion I've never seen before.

She extends a hand, bangles jingling in the breeze, toward, "Our new spa."

"Spa?" I'm not sure I heard her correctly. This thing is just a roof held up by a few telephone poles.

"It's heavenly. Come." With a sweep of her leg, Crystal slides off the horse, yards of bright fabric billowing around her before she lands.

I try to get off the same way, but my dismount looks—and feels—more like a slow fall from a high place.

Inside the pavilion, there aren't even picnic tables—just a huge wooden sandbox-like frame that takes up the entire space. And has been filled with, "Corn?"

Crystal slips out of her sandals. "Take your shoes off, darling."

"Is this like one of those fish tank pedicures, only instead of fish, it's giant, plague-infected rats?" I ask, kicking off my Converse.

Crystal steps into the corn and moans appreciatively.

I try not to roll my eyes as I follow her in, but the moment my feet sink into that sea of dried kernels, my eyes roll all by themselves—up into the back of my head. "Oh my God, why does this feel so goooood?"

Crystal turns to face me with a grin. "Wait until you lie down. It's like being cradled in the bosom of the Divine Mother herself."

She doesn't have to tell me twice. I practically swan-dive into the vat of corn, turning onto my back as a million little kernels wrap me up in one giant hug.

My mom kneels beside me, smiling and humming to herself as she piles more corn on top of me, burying me up to my face. "It's nice, right?"

"It's amazing." The sensation is unlike anything I've ever felt. It's like floating on water, but the water is perfectly still. And it's heavy. And it's corn.

"I know what you're going through, Lou Bear," my mom says without looking up from the pile of kernels she's amassing on my chest. "You might not remember, but I lost my real estate business right before we came here."

"I remember you crying a lot," I admit.

"It was awful. First, I lost your father, and then four years later, the housing market crashed."

"And then you ran away to a hippie commune," I bite out. "I definitely remember that part."

The memory of those years takes whatever bliss I was feeling and lights it on fire.

"It took losing everything for me to finally find myself," Crystal says with a wistful smile.

And that smile is the kerosene. I sit up on my elbows, rage pumping through my veins, as a giant pair of corn boobies slides off my chest and into my lap.

"Yourself," I snap. "That's all you think about. What about me? I lost Dad, too, but at least I had friends back home. Did you ever stop to think about what it would be like for me to lose them too? To be the new kid at a high school where the parking lot had more tractors in it than cars? Did you ever stop to think about George? Or Dad? What about all the other people like him who need help too? Do you ever think about them?"

My mom's face turns to stone as she jams a finger into the corn next to her hip. "I think about the entire world, Luna. I don't eat animal products. I don't burn fossil fuels. I don't even use paper! Have you ever tried wiping your vulva with an oak leaf?"

I wince.

"It's a real sacrifice!"

Crystal closes her eyes and takes a deep, steadying breath. In through her nose, out through her mouth. When she looks at me again, her features are softer, less stabby.

"But that's my path," she continues, placing a hand on her chest. "I'm sorry that my self-discovery came at such a bad time for you, but the goddess intervenes when the goddess intervenes. And right now, it's your turn. That doesn't mean you have to start using lemon rinds as menstrual cups and become a beekeeper—although we do have an opening. I'm just saying that all this loss … it's a gift, sweetie." Her eyes begin to glisten with unshed tears. "It's an opportunity for you to find *your* path. Start using your goddess-given talents again."

Crystal's apology washes over my ancient, festering, enflamed wounds, like cooling rain over hot lava. With my anger finally extinguished, I feel like I'm able to see her clearly for the first time in my life. Her journey, her struggle, the enormity of her loss. The desperation she must have felt to bring us here. And also, the relief. I open my mouth to apologize as well, for being such a little shit all these years, but Crystal silences me with a henna-painted palm.

"I know you think that the only way to honor your father is to become a psychologist—and he would be so proud—but you know what he would want even more? For you to do what's right for *you*." She taps my hoodie-covered chest with a delicate finger. "All he ever wanted was for us to be happy." Her voice breaks on that last word, as does what's left of my heart, as tears spill down her makeup-free cheeks. "He tried so hard to be happy."

"I know, Mom." I sit up and wrap my arms around her, realizing that it's the first time I've seen her cry since we moved here.

She used to cry every day back home, but ever since we came here, there's been a lightness about her that I envy. I want to feel that free too.

My eyes pop open.

Thomas said almost the exact same thing after our second group therapy session. The only time he feels truly free is when he's writing about psychopaths, which is how I feel about drawing. But I need a subject in order to draw. So, maybe Thomas just needs …

Oh my God.

Sitting up, I hold Crystal at arm's length. "What day is this?"

Suddenly, the corn on the other side of the pit begins to shift as a shirtless Jethro emerges from beneath the surface, swim goggles covering his eyes and yellow kernels dotting his wiry white beard.

"It's Sunday, man," Jethro says with a stoned drawl. "I know 'cause we sold apples at the farmers market this morning. It was beautiful."

"Shit!" My eyes cut back over to Crystal. "I gotta go!"

I give her a peck on the cheek and a quick, "I love you, Mom," before I leap to my feet and start wading through the corn.

My foot lands on something large and soft, eliciting a yelp from both me and the woman whose body part I just stomped on. She comes springing out of the corn like a topless jack-in-the-box, cucumbers tumbling from her eyes and kernels pouring from the gray curls on top of her head as she cuts me a dirty look.

"Sorry! So sorry!" I grimace, stepping out of the pit and into my shoes.

"Luna, where are you going?" Crystal calls out.

"You guys still share everything here, right?"

Lou

THE RV TIRES SPIN, kicking up soft Georgia clay and wet pine needles before finally gaining traction. I bounce in the driver's seat and grip the steering wheel harder as the Technicolored behemoth lurches out of its permanent parking spot and hops over tree roots on its way to the gravel road leading down the mountain.

"Lou! Lou, wait up!"

I glance in the side mirror and see George running after me, waving his arms.

I roll down the window and lean my head out. "Sorry, George! Can't stop!"

"Hey, pick me up a Quarter Pounder with Cheese meal while you're out! With the pickles on the side and a Diet Coke!"

George stops running and braces his hands on his knees, catching his breath.

As he gets smaller in my rearview mirror, the other hippies come into view. They've gathered around to glare at him in disgust over that McDonald's request, but George just waves them off.

That poor guy belongs here about as much as I do, but for the first time since we stepped foot on this soil, I understand why he stays. Why he put her needs before his own all those years ago and continues to do so every day of his life. Because she makes him happy. No amount of saturated fat or air-conditioning or ESPN could ever fill the void that she fills. And no job or accolade or shitty little rental house will ever fill mine.

I know what will make Thomas happy, what will make him feel *free*, and if I have to sacrifice everything in order for him to have it, then so be it.

I pull my phone out of my pocket and find April's name on my Contacts list and hit the green Call button next to it. Putting it on speakerphone, I drop the device into my lap as the highway appears up ahead. As soon as the RV lurches out from under the canopy of the woods, big, fat raindrops begin to splatter on the windshield.

Dammit.

I've never owned a car, and I can't even remember the last time I drove one, so finding the windshield wiper controls proves to be more difficult than I expected.

"Hey, Dr. Sterling!" April's voice chirps from between my legs.

"April! Have you told my clients I got fired yet?" I flip the first switch I see, and air-conditioning blasts me in the face.

"Oh my God, you got fired?"

"Uh, yeah." I push a button, and the oldies station comes blaring out of every speaker. "Don't you remember Security Steve escorting me out on Friday?"

"I thought he was just being creepy!"

"Seriously? I was carrying my degree and a box full of my stuff." I flip another switch, and the entire back of the RV turns

214

into a dance party. Swirling green pot leaves, peace signs, and smiley faces are projected onto every surface, including the instrument panel that I now see has a blinking yellow light right next to a picture of a gas tank.

Awesome.

"April, I need you to do me a huge favor ..."

I hold the phone between my shoulder and ear as I stick the gas pump into the RV tank, which took me a solid ten minutes to locate on this rolling monstrosity. In the rain.

A robotic female voice answers on the fourth ring. "You have reached the voice mail for ..."

"Thomas." I swallow. "Hey, it's, um ... it's Lou. You told me to ring when I got on your level, so ... ring, ring." I cringe at my awkwardness as I return the pump to its cradle.

"Listen, I'm ... so, *so* sorry about the way I left on Friday. I freaked out. I freaked out, and I completely understand if you never want to see me again, but ..."

I close the door and climb back into the driver's seat. "I really want you to come to group therapy tonight. Please? I owe you a proper groveling. Please come. Okay? Okay, bye."

I bang my forehead against the steering wheel a few times before cranking the engine and pulling away from the curb.

"Hey! Stop! You have to pay for that!"

I glance out the passenger window as the gas station attendant comes flying out of the convenience store, waving his arms and pointing at the gas pump in anger.

Shit. I forgot.

I pull a fistful of wadded up bills out of my purse and toss them out the window. "I have to go! I'm sorry!"

I search the center console for spare change in case what I threw wasn't enough, but what I find instead is a silver Altoids tin containing at least five expertly rolled joints.

Thanks, Mom.

"Here!" I shout, letting the little metal box fly. "Namaste!"

"Court! We're still on for tonight!"

"But you got fired."

"Nobody knows yet!"

"I don't know, Lou. Brian is pretty upset about my door, and the group hasn't exactly been goin' well ..."

"If I say I'll pay to fix your door, will that make it better?"

"You're gonna pay to fix my door?"

"Of course not. I just got fired."

I pass a cute little farmhouse with its front porch all decked out for fall and get an idea. Slamming on the brakes, I pull over onto the shoulder of the road with a screech and a skid. "Hey, Court, I gotta go, but I'll see you tonight."

"But I didn't—"

"And try to get there early, okay? Thanks so much!" I hang up and dial another number as I climb out of the mobile eyesore and tiptoe across the wide, muddy yard. I get to the side of the house and lean against it, whisper-shouting into my phone like I'm some kind of secret agent behind enemy lines.

"Mark, please tell me you're not at rehab yet. I need you to let us into the bar tonight. You owe me, asshole."

I pocket my device and peek around the side of the house. Then, when I'm sure the coast is clear, I dash over to the front porch, snatch a pot full of pretty orange chrysanthemums off the bottom step, and take off running back to the RV.

As I drive away, I make a mental note of the address so that I can return them tomorrow.

If I survive tonight, that is.

Thomas

"THOMAS. HEY, IT'S, UM … it's Lou. You told me to ring when I got on your level, so… … ring, ring."

Lou's voice mail has been playing on a loop in my head for the last four hours.

I sat by my mobile for two and a half days, waiting for that call, and when it finally came, I couldn't pick it up. I'd touched Lou not once, not twice, but on three different occasions, and every time, she shoved me back into the client zone and made it clear that her job comes first. And now, I'm supposed to believe that she's had a change of heart? No one touches a hot stove four times without being committed to Broadmoor. No one.

"I really want you to come to group therapy tonight. Please? I owe you a proper groveling. Please come."

Her begging is what pisses me off the most. After being under the thumb of three overbearing women my entire childhood, I swore that I would never let another person control me again. I live alone. I work alone. I do what I want, when I want, and with whomever I choose. But with one little *please*, Lou has me pulling into The Yacht Club car park at ten o'clock at night in the pouring rain, just to get my heart stomped on all over again.

I pull the car into an open spot in the back and grip the steering wheel.

Let's get this over with.

Lightning slices across the black sky overhead as I jog through the rain toward the building. It feels like an omen. One that I don't ignore.

With a deep breath and a heart full of bitter resignation, I pull open the wooden door with the porthole window for what I'm positive will be the last time.

"Mr. O'Reardon, welcome." Mark sweeps a hand out like a proper maître d'. His demeanor is more professional than usual, but he's wearing a sweatsuit with the arms and legs cut off, so professional is relative.

He extends the phone basket to me, and I drop mine in, knowing I'll just be snatching it back out in about forty-five minutes when Lou finds another publicly humiliating way to send me packing.

Mark sets the basket on the host stand and clamps a hand on my shoulder. "For what it's worth, you take a mean right hook."

"Don't you mean *throw*?"

"Mmhmm ... so listen ..." Mark steers me through the pub, and I can feel the covert stares of everyone we pass. "I know you love my group," he continues, "but I'm under strict orders to send you to Dr. Sterling's group tonight."

With both hands on my shoulders now, Mark deposits me at the end of Lou's booth, but it's been transformed. The table is covered in an assortment of glowing candles, potted flowers, and a jack-o'-lantern that looks like it was carved by a child. The ceiling above it is dripping with golden patio lights. And sitting in her usual spot is my mindfuck of a therapist. She's dressed in a pair of ripped jeans and an oversize band T-shirt, the hem of which is balled up in both of her tiny fists, and somehow, she's never looked sexier.

Two plump, peachy lips brighten her otherwise miserable face, reminding me exactly why I've been so bloody bad at not kissing her lately.

Lou's cheeks flush the same color as her perfect mouth when she looks up and sees me. Her hand immediately flies to her hair. She tucks her thick, wavy mane behind one ear—a nervous habit—but when her fingers brush over the feather hidden there, it brings a very different memory to mind. The one of me brushing that hair behind her ear two days ago, right before she walked out of my life.

"You came," she says, forcing a smile.

"You rang," I reply, taking my designated seat across from her like the summoned puppet I've allowed myself to become.

Lou lifts her eyes again—a warm, welcoming amber, rimmed in black lashes—and the sizzle I feel when they lock on to mine is answered with a rumble of thunder from the storm outside. Or perhaps it's the sound of my defenses rebuilding themselves as quickly as possible before this beautiful, evil woman has the chance to strike again.

"I leveled up." Lou gives me a small smile before pulling her fat bottom lip between her teeth.

I nod slowly. "And what's all this?" My eyes cut over to the rather random arrangement of fall decor at the end of the table.

"It's … a date?" Her dark eyebrows lift along with her shoulders, but when I don't respond, they plummet. "I want to start over, Thomas. I want to call this exactly what it is. It's not a therapy group. It never was. It's an unethical, mismanaged, poorly organized excuse for me to spend more time with you, and now, everybody knows it."

I glance past her at the other two groups in the room. They're watching us shamelessly, but they do at least have the common decency to try to look busy when I catch them staring.

"Thomas, you asking me out was the best thing that ever happened to me. This is me saying yes. I'm sorry it took me so long."

Another clap of thunder shakes the building, and this time, I know it has nothing to do with my defenses. Because I have none. They're gone, demolished, ground to dust, and they have been since the moment I walked into this woman's office.

"So … what happens on this *date*?" I ask, eyeing her sideways.

Lou grabs something off the seat next to her and shimmies her way out of her side of the booth. My heart begins to pound like a proper schoolboy's as she stands, holding a laptop, and slides in next to me. She scoots over until her thigh brushes mine, and warmth oozes from the spot where we touch. She smells different. Earthier. Like fresh air and campfires, fall leaves and pine forests. I want to bury my nose in her hair and inhale the freedom that scent evokes. It's wild and alive, and I want to catch it with both hands and never let it go.

But on the outside, I'm the picture of composure—unfazed and unimpressed. It's a mask I wear well.

Lou places the laptop on the table and opens it. The screen illuminates, revealing the Netflix home page. She turns to me with a shy smile, balling the hem of her shirt in her fist again.

"What happens is … you pick any scary movie you want, and I promise to make out with you through the entire thing."

Her tongue sweeps across her pouty peach lips, and as badly as I want to follow it with my own, I can't help but think that this feels like a trap.

"As I recall," I say, my eyes drifting to her parted mouth, my arteries surging with every beat of my racing heart, "the last time I kissed you in front of all these people—"

Lou's lips crash into mine, and the rest of that sentence, as well as the fear behind it, melts away on contact. My hands dive into her wild, dark hair, and I'm lit up from the inside out. Kissing this woman feels like taming a flame. I suddenly don't mind the few times I got burned in the process.

Another clap of thunder rattles the walls, and gasps fill the room. I open one eye to see that the entire pub has gone dark, except for the candles and laptop on our table. Lou is unconcerned.

"It's probably just a downed power line," she whispers, brushing her lips against mine again.

In the darkness, it's even harder to remember that we're surrounded by people.

That is, until one of them screams.

Lou pulls back and locks eyes with me as more screaming erupts throughout the pub, this time from multiple sources. Maniacal laughter rises above the cacophony, followed by glass breaking and general bloody chaos.

A muffled squeal pierces the sudden madness, and Lou jumps to her feet. "Courtney!"

She disappears from the table, and I follow immediately. I have to stay close to keep from losing her in the darkness. The only source of light beyond our table is the Emergency Exit sign above the front door.

The sounds of mass hysteria continue to fill the pub as Lou and I come to a stop at the Anxiety table.

On the right, a slight man wearing large glasses is rocking back and forth with his hands over his ears, repeating, "Ignore that which you cannot control. Ignore that which you cannot control …"

To the left, a tall, wiry woman frantically brushes the salt off the table while cackling like a witch.

Another woman pokes her head out from under the table near Lou's feet, startling her.

I wrap my hands around Lou's upper arms to steady her when a man with a mustache pops up from behind the table, pointing a water pistol at us and shouting, "Stay back!"

In a rather impressive burst of evasive action, Lou darts around the side of the table, leaving me to take a full blast right to the chest. While the water sniper pumps the plastic shotgun in preparation to spray me again, I do something I've only seen in American cop movies—I slide across the table like it's the bonnet of a police cruiser and snatch the gun out of his hand. Before I can retaliate, the mustached gunman retreats below the table. I stand and marvel at the plastic toy in my hand.

Did I just—

"Oh my God, Court!" Lou cries from a few feet away.

I turn and find her staring down at her friend, who is lying on the floor with two salt shakers shoved in her mouth.

As soon as Lou pulls the plastic shakers out of her mouth, the woman from under the table decides to make her presence known, leaping onto Lou's back and screaming, "Life is chaos! Hahahahaha! Life is chaos!"

Without a second thought, I shove Courtney's vacated chair out of the way and press the water pistol against the flailing woman's ear. "Let her go," I say, "or your brain gets a bath."

The woman sneers at me but shoves Lou to the side and slinks back under the table with a hiss.

I go to help Lou get back on her feet, but she waves me off and points at Courtney, who is coughing and trying to sit up. Lou and I each take one of her arms and pull her to a standing position.

"Behind the bar!" Lou shouts. "Now!"

As she and her friend stumble through the pub, I walk backward behind them, holding the maniacs at the Anxiety table off with the threat of high-pressure, room-temperature water.

Over at the bar, the Depression group is less aggressive but equally unhinged. An older gentleman is standing on the counter, singing a loud, warbling rendition of "Danny Boy" while dropping wineglasses on the floor, one by one. A middle-aged woman next to him cheerses herself with a bottle of whiskey and a bottle of gin before pouring them both into her mouth at the same time. And a girl who looks far too young to be in a pub is kissing a fellow in a business suit, who probably has gambling debt older than she is.

"Oh my God!" Lou calls out once she and Courtney make it to the other side of the counter. "Dee! Dee, what happened?"

I make it round in time to see Lou's friend Dee lying on the floor in a bed of broken glass. She reaches up and touches her head, and even in the dark, I can tell that her fingertips come away shiny and red.

Extending one shaking, bloody digit in the direction of the Employees Only door, Dee sits up and croaks, "White bitch."

I grab a dishcloth off the counter and wet it in the sink, careful to avoid a falling beer stein from Danny Boy up there, and crouch back down behind the bar.

"It's true!" Courtney says, finally regaining her wits enough to speak. "After the power went out, some crazy woman burst in here and attacked me."

Courtney pauses to dry-heave as I press the towel against the side of Dee's forehead. She takes it from me with a glare and holds it in place herself.

"She choked me and threw me to the ground, Lou. Why would she do that?" Courtney's voice climbs an octave as she reaches up and touches the back of her head. "The fall musta knocked me out ..."

"Did you see who it was?" Lou asks.

Courtney shakes her head. "No, but..."—she presses a fist to her mouth, and her cheeks puff out as she dry-heaves again— "I think she's lookin' for *you*."

"Me? Why?" Lou asks.

"Are you okay?" I ask Courtney.

She shakes her head again. "I think I might have a concussion. Or what if I'm overdosin' on sodium? I read once that—"

Without warning, Courtney turns and pukes on Dee's arm.

"What the fuck?" Dee cries, shoving Courtney.

She uses the cloth from her head to wipe off her arm, but Courtney tries to take it from her.

"I'm so sorry, hon. Let me do it."

A scream so loud that it rises above the chaos of the pub rings out from the back. A male scream.

Lou locks eyes with me. "That was a—"

"Bad scream," we say in unison.

The two of us leave Courtney and Dee squabbling behind the bar and creep over to the Employees Only door a few feet away. The closer we get, the louder the shouts and crashes inside become. I wrap a firm hand around Lou's forearm and feel the same surge of electricity I felt when I touched her for the first time, only amplified. I feel the same primal need I felt when I saw her draped in my shirt, smelled my cologne on her skin, only stronger. I feel a sense of purpose I've never known. It's as if the reason why I came here is finally clear.

I have to protect this woman.

Lou's lips part, and her eyes lift to mine.

"I'll go in first," I say, pressing my forehead to hers, "but stay close. I don't want you out of my sight."

Lou nods and presses a soft kiss to my determined lips.

Tucking her behind my back, I take a breath and push the door open, just a crack. What I see has me pulling it shut again.

"What?" Lou whisper-shouts over the noise in the pub. "What's happening?"

I turn to face her. "The inmates have taken over the asylum."

Lou reaches around me and pushes the door open to see for herself. Her eyes go wide as she takes in the shirtless, four-way MMA fight happening on the yoga mats in the center of the storage room, and they practically pop out of her head when she sees Mark strung up on a forklift by the back of his sleeveless sweatshirt in the corner of the room.

Lou and I push through the door, dodging swinging fists and flying feet as we make our way over to Mark. His cheek has three bloody scratches on it. Two have a gap in between them, as if whatever animal did this to him was missing a claw.

Mark tugs at the neck of his sweatshirt with both hands to keep from choking. "I told 'em no fightin', Lou! I did what you said! But then the fuckin' Drama Llama burst in here, screamin' about not being invited, and clawed me up!"

"Kimberly?!" Lou asks, searching his dangling body for other injuries. "Is she the one who put you up here?"

"No," Mark chokes out. Even in the dim glow of the Emergency Exit sign, his face is noticeably red. "These heathens saw the blood and lost their gotdamn minds. It was like Shark Week up in here!"

Lou ducks, and Mark gets hit in the face with a pickle.

"Did you see where she went?" I ask, but my question is immediately answered by screams coming from the kitchen.

Lou turns toward the sounds. "Shit!" She swivels back to Mark, looking helpless. "How do I get you down?"

While Lou messes with the forklift controls, to no avail, I crouch down and put Mark's dangling legs over my shoulders.

"Hold on," I say, taking a few labored steps forward until his sweatshirt slides off of the raised forklift platform.

Mark sits up straight and spreads his arms wide. I have to wrap my hands around his furry shins to keep from dropping him as he shouts, "I'm flying, Jack! I'm flying!"

Just then, Coach Beth runs in from a back hallway that I assume leads to the kitchen. "Lou," she pants, "come quick!"

Lou takes off running behind Beth, leaving me holding her traumatized roommate. I try to shrug him off, but Mark resists, clinging to my head like a spider monkey as he shouts, "No! Don't put me down! They're savages!"

I begin to panic. I have to get to Lou. That woman could be in the kitchen, the one who's looking for her, and—

I grab Mark's hands, prying them off my head as I bend at the waist, trying to throw him off.

But Mark tightens his knees around my ribs, holding fast. With a primal growl, I reach behind me and grab his upper arms, yanking harder, but Mark won't budge.

The Anger Management group circles around us, chanting, "Fight! Fight! Fight! Fight!" as I grunt and struggle and Mark slaps my hands away.

"Oh, for God's sake!" I shout, shoving a hand in the direction of the door. "The bar is unattended!"

All four shirtless barbarians stop and share a glance before thrusting their fists in the air with a new battle cry on their bleeding lips. "Shots! Shots! Shots! Shots!"

They file out the door and into the dark chaos of the pub.

With Mark distracted, I successfully manage to yank him off on my next attempt. He rolls over the top of my head and lands on his back in the middle of the yoga mats.

I take off running down the corridor as he calls out after me, "I won't let you go, Jack! I'll never let go!"

There's only one door at the end of the short hall. I burst through it without stopping to consider whom or what I might find on the other side. Not that it matters. Nothing I could have imagined would have prepared me for the sight of Lou's rigid, petrified body pressed against the length of a tall blonde woman with a kitchen knife being held to her throat.

Lou's eyes dart to mine, but the rest of her remains paralyzed by fear.

Beth stands on the other side of the kitchen, blocking her huddled, trembling life-coaching clients with her body.

"Good job, piggy," the blonde holding Lou at knife-point says to Beth. "You and your little friends are free to go."

Her clients turn and sprint out the door leading into the main bar area without a second glance.

Beth grimaces as she walks backward behind them. "Sorry, bro. It was four for the price of one. But hey"—she gives Lou two thumbs-up—"you got this!"

"Call the police!" I yell after her just before she disappears through the door.

The woman I assume is Kimberly abruptly turns to face me. "With what?" the blonde coos, tilting her head toward a familiar-looking basket on the counter. "One of these?"

"The bar has a phone," Lou says, a twinge of hope in her trembling voice.

"I cut the phone lines when I cut the power, duh." Kimberly rolls her eyes. "I thought psychologists were supposed to be smart."

I recognize her now. I've seen her on billboards around town.

"Hey, aren't you …"

"If you say the Drama Llama, I swear to God, I will end this bitch faster than they canceled *Boss Wives*, season two!"

I hold my hands up defensively. "What do you want?"

"I want to make Dr. Sterling pay for not inviting me to her little fight club."

"Kimberly," Lou pleads, "I swear this is not a fight club. Why does everybody keep calling it—"

"Shut up!" Kimberly screams, pressing the knife against Lou's throat until she whimpers and squeezes her eyes shut.

Fuck!

"It's true!" I say, taking a step forward. "It's a therapy group. For the deeply disturbed. Dr. Sterling told me she only invited her most deranged clients. That's probably why you weren't—"

"Liar!" Kimberly digs the blade in deeper, and Lou winces. Blood appears along the edge of the knife. Just a smear, but it's enough to make me see red. "She didn't invite me because she doesn't like me! Nobody likes meeee!"

Don't react. Don't react. Fuck. Just ... stay calm.

"Hey! Kimberly, right?" I smile, the same one I use for talk shows and interviews and women that I wouldn't mind getting into bed, as I take another step forward. "Why don't you and I make our own club? Just the two of us."

I hold out my hand, but Kimberly looks at it with a disgusted sneer.

"Have you ever ridden in a Maserati before?" I ask, lowering my outstretched hand to the counter beside me. My fingers graze the handle of a metal serving spoon and curl around it on instinct.

"Oh, please." She rolls her eyes. "I got three in my divorce."

"Right. Well, have you ever—*expelliarmus!*"

Time slows to a crawl as I throw the utensil, and for a brief, suspended moment, I am seventeen-year-old Harry Potter, pointing a wand at She Who Shall Not Be Named before I release it and watch it soar.

The metal spoon hits Kimberly's thumbnail with a sickening crunch. She drops the knife with a shriek and jams the injured digit into her mouth, mumbling something that sounds a lot like, "You broke my fucking nail, asshole!"

With Kimberly temporarily disarmed and distracted, I lurch forward and grab Lou by the wrist. We take off running through the kitchen as Kimberly screams like a banshee behind us. Pots and pans sail past our heads as she gives chase, but we burst through the door before she can catch us.

The main bar area is in full-on *Gremlins* mode. People are fighting, kissing, singing, crying, dancing on the tables, and several shirtless Anger Management blokes are pounding shots with their arms linked around each other's necks over at the counter.

I shove my way through them all, dragging Lou behind me, as the howls of a woman possessed emerge from the kitchen behind us. I make it to the door, bracing myself for the cold, wet air of freedom when Lou suddenly screams and stops running.

I turn and am confronted with my worst nightmare come to life. I've written gruesome, horrible things. Things that give my readers night sweats. Images that will haunt them for the rest of their lives. Perhaps this is my penance. Perhaps I'm being punished for all the psychological damage I've inflicted because there is no other logical explanation for why Lou—my Lou—is staring at me with wide, stunned eyes as she clutches her side through the blood-soaked fabric of her T-shirt.

With a jerk, Lou's mouth falls open as Kimberly grins behind her, retracting a red-streaked knife for me to see.

Lou's knees buckle, and I catch her. The moment I pull her against my chest, Beth swings in on a light fixture fashioned from an old nautical rope and kicks the knife out of Kimberly's hand. She lands on her shoulders, crotch to face, and both women fall to the floor.

Beth pins Kimberly in a half nelson and pulls her arm back until she screams.

"I got her!" Beth shouts. "Run!"

Cradling Lou's unconscious body to my chest, I push through the front door and stumble out into the rain.

"Help!" I shout, scanning the car park and street beyond for any signs of life. "Please! Someone help us!" My voice cracks as I glance down at Lou's side. The dark spot seeping through her shirt is enormous.

"Fuck. Stay with me." I clutch her tighter as we approach the street, rain blurring my vision.

"Help!" I shout again as two cars approach, but with my hands full, I can't wave them down.

I manage to get a hand around Lou's arm though, so I wave that in the air as a few more cars pass. A wall of rainwater sprays us from their tires, but no one stops.

"Help us! Please!"

Just then, an ambulance passes us on the other side of the street and immediately turns on its lights.

"Oh, thank God." I sink to my knees in relief, cradling Lou's lifeless body to my chest.

I try to estimate the number of minutes it's been since she was stabbed. Two? Maybe three? In my research for *The House Guest*, my third book, I learned that it takes about five minutes for … for something like this to …

"Stay with me, Lou." I clutch her tighter, giving her a gentle shake. "Please. Help is coming. Please stay with me." I rock her back and forth as the ambulance turns round in the middle of the road and heads back toward us. "What can I do? Tell me what to do."

Lou whispers something inaudible and coughs.

"What?" I sit up straighter. Smoothing the wet hair from her face, I lift her head closer to my ear. "What was that?"

The ambulance pulls up to the curb, splashing us from the waist down with rain as it does.

The moment that freezing cold water hits Lou, her entire body shudders, and her eyes flutter open, landing on me. She tries to smile, but it quickly turns into a wince of pain.

"What did you say?" I ask again, my voice growing frantic as a paramedic comes around and yanks open the back doors of the ambulance.

Lou's lips graze the edge of my ear, and I can hear her teeth chattering beneath them.

"Write," she whispers, her breath barely warm. "Write me a scary story, Thomas."

I turn and press my lips against hers, hard enough to stop them from trembling. Her body is so cold. Her shivering so violent. I hear the clanking and rattling of a stretcher being pulled over to us, but I don't let her go until she is physically removed from my arms.

"She's bleeding out!" the paramedic shouts. "We've got to get her stabilized—now!"

"Her name is Dr. Luna Sterling," I say to the nameless, faceless man taking her away from me. "She goes by Lou."

"We'll take it from here!"

And with the slamming of two doors, she's gone.

Thomas

I RISE TO MY feet and watch as the ambulance pulls away from the curb, realizing a moment too late that I didn't ask where they were taking her. Even if I call every hospital in the Atlanta area tonight, they probably won't disclose who their patients are to non-family members, and I can't call her directly because her mobile is still in the fucking pub.

A split-second decision sends my feet scrambling toward my car. I stood by and watched her disappear from my life once this weekend. I can't do it again. I won't.

The key fob in my pocket unlocks the door just before I dive into the driver's seat and throw it into reverse. I peel out of the car park and catch up to the ambulance just before it turns right a few blocks down.

My body is mechanically steering and shifting, but my mind is back at the pub, reliving every moment in high-definition, trying to work out what I could have done differently, what I should have done but didn't.

Lou's words from two days ago echo in my mind.

"I failed you. And now, you're gonna lose a million-dollar book deal because of it."

Tonight, I failed her. Spectacularly. And the price ... the price could be much steeper.

My mind presses pause on an image of Lou, lying in my arms, blood soaking through her shirt, rain washing away her makeup, and all I want to do is get her back. I want to feel the weight of her in my arms again, tonight and every night, from now until the last. And even after that. For what is death but an eternal night?

Death.

The ambulance slows to a full stop before turning right at the next intersection, and I realize that its lights are no longer flashing. Its siren isn't on. In fact, it doesn't seem to be in a hurry to get anywhere at all.

And that's when it hits me.

I'm not following an ambulance anymore.

I'm following a hearse.

"No," I say out loud, declaring it. Demanding it. "No!"

But there, directly in front of me, is my proof, driving the exact speed limit and obeying all traffic laws.

It's been over five minutes, a voice inside of me announces.

"Fuck!" I slam my palm into the steering wheel. Then again, and again, and again. "Fuck, fuck, fuuuuck!"

My heart is racing, my throat feels like it's closing completely, and my body must have switched over to autopilot because when the ambulance turns again, I realize that I've been driving on the left side of the road.

But still, I follow because I can't do anything else. Because my heart has flatlined inside that car. Because I can't even remember which side of the road they drive on here anymore. All I can do is stare out the rain-streaked windscreen and count the ways that I pissed on Lou's career, love, and now, life in the short amount of time since I met her. If I hadn't asked her out, she never would have created that fucking group. If I had taken Courtney more seriously when she said her attacker was looking for Lou, I would have gotten her the hell out of there instead of following her into danger like a bloody git. If I had been braver, I would have subdued Kimberly the second I saw that fucking knife instead of diddling around like a goddamn twat.

But it doesn't matter now. What matters is that the vehicle in front of me is driving twenty-five miles per hour down a residential street without a single sign of urgency.

Because there is no more emergency.

The ambulance turns right again. And pulls me right along with it.

This is what happens when you fall in love, I think, a self-protective numbness falling over me like a shroud. *It destroys everything.*

The road goes blurry, and I don't know if it's from the rain on the windscreen or the tears in my eyes, but I don't care. It doesn't matter. If Lou is gone, nothing matters anymore.

The ambulance pulls into a car park, and despite their grip on the steering wheel, my hands begin to shake. I'm not ready. I just found her. I just got her back. I'm not ready to say good-bye.

But my arms and legs cooperate, steering and braking and depositing me right next to the vessel that contains my deepest, darkest fear. I'm not afraid of love—I'm afraid of *after* love. What becomes of you once it is gone. The husk of a human you wither into, the endless years of joyless existence that stretch on further than the eye can see. I thought I could avoid it.

But I failed at that too.

Get out. Get out of the car, dickhead. Face what you did.

As I open the door, cold air whips around me, as if coaxing me out into the night. Pulling me toward the inevitable.

Left foot, right foot. Stand up, close the door.

My chest is so tight I feel like I can't breathe, and for a moment, I wish that were the case. I wish my breaths would cease right along with Lou's so that we could go ahead and spend the rest of eternity picking up where we left off.

But I'm not that lucky.

I force myself to take a few more steps toward the ambulance, but when I finally look up and observe my surroundings, I discover that we're not at a hospital. We're right back where we started—The Yacht Club car park.

Which only makes my heart sink further.

They probably came back to wait for the coroner.

And the police.

Because this is now a murder scene.

And it's all my fucking fault.

The sound of a dozen laughing arseholes pulls me out of the coal-black cesspool that is my head, if only temporarily. Harnessing what's left of my lucidity, I look toward the entrance of the pub and watch as the remaining group therapy members file out of the main entrance with their faces tipped back in drunken delight and their arms linked round one another's necks.

The woman who was brushing salt off of the Anxiety table turns and calls over her shoulder, "Kimberly, you were amazing!"

The woman next to her, who I'm pretty sure is the one who jumped on Lou's back, adds, "Oh my God, girl. I had no idea you were such a good actress!"

My hands form involuntary fists as the psycho who stabbed Lou comes strutting out behind them, wearing a smirk.

"Me?" Kimberly laughs. "Did y'all see Dr. Baker? Homegirl can puke on cue."

Puke on cue?

Courtney walks out next to Beth, sporting a bashful smile. "It's no big deal." She shrugs. "I just have a really sensitive gag reflex."

"Lucky Brian." Beth chuckles sarcastically, shoulder-checking Courtney. "Yo, Kim. Sorry about the whole *Tarzan/crotch in your face* thing. I kinda got caught up in the moment."

Caught up in the moment? Lou was fucking stabbed!

Kimberly rolls her eyes as one of the women from Anger Management bounces over to her, still shirtless. "Can we get a selfie before you go?"

Mark holds the door open as Dee and the last few stragglers walk through.

"It's cool, guys," he calls out to no one in particular. "I'll just clean up the entire bar *by myself*."

A woman from Dee's group gives him a second glance on her way out. "Wow, did Lou paint those scratches on your face? The head wound she gave Dr. Dawson looks so real."

"Hell no," Mark huffs. "I had to look pretty to greet everybody. Bill did it with some ketchup."

Courtney turns to face the other group leaders. "So ... do y'all think it worked?"

Mark's eyes drift across the parking lot, landing on me, and his face goes pale. "Uh, gotta go!" He pulls the door shut as another door opens—the one on the back of the ambulance.

My mind is reeling as a person I never thought I'd see again without quarters on her eyes and a name tag on her toe hops out—very much alive, very much unharmed, and very much surprised to see me.

"Thomas?" she exclaims, looking around as if the parked cars nearby might hold some kind of clue as to how much I've figured out. "I ... uh ..."

"This was all ... an act?" My blood feels like molten-hot battery acid pumping through my fragile brain, burning away everything I thought I knew. Everything I thought I felt. Experienced.

I can't stop shaking my head.

"Shit." Lou rubs her bare arms with both hands. "Can you just ... pretend like you didn't see this part?"

"What?"

Without taking her eyes off me, she slaps the back of the ambulance twice. "Thanks, Paul!"

The emergency vehicle honks cheerfully and drives away, leaving me with a ghost.

"I thought you were dead," I hear myself say. I sound so calm. I want to fall at her feet and fucking weep. I want to scream at her. I want to grab her by the shoulders and shake her and kiss her and shake her again, but here I stand, a captive in my own prison of self-composure.

"Hey …" she says, taking a tentative step forward as her eyes dart back and forth between mine. She sees something there, something I thought I was hiding, and it makes her look as gutted as I feel.

Lou reaches for my face, and I turn away, but she caresses my cheek anyway, wiping away an errant drop of rain.

It's definitely not a tear.

And I definitely don't close my eyes and lean into her touch either.

I feel so many things at once that I'm paralyzed by them all. I'm humiliated and enraged that she would fake her own attack, dumbfounded as to why, a little impressed that she pulled it off, if I'm being honest, but mostly, I'm overwhelmed with relief. It hits me like a tidal wave. My knees threaten to buckle under the enormity of my joy.

I cherish every hot exhalation that pours from her lips; I admire the way they swirl between us in the crisp night air because they're visible proof that she's still here. She's still breathing. Just like me.

I can't resist the pull anymore. With her hand on my jaw and her shivering body mere inches from mine, not holding her is excruciating.

"Thomas, I'm so—"

I silence her apology with a kiss. Right now, I need her in my arms more than I need an explanation. I need proof that she's alive and going to stay that way. I need to feel the goose bumps on her flesh and the weight of her rain-drenched hair in my fist. I need to feel the heat of her mouth and the rise and fall of her chest against mine. If the last two days spent without her were a revelation, thinking I lost her forever was a revolution.

"S-s-s-sorry," she finishes, whispering the word against my lips as her teeth begin to chatter again. "You weren't s-s-supposed to ... I didn't think you ..." Lou's soaking wet body shivers in my arms. "Can we talk about this ins-s-side?"

"I am *not* going back in there." I smirk, tilting my head toward the pub. It's a terrible lie. I would go with her anywhere. I just want to see her smile.

But Lou takes me seriously. Remorse flashes across her face, and she nods in understanding. "I have another place we can go."

Lou takes my hand, and feeling her tiny, freezing digits mold to the shape of my palm thaws what little ice was remaining around my heart. Then, she takes off in a sprint, dragging me behind her past the few remaining luxury cars and through a half-dozen surprisingly deep puddles as she heads directly toward a giant recreational vehicle painted to look like the official death of my sanity.

My eyebrows shoot up when Lou pulls a set of keys out of her pocket and unlocks the door. I add, *Why are you in possession of a psychedelic motor home?* to the growing list of questions I never thought I'd have to ask another human being and climb aboard.

Lou flips a few switches and curses under her breath as a disco ball suspended from the ceiling begins to spin and a projector shines swirling pot leaves, peace signs, and smiley faces all over the interior of the vehicle. Lou manages to find the correct switch, and the party atmosphere is swiftly replaced by a soft, warm glow that feels like a torch pointed at the ceiling of a blanket fort.

Next, Lou darts across the sitting area and turns on a space heater in the corner of the room. Her entire body shudders as the warmth hits her legs. She drops into a squat in front of the glowing orange contraption and immediately winces in pain. Lifting her soiled T-shirt, she pulls a squirt bottle of sriracha out from the waistband of her jeans and sets it on the counter above her. Then, after looking down at the mess she's wearing, Lou pulls her soiled, sopping wet T-shirt off over her head, uses it to wipe her stomach clean, and tosses it up on the counter as well.

Bloody. Fucking. Sriracha.

I want to be livid. I want to be insanely, table-flippingly mad at her, but right now, all I can do is stare at her beautiful, breathing, wound-free body and try not to weep.

Lou extends a hand toward me with a worried V between her eyebrows. "Come here. *Please?*"

There's that word again. The one that turns me into her puppet. My legs move without a second thought, and in a handful of strides, I'm crouched next to her in front of the space heater, staring into those whiskey-colored eyes and thanking every deity in existence for letting me see them again.

"You're drenched."

She reaches for the top button on my shirt, and I let her unbutton it, unable to tear my eyes away from her lips as she works.

"You're so quiet," she adds, lifting her gaze to mine for a split second. "I know you probably hate me right now, but just ... hear me out. Please?"

Hate. She has no idea how wrong she is.

Lou's trembling hands move down to the next button—the one right beside my heart. "A lot has happened in the last two days."

Tell me about it.

"I lost my job."

"What?" I exclaim.

"I lost my house." She makes a circle in the air with her free hand, gesturing to our surroundings. "And I lost you."

"You didn't lose me."

Hot air from the space heater caresses my damp, exposed chest as Lou's fingers slide their way down to the next button.

"I lost everything," Lou says, refusing to look me in the eye. "But I couldn't stand by and let you lose everything too. You're my favorite, Thomas. My favorite writer, my favorite person, my favorite thing to touch." She traces a single featherlight line down my sternum, making me shiver. "You're not empty. You just needed—"

"A story."

Lou looks up at me, watching with silent affirmation as everything clicks into place.

"A story," I say again, nodding slowly as my mind begins to whir with possibilities. Settings. Characters. Arcs. Plot twists. My eyes look through her now, unseeing, as I try to wrap my hands around one train of thought long enough to follow it to the end. "An author with writer's block falls in love with his therapist," I say, chasing the idea out loud. "But they can't be together, so he goes to her weekly therapy group as an excuse to spend more time with her. Only his presence at the group proves to be too much of a distraction, and the therapist loses control of her clients. They become increasingly jealous and violent until one member—a psychopathic former reality star—convinces the group to mutiny and kill the therapist. In the end, the author has to make a choice—confront his deepest fears and rescue the woman he loves or leave it to the authorities and retreat back into the safety of isolation."

When Lou's face comes back into focus, her lips are parted, and her eyes are glistening. "Something like that." She smiles, unbuttoning my last button.

I tear my damp shirt off the instant it falls open and pull Lou into my lap. She lands astride me with a yelp, followed by a moan as I claim her mouth, pouring every overwhelming ounce of emotion she's made me feel tonight right back into her. I want to kiss her everywhere, to anoint every inch of her living, breathing body with my gratitude. My adoration. My endless, hopeless devotion.

Sucking a trail of wet kisses down the side of her neck, I pause and ask, "How many books has Stephen King published since he got married?"

"Almost a hundred," she rasps, rolling her hips as I sweep my tongue along her delicate collarbone.

"Think we can beat it?"

Her body stills, and her breathing ceases as she takes in my words.

I sit up and cup her jaw in my hand, forcing her to accept my sincerest gaze. "You're my Tabitha, Lou. I can't do this without you. Not anymore."

Her throat pulses against my palm as she swallows, sending another surge of blood to my already-engorged manhood.

"But next time you have a story idea, maybe just tell me."

Her worried lips widen, and a soft laugh escapes from somewhere deep and hopeful and true. I capture it with my mouth, loving the way her body melts into mine the moment our lips meet. But I also love the way she shrieks when I turn and toss her onto the couch next to us.

As I peel the rest of her wet clothes off, revealing perfect, supple curves wrapped in smooth, unharmed skin, I feel my chest tighten with another surge of emotion. The night I spent exploring this body—tasting it, filling it, memorizing every arch and freckle and sound it makes—was the night I realized I never wanted another. Sex has never made me *feel* before, not like that, and staring down at Lou, knowing I might get to experience that feeling for the rest of my life, sets my soul on fire.

The rest of my clothes quickly join hers on the floor, and I crawl into the space between her and the back of the couch. Lou turns toward me, using my bicep as a pillow, and gazes into my eyes as she wraps a thankfully warm hand around my shaft.

"I missed you," she says, working me with slow, swirling, mind-numbing movements.

"I've been missing you my entire life," I admit, slipping a hand between her smooth thighs, which part to welcome me in.

I explore her silky flesh with two fingers, sliding them in, up, and around at a languid pace that has her writhing against my palm and panting against my lips within seconds.

"You like that." I smile, watching her skin flush and nipples peak with pleasure.

Lou bites her lip and nods in response.

"Roll over then."

Without hesitation, Lou releases me and turns so that her back is pressed against my chest, her head is once again propped up on my arm, and her ample arse is nestled against my rigid cock. I palm and knead her generous backside before sliding that hand down between her thighs again. She spreads them for me once more, and the sight makes my mouth water.

I kiss her shoulder as I position my crown against her slick center. A shudder ripples down her spine as she reaches between us to touch me. Only she doesn't guide me in. She tilts her hips so that I'm cradled against her throbbing flesh and begins to stroke me again, this time with her body. The sensation is blissful torture, which is exactly what I intended on inflicting upon Lou.

Pulling away momentarily, I catch my breath, grab her hip, and fill her until I find the absolute depth of my newfound obsession. All sensations fade away, except for the ones involving Lou. The way she feels, inside and out. The way her back arches and breasts bounce with every exquisite push and pull. The way her woodsy scent is now mixed with rain. The way her lips taste when she turns her head sideways to kiss me. And the way her soft moans turn to desperate gasps when my fingers resume their fluid rhythm.

Up and around, just the way she likes it.

Lou becomes a tense, panting, kinetic thing as I push her higher. "Thomas," she whispers, wrapping a hand around the back of my head.

Her eyes open, and the moment they connect with mine, I'm lost. Sparks shoot through my blood as I swell inside of her, gritting my teeth until I feel her body contract and tighten around me.

Her cries of pleasure are my undoing. Sinking my teeth into her shoulder and wrapping my arm around her waist, I thrust harder, hold her tighter, until her ecstasy becomes my own. Our bodies pulse in unison as we cling to one another, not in fear, but in awe. It is a bliss I wish I could float in forever.

But I can't.

I have a book to write.

Lou

I HAVEN'T LEFT THOMAS'S apartment in ten days.

Thomas hasn't left Thomas's apartment in ten days.

He didn't even let me return the RV to the commune. After the night that had almost killed us both—me from hypothermia, him from driving on the wrong side of the road while traumatized—we'd brought the psychedelic motor home back to his apartment building, where, at one thirty in the morning, Thomas helped me unload all of my stuff under the covered portico out front and paid an exorbitant amount of money to a valet driver to take it back to Indigo Hills for me. The next day, he paid a different one to go get his Maserati from The Yacht Club.

It's been sitting in the parking garage below the building ever since.

And Thomas has been parked in front of his computer just as long. He is a man possessed. Making sure he doesn't die of starvation, dehydration, or sleep deprivation has become my new full-time job.

The treadmill—that he really did order, evidently—arrived last week, so every few hours, I've been dragging him out of his high-tech computer chair and forcing him to get on it. I found a really cool dictation program that allows him to keep working while he's jogging, but the typos are atrocious, so just as fast as Thomas has been writing, I've been editing.

And I can honestly say, it's the best book I've ever read. Not just because of the brilliant way he weaves the lives of each character and client in and out of the story, or the way he places every breadcrumb and red herring so that they're perfectly hidden in plain sight, or the way he can build the suspense or sexual tension to a fever pitch with just a few stolen glances and a handful of short, staccato sentences, but also because it's the story of us.

Getting to see myself through Thomas's eyes has been … life-changing. It's the only thing that has quieted the voice in the back of my mind. The one that tells me to run, that whispers I'm not good enough for him, that insists he's going to leave me. Every night, when he hands me a new stack of chapters, exhausted and delirious, he's really handing me his fleshy, beating heart. And what I find inside is so beautiful that it makes me cry.

Despite all the typos.

Or maybe because of them.

I tiptoe into his office with a new mug of tea, careful not to step on the piles of chapters he's printed and laid out all over the floor. It's hard to believe that this room ever looked unused. The desk is littered with food wrappers, half-empty teacups, a small white board with plot points charted like a timeline, a notebook filled with manic scribbles, and markers and pens and pencils everywhere you look. No matter how many times I come in here and straighten up, it looks like this again within hours.

One thing does look different though. Instead of being hunched over his laptop, chewing on his lip or squinting into the distance, Thomas is flopped back in his chair with his arms dangling lifelessly over the sides.

His bloodshot blue eyes travel slowly from his computer screen up to mine. I've been making him shower semi-regularly, usually while holding his phone just outside the cracked door so that he can dictate while he's in there, but he hasn't shaved in a week and a half. I kind of love it. His beard is short and reddish, an outward extension of his inner madness.

As soon as his gaze locks on to mine, my breath catches and my heart skips a beat. I thought Thomas was intense before, but that was nothing. That was Vacation Thomas. This is Inspired Thomas. Inspired Thomas is an entirely different beast. I was right when I compared him to an Olympic athlete during our first session. The extreme, unwavering level of concentration and mental stamina he's managed to maintain for the past ten days is almost superhuman.

But when the hard line of his mouth curves up on one side and his laser-focused eyes soften around the edges, I know that Vacation Thomas is coming back to me.

Suddenly, Thomas reaches out and pulls me into his lap. I squeal as he spins us around one, two ... twenty times in his chair, nuzzling my hair and kissing the side of my neck. His hand slides up under the bottom of my tank top, and I swat it away.

"Not until you type *The End*, mister."

"I just did."

"What?" I sit up so that I can look him in the eye. "Thomas ... oh my God!"

He beams.

"I can't wait to read it! Oh my God, oh my God, oh my God! Tell me the last line! Just tell me the very last line."

"It's"—Thomas glances over my shoulder at his laptop screen—"*Patrick, nooooo!*" He reads the line in his best American female accent, impersonating me.

I throw my head back and laugh. "*That's* how you ended it? You're such a tease!"

"You're the one withholding sex."

"And look, you wrote an entire book in ten days. I told you it works," I gloat.

If you don't count that one time in the shower. And that other time in the kitchen. And yesterday morning while we watched the sun rise in bed, but I blame God for that one. That sunrise was unfairly romantic.

Thomas shakes his head in disbelief. "We'll get these final chapters polished up, send the whole thing to my editor, and you'll be back at work by Monday."

"You did it, baby." I cup his scruffy cheek with my hand, watching the light return to his eyes with every passing second. "You fucking did it."

"We did it," he says, tucking a lock of hair behind my ear.

"Well, *we* need to go celebrate." I go to stand up, but Thomas holds me tighter.

"I believe you owe me a reward first."

I smile and kiss him with every ounce of love and admiration my limited human body can muster, and this time, when Thomas's hands slide under my tank top, I let them.

"You were approved for that tourist visa," I say, lifting my arms so that he can pull the thin camisole off over my head. I knew he was close to finishing his book, so I didn't wear a bra today, hoping the sight of my hard nipples bouncing in and out of his office would light a fire under him.

Guess I'm not such a bad psychologist after all.

"Really?" Thomas murmurs, his hands cupping and caressing my breasts while his teeth and lips graze my jaw.

"Mmhmm ..." I moan. "It's valid for six months, longer if they grant you an extension." I tilt my head back and thrust my hands into his hair as his tongue dances along my collarbone and burns a trail of hot kisses down the center of my chest. "But I don't know what we'll do after that."

"I do," Thomas says.

The certainty in his voice penetrates through my breastbone and echoes in every chamber of my heart.

I do. I do. I do. I do.

My lips part, and my head tilts down to find a pair of guarded, steely eyes staring up at me. Thomas responds to my gasp with that half-smile I love so much, made infinitely sexier by the addition of facial hair and the promise of forever dancing on those wicked lips.

So, I seal them with a promise of my own.

And relish the way they split into a grin when I reach out and knock over a decorative bowl of fruit on the bookshelf beside us.

Epilogue

Ten Months Later

WITH HER HAIR DONE, shoulders back, heels high, and dress practically painted on, Kimberly Kline moves through the smoky Atlanta nightclub with a purpose. Two security guards size her up outside of a VIP room, but Kimberly knows the password. It's spilling out of the top of her low-cut dress.

The room is filled with men in suits, handling stacks of either cash or coke; cocktail waitresses who serve them drinks and swat their roaming hands away; and one man who stands out from the crowd by not standing at all—the kingpin. He's seated at the head of the farthest table in the back, holding court.

His beady eyes land on Kimberly as she struts through the room, headed straight toward him.

"Hey …" He shoves one of his goons and gestures toward their newest visitor. "Who let the blonde in?"

Kimberly tosses her hair over one shoulder as she stops directly across from him. "I'm not just any blonde...," she says, reaching into her cleavage and pulling out a shiny golden shield. "I'm a blonde with a badge. You're under arrest!"

NARRATOR: In the war against crime, the APD has a new secret weapon ...

Kimberly walks down an Atlanta sidewalk, wearing a skintight police uniform and aviators. Next, she's karate-fighting a burglar in broad daylight, sprinting after a group of criminals while wearing high heels and pointing a gun, and finally, she's knocking a man out cold with a single head-butt before calmly reapplying her lipstick in a shop window.

Now, Kimberly sits in an interrogation room. Across the table, glaring at her, is the kingpin she helped to bring down.

"So, what are you," he asks with a thick Russian accent, "the good cop or the bad cop?"

"I'm not a good cop or a bad cop," Kimberly says, flipping her hair as she turns to pout for the camera. "I'm a—"

NARRATOR: Hot cop.

The title of the show, *Hot Cop*, appears below Kimberly's face, followed by the words, *Starring Kimberly "The Drama Llama" Kline.*

NARRATOR: Watch the season premiere tonight, only on NBC.

The NBC logo fills the screen and then flies off, transitioning back from the commercial break to the show I've been counting down the minutes to see for over a month now.

Kelly Clarkson sits onstage in front of a studio audience. The word *Prerecorded* flashes in the lower-left corner of the screen and disappears, but I already knew it was prerecorded. I was there.

"Our first guest today is a *New York Times* best-selling author whose latest book, *Murder Therapy*, is one of the most talked about this year, especially if you've been within the vicinity of me." Kelly holds up a copy, and I have to bite my lip to keep from squealing.

"Please welcome ... Thomas O'Reardon!"

The camera pans to the side of the stage, where my tall, brilliant, beautiful boyfriend walks out, looking like a goddamn movie star. The crowd cheers, maybe even louder than usual, as Thomas crosses the stage with his signature calm, self-composed confidence and hugs Kelly, who is waiting for him with open arms. They have a seat.

"It's so nice to finally meet you." Thomas gives Kelly that subtle half-smile, and even though I've been living with the guy for almost a year now, that look still makes me swoon.

"It's so nice to meet *you*. As you know, I read an early copy of the book and have not been able to stop talking about it since." She turns to the audience. "Right, y'all?"

They cut to a shot of the audience, laughing and nodding.

"So, for the five people left in America who haven't read it, why don't you tell us a little bit about the book?"

Thomas smiles, genuinely touched. "Well, thank you. That's very kind. As you know, I can't say much about the plot without spoiling something, but I can tell you that it's based on an actual therapy group I attended last year, which devolved into something resembling the Seventh Circle of Hell. I'm lucky I lived to tell the tale." He flashes her a wicked grin, and my heart stops.

"We're all lucky," Kelly says, gesturing to the audience.

"It was touch and go there for a minute," Thomas jokes.

"So, you dedicated this book to somebody named Dr. Sterling, which makes me think that she must be the real-life inspiration for Dr. Golding. Is that right? Please tell me this person is not still out there, practicing psychology, after this."

Thomas laughs silently, and I feel like I might sprain my face from smiling so hard.

"Actually," he says, looking into the camera.

"Dr. Sterling?"

"Hmm?" I look up and find Michaela, my four o'clock client, standing at my desk, staring at me expectantly.

I click the pause button on my laptop and yank the earbuds out of my ears. "You all done, sweetie?"

She nods.

My new office isn't as fancy as my old one. The textbooks on the shelves are actually current; the walls are covered in cheerful, abstract art prints instead of expensive textured wallpaper; and the furniture is low to the ground and easy to clean, which is super important around here.

I sit next to Michaela in a chair made for someone two feet shorter than me and take a look at her finished work. "I love it," I say. "Tell me everything."

The seven-year-old nods. "Well, this is me and Mommy and Baxter"—she points to two people and a cat standing in the grass at the bottom of the page—"and up here is where Daddy and my goldfish, Harry, live now. It's called heaven." She points to a man standing on a cloud next to an orange fish.

"He's got some ice cream, huh?" I point to a cone-shaped thing in his hand.

"Yeah. Mommy said you can eat ice cream whenever you want in heaven."

"He looks happy," I say. "And what about you? How do you feel in this picture?"

Michaela drops her eyes and plays with the eraser on her pencil. "Sad."

"I can tell. You have your own little rain cloud up here, huh?" I gesture to a gray cloud hovering lower than the others.

She nods.

"Hey, you know why I always draw in pencil?" I ask, earning a glance from Michaela. "Because things can change. Right now, you feel really sad, and that's okay, but one day …" I pluck a pencil out of the cup in the middle of the table and hover my eraser over that little gray cloud. "May I?"

The little girl nods, and I erase the rain cloud.

"You're going to find something that makes you feel happy again."

I replace the cloud with a shining sun, peeking out from behind the clouds.

"And when you do, you don't have to be scared of it, okay? You might think that you don't want to feel happy because it could go away again, or you might worry that your daddy won't think that you miss him anymore, but he wants you to be happy. Look."

I draw another hand on her father, this one waving down at her.

"He can see you so much better without that rain cloud in the way."

Michaela smiles up at me with big, sweet eyes before wrapping her arms around my waist. "Thank you, Dr. Sterling."

I give her shoulder a little squeeze. "What do we say?"

"One day at a time."

"Yes, ma'am. Now, sign that masterpiece, and I'll make a copy for you to take home."

Michaela's mom is the only person waiting in the front lobby, which is also smaller and less swanky than the one at Atlanta Psychology Associates. But the furniture is new, the walls still smell like fresh paint, and nobody here can threaten to fire me, considering that I own half of the business.

Thanks to a generous, interest-free loan from my boyfriend.

I tried to refuse him, but Thomas said that he would have lost a million dollars if it wasn't for me, so the least he could do was loan me a few hundred thousand. It's hard to argue with that kind of logic.

As soon as the lobby door chimes, signaling that Michaela and her mom are gone, Dee comes flying out of her office. She's topless, wearing a battery-operated breast pump backpack and a hands-free bra that holds the suction cups and bottles in place. I wish I could say that I was surprised, but this is a regular occurrence around here.

"I just saw Thomas on *Kelly Clarkson*!"

"Me too!" I beam. "Wasn't he so good?"

"Good? He didn't even mention me! After that Oscar-worthy performance I gave, what the fuck?"

"Uh, I'm pretty sure all you said was, 'Uggghhh ... white bitch.' "

"And I killed it."

I laugh, ducking back into my office to grab my purse. "Well, I'll be sure to tell him he fucked up when I get home," I call out, switching off the light and locking my door.

Turning toward Dee, I ask, "You sure you don't want to come tonight? I know you love a good train wreck."

Dee motions to her nipples, which are shooting milk all over the inside of two clear plastic suction cups at a rate of one spray per second. She must really have that thing cranked up. It sounds like the machine Frankenstein's monster was hooked up to. "Look at me, Lou. What about this look says, *I want to drive into the mountains and do peyote with a bunch of folks who don't believe in modern plumbing?*"

I smirk, letting her vent a little longer.

"In the last three months, I opened a private practice *and* gave birth to a tiny human parasite, so if you think I'ma do anything other than go home and leak on everything I own—"

"You're gonna use 'tiny human parasite' as an excuse for the next eighteen years, aren't you?" I ask.

Dee shrugs. "It's literally the only perk."

"Well, enjoy your leaking," I tease as I head toward the front door.

On the other side of the glass, in bold black stick-on letters, it says *Autonomous Art Therapy, LLC* with the names *Deborah Dawson, PhD* and *Luna Sterling, PhD* in fine print underneath. I smile every time I see it.

Pulling the door open, I call over my shoulder, "See you Monday, boss."

"Happy birthday, bitch."

Four hours later, Thomas, Beth, Mark, Courtney, her husband, Brian, and I are gathered around the splintery outdoor dining table at the commune, trying our best not to offend the Indigo

Hills hippies who have served us a meal so health-conscious and flavorless that bacteria probably won't even eat it.

"And this is?" Thomas whispers, lifting a spoonful of gloopy, rust-colored broth out of his earthenware bowl.

"Gazpacho," I whisper back. "It's like cold vegetable soup."

Thomas raises an eyebrow at me, and I have to bite my lip to keep from laughing. "We'll get pizza on the way home."

Clink, clink, clink!

Leif stands up at the end of the table, and I feel myself cringe preemptively.

Raising his cup to me, he says, "We are gathered here tonight to celebrate the anniversary of the day that *Crystal* "—he swivels toward my mother, and I roll my eyes—"became a bridge between realms. Her body a literal channel through which Spirit could enter our world." Leif makes a circle with his fingers on the word *channel* and sticks another finger into it on the word *enter.*

I can't even make this shit up.

"And what a spirit she is!" Leif turns back toward me, and I lean away from him instinctively, bumping into Thomas's arm.

Before Leif can finish saying, "Happy birth—"

Thomas jumps to his feet, taking Leif's creepy attention off of me, but now, *all* of the attention is firmly on him.

Thomas rubs the back of his neck as he glances around the table at all the eyeballs pointed in his direction. "I, uh, have a few words I'd like to say as well, if I may."

Leif bows and gives him the floor. Then, he returns to his seat and resumes his never-ending flirtation with my mother.

Thomas looks down at me with a tight smile.

Is he nervous? I've never seen Thomas act nervous before.

"Luna. Lou," he says. "Hi."

"Hi," I reply, reaching out to squeeze his hand.

He squeezes it back, holding on tight.

"I just want to say ... in front of all these strangers ... how happy I am that Crystal did bring you into this realm."

That earns him a smile from my parents.

"You and I might have been born on different continents," he says, taking my hand in both of his, "but I think we could have been born on different planets, and I still would have found you. It wasn't chance that led me across the ocean and into your office, and I knew it the moment I saw your fucked up drawings."

I laugh, and he seems to relax, the tension leaving his eyes as they sparkle blue in the flickering candlelight.

"You're my soul mate, Lou," he says with a matter-of-fact shrug. "And if it's all right with you …"

My heart leaps into my throat as Thomas sinks down onto one knee beside me and pulls a ring box out of his pocket.

"I'd like you to be my wife as well."

He opens the lid, but I can't pull my eyes away from his. I can't even remember how to breathe, let alone speak.

But the hippies at the far end of that table seem to have no problem with it.

"I can't watch this patriarchal bullshit."

"Might as well put a collar around her neck like a dog, man."

"You know that's probably a blood diamond. Murderer!"

I bristle as Mark—who I can see out of the periphery of my frozen, shocked stare—turns to address the peanut gallery.

"Actually," he announces, "that ring is made from sustainable, free-range porcupine quills that were allowed to fall off the animal naturally, so … yeah."

That shuts them up and finally pulls a sound out of me. It isn't a *yes* or a *no* but a deep, cackling laugh. It's all so ridiculous. This place, these people, the fact that this man is here at all, let alone asking me to be his wife.

I shake my head as tears fill my eyes, which is evidently the wrong thing to do after someone asks you to marry them because it makes Thomas's eyebrows pull together and his mouth turn down at the corners.

I laugh even harder and switch from shaking my head to nodding it. "Yes," I finally say, grasping his handsome, frowning face and kissing him until his lips curve up again. "Yes." Kiss. "Yes." Kiss. "Yes."

Somewhere across the table, a flash goes off, and I crack my eye open just in time to see George pointing the cell phone I got him at us. Crystal shoves his hand down to hide it but smiles at him tearfully. He wraps an arm around her and kisses her on the head.

While I'm distracted, I feel Thomas slide something onto the ring finger of my left hand. With a deep breath, I force myself to look at it … and start laughing all over again.

I cover my eyes with the hand that *isn't* adorned with a ten-pound, cushion-cut precious stone and whisper, "Holy shit."

Also probably not the reaction Thomas was going for.

The group stands and cheers, a bonfire roars to life, and the table clears, leaving me alone with my future husband.

I wrap myself around Thomas's torso, as if his physical presence were the only thing keeping me tethered to the earth, and look up at his beautiful face.

"I love you," he says, tucking my hair behind one ear.

"I loved you first," I brag.

Thomas gives me that book-cover smirk, and I really wish he wouldn't be so pornographic with my parents present.

Speaking of parents, a loud throat-clearing alerts me that George is lingering nearby.

I turn and find him standing behind me, holding his Mets cap in both hands. "May I have this dance?"

I don't know why I expected him to stiffly slow dance and twirl me like a normal awkward dad would do. Nothing about my life has ever been normal. Instead, George spins and undulates around the bonfire to the surprisingly random, non-rhythmic music-like sounds being supplied by the Indigo Hills drum circle.

"It's good to see you happy, kiddo," George says, doing something that resembles the wave at a baseball game.

"Thank you." I smile, doing the *uncomfortable girl at the club side-to-side step* thing.

"Listen, no pressure," he says, spinning in place, "but if you and what's-his-name wanna get married in New York... ... maybe your old man could see a Mets game while we're in town. You'd just have to buy me a plane ticket. And also a Mets ticket."

"George …" I laugh, giving him the side-eye.

"What?" He shrugs, rolling his hips like he's doing The Worm but vertically.

My mom sidles up next to me and wraps her arm around my shoulders. Her other arm is being used to pat her leg with a tambourine. "The goddess is happy with you," she says, kissing me on the cheek. "Just look at all of your blessings."

It's her way of saying *I told you so*, and for once, I don't mind at all. As we gaze over George's shoulder at the man I wished for all those years ago, I picture my father sitting on a cloud above me, smiling and eating ice cream and sharing this moment with us.

Thomas laughs at something Mark or Beth said, and I know without being able to hear him that he didn't make a sound. I know all of Thomas's laughs now. But I might discover a new one tonight because my future husband just raised a half-empty glass of punch to his lips and took a sip.

"Thomas, nooooo!"

Thank you for reading Group Therapy*! I hope you enjoyed it! If you did, I think you'll love* 44 Chapters About 4 Men. *It's my shockingly sexy, heartwarmingly sweet, hilariously self-deprecating memoir, and it's also the inspiration for the Netflix original series* Sex/Life*! Read on for a sneak peek or download a sample at*
https://mybook.to/44chaptersabout4men

44 Chapters About 4 Men
Chapter One

August 16

DEAR JOURNAL,

This motherfucker is killing me. Fresh out of the shower. He's so close I can smell the Irish Spring on his skin. His hair's all damp and sexy, and his beard scruff is at that perfect length—just long enough to be soft to the touch, but not so long that it hides his perfect chiseled features. And the way his undershirt clings to his biceps and stretches across the hard planes of his chest ... I could look at him all night. Actually, I have been—through the corner of my eye. But that's not enough.

I want to touch him.

In the half hour since he plopped down next to me and flipped on the Braves game, I've thought of a thousand and one ways to reach over and caress this man. I could lace my fingers through his or run my knuckles along his rough, square jaw. Maybe I could be playful and walk my mint-green nails up his sculpted abs; then, once I have his attention, I could straddle his damp, clean, hard body and thrust those same fingertips into his wet hair.

But I don't do shit because I know all it will get me is a sideways glance and a shift in the opposite direction.

My husband is a rock. Not as in, *He's so strong and supportive. I don't know what I'd do without him.* But more like, *He's so fucking cold; I wonder if he still has a pulse.* Ken has never even held my hand, Journal. Not on purpose anyway. He has had his hand held by me while unconscious, but whenever I've tried that move during waking hours, Ken has politely endured the discomfort of human contact for … oh, say, five and a half seconds before smoothly removing his soft, limp flesh from my grasp.

Sex is pretty much the same story. Ever the gentleman, Ken will lie on his back and allow me to have my way with him while he quietly engages in minimal and obligatory petting. (Even when I try to be fun and reenact the ice cream scene from *Fifty Shades Darker*. In his defense, I do have to play the part of Christian because Ken *obviously* doesn't know his lines. And I admit, the white noise of a baby monitor isn't exactly Al Green. And for some reason, we never seem to have vanilla ice cream, like in the book. We only have Cherry Garcia, which is pretty awkward to lick off, what with all the chewing required. But still. A *little* participation would be appreciated.)

Regardless of the level of theatrics involved, afterward, I always kiss and cuddle Ken's lean, beautiful body, trying to squeeze a single degree of warmth from the man-shaped boulder that is my husband. All the while, I can almost hear him counting to himself—*one one thousand, two one thousand, three one thousand*—before he taps me on the ass. My cue to get the fuck off of him.

At least, that's how it seems.

Ken's problem isn't his coldness—his complete lack of need, want, or capacity for intimacy. Those attributes actually keep our marriage quite stable and drama-free. That, and the fact that the man never does *anything* wrong.

Kenneth Easton is a lawn-mowing, bill-paying, law-abiding, defensive-driving, trash-toting *husbot*—a cyborg built specifically to withstand seventy to eighty years of gale-force matrimony. I've *never* caught him looking at another woman. Hell, I've never even caught him in a lie.

No, the problem with Ken is that he's married to me.

Journal, before meeting Ken, I'd been contorted into at least seventy-three percent of the positions in the *Kama Sutra*. I'd shaved most of my head and had all my lady bits pierced before I was old enough to see an R-rated movie. I'd spent my free time being handcuffed to things by boys with more combined tattoos than a Guns N' Roses reunion concert. Ken simply can't compete.

So, why, you might be wondering, did a slutty little punk like me go and marry someone so straightlaced?

It was because of *them*. Because of the way my adrenaline spikes and my pupils dilate in a fight-or-flight-or-fuck response every time I smell the sickly-sweet musk of Calvin Klein's Obsession for Men. Because of the way a pierced bottom lip makes me want to take up smoking again. Because of the way a full sleeve of tattoos makes me want to hitch a ride on a tour bus and leave everything I worked so hard to achieve in a gutter at the side of the road. Because my nerves were fucking shot by the time I met Ken, my heart was riding in on fumes, and the stability and security and sanity he offered was a soothing balm to my spent, scorched soul.

Those inked-up men-children from my past might have been ferocious lovers, but they couldn't keep their dicks in their pants, their asses out of jail, or a positive balance in their bank accounts to save their lives. Ken, on the other hand, was just so … safe. Responsible. Easy. He wore Nikes and Gap T-shirts. He owned his own home. He *jogged*. His criminal record was as ink-free as his freckled skin. And, to top it all off, he had a degree in … wait for it … *accounting*.

I might have overcorrected a bit.

Don't get me wrong. I love the shit out of Kenneth Easton. He is my best friend, the father of my children, and we are actually ridiculously happy together. Or at least, I'm happy. I am. Really. You can be bored to tears and happy at the same time, right? They call those happy tears. Happy, bored, oh-so bored tears. Ken is pretty anhedonic and deadpan, so it's hard to tell how he's feeling. I choose to think of him as happy, too. But let's be honest. Ken may not really have feelings.

What he does have is a Captain America–style square jaw with a subtle cleft and a permanent five o'clock shadow. And enviably high cheekbones. And aqua eyes, hooded with espresso-colored lashes, and sandy-brown hair that is just long enough on top to do this cute little flip thing in front. His physique is lean and muscular. His sense of humor is dry. He is brilliant, self-deprecating, and tolerant of my bullshit.

The man is at least ninety percent perfect for me, but lately, all I can think about is the less than or equal to ten percent that's missing—passion and body art. Two things I need to mourn and move on from in order to protect my lovely, monotonous marriage.

But I can't.

Tattooed bad boys are like a drug I can't quit. I devour antihero romance novels like they're an essential food group. My iPhone runneth over with the songs of a thousand breathy, angsty, tattooed alt-rockers, ready to fill my head at the press of a button whenever I need to escape. My DVR is brimming with mysterious vampires, renegade bikers, hedonistic rock stars, and zombie apocalypse survivors—alpha males into whose ink-covered arms I can run whenever things around here get a little too ... domestic.

And do you know what I realized during my escapes to these imaginary dystopian societies and fictional underground fight rings? I know these men. I dated these men—the high school bully with daddy issues and childhood trauma, the US Marine who just needs the love of a good woman to help him through his PTSD, the tattoo artist turned motorcycle club outlaw, the ex-convict/underground hot-rod racer, the sensitive guy liner–sporting heavy metal bassist ...

I had them all, Journal. How did I not see the parallels between my fantasy men and my ex-boyfriends before? And I call myself a psychologist!

In fact, Knight, my high school boyfriend, is probably the reason I became a psychologist in the first place. Fucking psycho. I'll tell you about him tomorrow. Ken's going to bed, which means I only have about a five-minute window to get in there and pounce on him before The History Channel lulls him to sleep. Wish me luck!

GROUP THERAPY

You can read the rest of my shockingly sexy, heartwarmingly sweet, and hilariously self-deprecating memoir, 44 Chapters About Men, *at* https://mybook.to/44chaptersabout4men

Books by BB Easton

44 CHAPTERS ABOUT 4 MEN

Inspiration for the Netflix Original Series Sex/Life

THE 44 CHAPTERS SPIN-OFF SERIES

Darkly funny. Deeply Emotional. Shockingly sexy.

SKIN (Knight's backstory, Book 1)
SPEED (Harley's backstory, Book 2)
STAR (Hans's backstory, Book 3)
SUIT (Ken's backstory, Book 4)

THE RAIN TRILOGY

A gritty, suspenseful, dystopian romance

Praying for Rain
Fighting for Rain
Dying for Rain

GROUP THERAPY

Hilarious, heartwarming psychologist-client rom-com

Acknowledgments

FUN FACT: I WAS supposed to start writing this book in March of 2020. Remember March of 2020? Yeah, good times.

I had just published the final novel in The Rain Trilogy, a dystopian love story that seemed inconceivably far-fetched while I was writing it, but within a few weeks of its conclusion, a shocking number of my apocalyptic plot points began coming true. A threat that we knew very little about was killing the oldest and sickest members of our society, grocery stores were being emptied, the political climate became frighteningly radical, people began stockpiling guns and ammunition, and our collective stress levels were building to a fever pitch.

I received dozens of messages from readers, accusing me of causing the pandemic.

The Rain Trilogy is coming true!

BB, what have you done?

If you have a Rain Trilogy vision board somewhere, you need to burn that shit ASAP!

Girl, make it stop!

They were kidding—*I think*—but I decided that, to do my part to prevent the downfall of man, I should probably write something lighthearted with a big, fat happy ending as soon as fucking possible. I came up with a loose idea for *Group Therapy* and was really excited about it, but the day I was supposed to sit down and start writing it … my kids' school closed due to COVID-19.

I went to bed a full-time author and woke up a full-time "digital learning" supervisor.

I tried to write when I could, but between the constant distraction of having my kids and husband home all day, every day and my brain's inability to concentrate on anything that wasn't the news, the best I could do was a few lines of dialogue here and there.

Being that unproductive for months on end was extremely frustrating, but I kept trying. And every time I did, the result would be the same—dialogue. Dialogue, dialogue, dialogue. And that's when it hit me—I wasn't writing a novel.

I was writing a screenplay.

But I didn't know how to write a screenplay. So, for guidance, I went directly to the source. The man who has written, produced, and/or directed all of my favorite female-led comedy films. The man who gave us *Bridesmaids*, *Trainwreck*, *Knocked Up*, and *This Is 40*. The man who has given me more hours of pleasure than most of my boyfriends.

Judd Apatow.

Suddenly, instead of stomping around the house, feeling creatively stifled and powerless to do anything about it, I felt excited again. I stayed up late every night, watching Judd's movies and his outstanding *MasterClass*, pausing every thirty to sixty seconds to take notes or find a pillow to laugh into so that I didn't wake my family. His story structure, his character arcs, and his portrayal of women as flawed, funny, complex creatures worthy of the spotlight gave me an invaluable model to go by, and I cannot thank him enough for providing me with the tools, inspiration, and example I needed to take on such a daunting new project.

The *Group Therapy* screenplay got me through some dark, uncertain times. By the time I finally typed *The End*, my kids had gone back to school, 2020 was coming to an end, and the world no longer felt like a misshapen lump of clay on a pottery wheel that was seconds away from splattering against a wall. I finally got my beloved full-time job back, and one year to the day after I intended to start this book, I finished it with a surprise baby screenplay in tow. Life is weird, man.

And speaking of the screenplay, I'd also like to extend my thanks to the actors whose magical performances helped shape some of the characters in this story:

> Zoë Kravitz, your portrayal of Rob's character in *High Fidelity* inspired so much of my Lou. Her androgynous, monosyllabic nickname; her effortless, thrift-store-chic style; her snarky apathy, deep well of loneliness, and pining, aching obsession with a certain handsome Englishman all snuck their way into my heart and into my girl. You absolutely crushed that role. Brava.
>
> Lisa Bonet, because your daughter inspired my heroine, Crystal was naturally inspired by you. You have set the bar for coolness impossibly

high, but on behalf of all womankind, we forgive you for it.

Kristen Wiig, your character in *Bridesmaids*—and the entire screenplay—was nothing short of brilliant. My goal was to bring that same big, flawed, funny female-ensemble energy to a mental health setting, and *Bridesmaids* was my bible. Thank you for your art.

Melissa McCarthy, you are a true comedic genius as well as my muse for Beth.

Tiffany Haddish, nobody could play Dee better than you. You weave this amazing combination of playfulness, badassery, and vulnerable honesty into everything you do, and I have had so much fun watching your star rise because of it.

Kristen Bell, you're my Courtney. All day, erry day.

Mark Kanemura, your incredible Instagram dance parties inspired Mark's *dance party intervention* scene. You are a gift to the world, and every time I see you, I can't help but smile.

Larry David, you also make me smile but for very different reasons. Your look and delightfully discontented persona were my foundation for George's character. I even named him after George Costanza on *Seinfeld* in your honor.

Chuck Palahniuk, I know you're not an actor, but thank you for writing both *Fight Club*, which inspired the *storage room fight* scenes and the idea of holding group therapy in a random, irrelevant location after hours, and *Consider This*, one of my favorite, most cherished books on writing. I bow down.

And Nicholas Hoult, although you were my physical muse for Thomas O'Reardon, I stole all of his cold, guarded, infuriatingly analytical traits from my husband. I'm sure you're as warm as a sunbeam in person.

Which brings me to Ken, my husbot. There is no one I would rather be stuck in a house with during a global pandemic than you and those two beautiful kids you let me have. Not only because you're the calmest, cleanest, easiest person to get along with on the planet, but also because your extreme-couponing and bulk-purchasing habits made it so that we didn't even have to panic when lockdown started, thanks to all the "bargains" you'd been stockpiling in our laundry room. I love you so much.

And a huge thank-you to Dr. Sara Snow for being my clinical psychology fellowship consultant and general ride or die.

Writer's block is a bitch, and nobody knows that better than Staci Brillhart and Tracey Frazier, only because I whined to them about it for a solid four or five months before the *Group Therapy* screenplay began to take shape. I love you, ladies. Thank you for being my own personal therapy group.

Colleen Hoover, thanks for being born.

To my copy editor, Jovana Shirley, my content editor, Traci Finlay, my beta readers, Sammi Lynn and Sara Snow, and my proofreaders, Crystal Blanton, April C., Michelle Beiger DePrima, Kayle Catlett, and Rhonda Lind, thank you for your sharp eyes, your gentle honesty, your precious time, and your much-needed enthusiasm. I hope you know just how much I appreciate you.

To my audiobook producer and narrator, Ramona Master—It's hard enough to find a great talent, but finding someone who is reliable, efficient, enthusiastic, *and* talented? Unheard of! I am so, so happy that I got to work with you again. Thank you for helping me bring Lou and Thomas to life.

And finally, to my biggest support group, #TeamBB—Thank you for taking this wild ride with me. Social media can be a nasty place, but it can also bring people together in a really beautiful way. It is how I met all of you, and you guys are the only reason I can do this incredibly solitary job without ever feeling alone. Thank you for making me laugh with your posts, for making me cry with your incredible reviews, and for making your friends read my books, often under threat of physical violence. I'm so happy we found one another.

About the Author

WALL STREET JOURNAL BESTSELLING author BB Easton lives in the suburbs of Atlanta with her long-suffering husband, Ken, and two adorable children. She recently quit her job as a school psychologist to write books about her punk rock past and deviant sexual history full-time. Ken is suuuper excited about that.

BB's debut memoir, 44 CHAPTERS ABOUT 4 MEN, is the inspiration for the #3 Most-Watched Netflix Original Series of all time, SEX/LIFE. Because she had so much fun writing it, BB went on to publish four more wickedly funny, shockingly steamy, and heartwarmingly honest books, one for each man in her memoir: SKIN, SPEED, STAR, and SUIT.

THE RAIN TRILOGY, an epic, immersive, end-of-the-world romance, is BB's first work of fiction. Or at least, that's what she thought when she wrote it in 2019. Then 2020 hit and all of her dystopian plot points started coming true. Hopefully, her feel-good romantic comedy *Group Therapy* will fix everything.

You can find BB procrastinating in all of the following places:

Website: www.authorbbeaston.com

Instagram:
www.instagram.com/author.bb.easton

TikTok:
https://vm.tiktok.com/ZMeEKRLyS/

Facebook: www.facebook.com/bbeaston

#TeamBB Facebook Group:
www.facebook.com/groups/BBEaston

Twitter: www.twitter.com/bb_easton

Amazon: author.to/bbeaston

Pinterest: www.pinterest.com/artbyeaston

Goodreads: https://goo.gl/4hiwiR

BookBub:
https://www.bookbub.com/authors/bb-
easton

Spotify:
https://open.spotify.com/user/bbeaston

Etsy: www.etsy.com/shop/artbyeaston

And giving away free e-books from her best-
selling author friends every month in her
newsletter: www.artbyeaston.com/subscribe